LOVERS OF THEIR TIME

Lovers of Their Time

AND OTHER STORIES

William Trevor

THE VIKING PRESS
NEW YORK

ACKNOWLEDGMENTS

These stories first appeared in the following publications: *A Book of Contemporary Nightmares, Best Irish Stories 2, Encounter, Irish Ghost Stories,* the *Irish Press, New Yorker, New Review, Spectator, Transatlantic Review, London Magazine.* The story 'Attracta' was first broadcast by BBC Radio Three as a radio play.

PUBLISHER'S NOTE

'The Tennis Court' was originally published in William Trevor's previous collection of stories, *Angels at the Ritz,* but is reprinted here as part of the trilogy of stories entitled 'Matilda's England'.

Published in 1979 by The Viking Press
625 Madison Avenue, New York, N.Y. 10022

LIBRARY OF CONGRESS CATALOGING IN PUBLICATION DATA
Trevor, William, 1928-
Lovers of their time and other stories.
I. Title.
PZ4.T8163Lr 1979 [PR6070.R4] 823'.9'14 78-23227
ISBN 0-670-44325-5

Grateful acknowledgment is made for permission to quote the following:

ATV Music Group: From "Yesterday" (John Lennon and Paul McCartney). Copyright © 1965 Maclen Music, Inc., c/o ATV Music Corp., 6255 Sunset Blvd., Los Angeles, Calif. 90028, for the U.S.A., Canada, Mexico & the Philippines. Northern Songs Limited for the rest of the world. Used by permission. All rights reserved.

Printed in the United States of America
Set in Monotype Plantin

CONTENTS

LOVERS OF THEIR TIME

Broken Homes

'I really think you're marvellous,' the man said.

He was small and plump, with a plump face that had a greyness about it where he shaved; his hair was grey also, falling into a fringe on his forehead. He was untidily dressed, a turtle-necked red jersey beneath a jacket that had a ball-point pen and a pencil sticking out of the breast pocket. When he stood up his black corduroy trousers developed concertina creases. Nowadays you saw a lot of men like this, Mrs Malby said to herself.

'We're trying to help them,' he said, 'and of course we're trying to help you. The policy is to foster a deeper under-standing.' He smiled, displaying small evenly-arranged teeth. 'Between the generations,' he added.

'Well, of course it's very kind,' Mrs Malby said.

He shook his head. He sipped the instant coffee she'd made for him and nibbled the edge of a pink wafer biscuit. As if driven by a compulsion, he dipped the biscuit into the coffee. He said:

'What age actually are you, Mrs Malby?'

'I'm eighty-seven.'

'You really are splendid for eighty-seven.'

He went on talking. He said he hoped he'd be as good him-self at eighty-seven. He hoped he'd even be in the land of the living. 'Which I doubt,' he said with a laugh. 'Knowing me.'

Mrs Malby didn't know what he meant by that. She was sure she'd heard him quite correctly, but she could recall nothing he'd previously stated which indicated ill-health. She thought carefully while he continued to sip at his coffee and attend to the mush of biscuit. What he had said suggested that a knowledge of him would cause you to doubt that he'd live to old age. Had he already supplied further knowledge of himself which, due to her slight deafness, she had not heard? If he hadn't, why had he left everything hanging in the air like that? It was difficult to know how best to react, whether to smile or to display concern.

'So what I thought,' he said, 'was that we could send the kids on Tuesday. Say start the job Tuesday morning, eh, Mrs Malby?'

'It's extremely kind of you.'

'They're good kids.'

He stood up. He remarked on her two budgerigars and the geraniums on her window-sill. Her sitting-room was as warm as toast, he said; it was freezing outside.

'It's just that I wondered,' she said, having made up her mind to say it, 'if you could possibly have come to the wrong house?'

'Wrong? *Wrong*? You're Mrs Malby, aren't you?' He raised his voice. 'You're Mrs Malby, love?'

'Oh, yes, it's just that my kitchen isn't really in need of decoration.'

He nodded. His head moved slowly and when it stopped his dark eyes stared at her from beneath his grey fringe. He said, quite softly, what she'd dreaded he might say: that she hadn't understood.

'I'm thinking of the community, Mrs Malby. I'm thinking of you here on your own above a greengrocer's shop with your two budgies. You can benefit my kids, Mrs Malby; they can benefit you. There's no charge of any kind whatsoever. Put it like this, Mrs Malby: it's an experiment in community relations.' He paused. He reminded her of a picture there'd been in a history book, a long time ago, History with Miss Deacon, a picture of a Roundhead. 'So you see, Mrs Malby,'

8

he said, having said something else while he was reminding
her of a Roundhead.

'It's just that my kitchen is really quite nice.'

'Let's have a little look, shall we?'

She led the way. He glanced at the kitchen's shell-pink
walls, and at the white paintwork. It would cost her nearly a
hundred pounds to have it done, he said; and then, to her
horror, he began all over again, as if she hadn't heard a thing
he'd been saying. He repeated that he was a teacher, from the
school called the Tite Comprehensive. He appeared to
assume that she wouldn't know the Tite Comprehensive, but
she did: an ugly sprawl of glass and concrete buildings,
children swinging along the pavements, shouting obscenities.
The man repeated what he had said before about these
children: that some of them came from broken homes. The
ones he wished to send to her on Tuesday morning came
from broken homes, which was no joke for them. He felt, he
repeated, that we all had a special duty where such children
were concerned.

Mrs Malby again agreed that broken homes were to be
deplored. It was just, she explained, that she was thinking of
the cost of decorating a kitchen which didn't need decorating.
Paint and brushes were expensive, she pointed out.

'Freshen it over for you,' the man said, raising his voice.
'First thing Tuesday, Mrs Malby.'

He went away, and she realised that he hadn't told her his
name. Thinking she might be wrong about that, she went
over their encounter in her mind, going back to the moment
when her doorbell had sounded. 'I'm from Tite Comprehensive,' was what he'd said. No name had been mentioned, of
that she was positive.

In her elderliness Mrs Malby liked to be sure of such
details. You had to work quite hard sometimes at eighty-
seven, straining to hear, concentrating carefully in order to be

sure of things. You had to make it clear you understood because people often imagined you didn't. Communication was what it was called nowadays, rather than conversation.

Mrs Malby was wearing a blue dress with a pattern of darker blue flowers on it. She was a woman who had been tall but had shrunk a little with age and had become slightly bent. Scant white hair crowned a face that was touched with elderly freckling. Large brown eyes, once her most striking feature, were quieter than they had been, tired behind spectacles now. Her husband, George, the owner of the greengrocer's shop over which she lived, had died five years ago; her two sons, Eric and Roy, had been killed in the same month – June 1942 – in the same desert retreat.

The greengrocer's shop was unpretentious, in an unpretentious street in Fulham called Agnes Street. The people who owned it now, Jewish people called King, kept an eye on Mrs Malby. They watched for her coming and going and if they missed her one day they'd ring her doorbell to see that she was all right. She had a niece in Ealing who looked in twice a year, and another niece in Islington, who was crippled with arthritis. Once a week Mrs Grove and Mrs Halbert came round with Meals on Wheels. A social worker, Miss Tingle, called; and the Reverend Bush called. Men came to read the meters.

In her elderliness, living where she'd lived since her marriage in 1920, Mrs Malby was happy. The tragedy in her life – the death of her sons – was no longer a nightmare, and the time that had passed since her husband's death had allowed her to come to terms with being on her own. All she wished for was to continue in these same circumstances until she died, and she did not fear death. She did not believe she would be re-united with her sons and her husband, not at least in a specific sense, but she could not believe, either, that she would entirely cease to exist the moment she ceased to breathe. Having thought about death, it seemed likely to Mrs Malby that after it came she'd dream, as in sleep. Heaven and hell were surely no more than flickers of such pleasant dreaming, or flickers of a nightmare from which there was no waking release. No loving omnipotent God, in Mrs Malby's view, doled out punishments and reward: human conscience, the last survivor, did that. The idea of a God, which had puzzled Mrs Malby for most of her life, made sense when she thought of it in terms like these, when she forgot about the mystic qualities claimed for a Church and for Jesus Christ. Yet fearful of offending the Reverend Bush, she kept such conclusions to herself when he came to see her.

All Mrs Malby dreaded now was becoming senile and being forced to enter the Sunset Home in Richmond, of which the Reverend Bush and Miss Tingle warmly spoke. The thought of a communal existence, surrounded by other elderly people, with sing-songs and card-games, was anathema to her. All her life she had hated anything that smacked of communal jolliness, refusing even to go on coach trips. She loved the house above the greengrocer's shop. She loved walking down the stairs and out on to the street, nodding at the Kings as she went by the shop, buying birdseed and eggs and fire-lighters, and fresh bread from Len Skipps, a man of sixty-two whom she'd remembered being born.

The dread of having to leave Agnes Street ordered her life. With all her visitors she was careful, constantly on the look-out for signs in their eyes which might mean they were diagnosing her as senile. It was for this reason that she listened so intently to all that was said to her, that she concentrated, determined to let nothing slip by. It was for this reason that she smiled and endeavoured to appear agreeable and co-operative at all times. She was well aware that it wasn't going to be up to her to state that she was senile, or to argue that she wasn't, when the moment came.

After the teacher from Tite Comprehensive School had left, Mrs Malby continued to worry. The visit from this grey-haired man had bewildered her from the start. There was the oddity of his not giving his name, and then the way he'd placed a cigarette in his mouth and had taken it out again, putting it back in the packet. Had he imagined cigarette smoke would offend her? He could have asked, but in fact he hadn't even referred to the cigarette. Nor had he said where he'd heard about her: he hadn't mentioned the Reverend Bush, for instance, or Mrs Grove and Mrs Halbert, or Miss Tingle. He might have been a customer in the green-grocer's shop, but he hadn't given any indication that that was so. Added to which, and most of all, there was the consideration that her kitchen wasn't in the least in need of attention. She went to look at it again, beginning to wonder if there were things about it she couldn't see. She went over in her mind what the man had said about community relations. It was difficult to resist men like that, you had to go on repeating yourself and after a while you had to assess if you were sounding senile or not. There was also the consideration that the man was trying to do good, helping children from broken homes.

'Hi,' a boy with long blond hair said to her on the Tuesday morning. There were two other boys with him, one with a fuzz of dark curls all round his head, the other red-haired, a greased shock that hung to his shoulders. There was a girl as well, thin and beaky-faced, chewing something. Between them they carried tins of paint, brushes, cloths, a blue plastic bucket, and a transistor radio. 'We come to do your kitchen out,' the blond boy said. 'You Mrs Wheeler then?'

'No, no. I'm Mrs Malby.'

'That's right, Billo,' the girl said. 'Malby.'

'I thought he says Wheeler.'

'Wheeler's the geyser in the paint shop,' the fuzzy-haired boy said.

'Typical Billo,' the girl said.

She let them in, saying it was very kind of them. She led them to the kitchen, remarking on the way that strictly speaking it wasn't in need of decoration, as they could see for themselves. She'd been thinking it over, she added: she wondered if they'd just like to wash the walls down, which was a task she found difficult to do herself?

They'd do whatever she wanted, they said, no problem. They put their paint tins on the table. The red-haired boy turned on the radio. 'Welcome back to Open House,' a cheery voice said and then reminded its listeners that it was the voice of Pete Murray. It said that a record was about to be played for someone in Upminster.

'Would you like some coffee?' Mrs Malby suggested above the noise of the transistor.

'Great,' the blond boy said.

They all wore blue jeans with patches on them. The girl had a T-shirt with the words *I Lay Down With Jesus* on it. The others wore T-shirts of different colours, the blond boy's orange, the fuzzy one's light blue, the red-haired one's red. *Hot Jam-roll* a badge on the chest of the blond boy said; *Jaws* and *Bay City Rollers* other badges said.

Mrs Malby made them Nescafé while they listened to the music. They lit cigarettes, leaning about against the electric stove and against the edge of the table and against a wall. They didn't say anything because they were listening. 'That's a load of crap,' the red-haired boy pronounced eventually, and the others agreed. Even so they went on listening. 'Pete Murray's crappy,' the girl said.

Mrs Malby handed them the cups of coffee, drawing their attention to the sugar she'd put out for them on the table, and to the milk. She smiled at the girl. She said again that it was a job she couldn't manage any more, washing walls.

'Get that, Billo?' the fuzzy-haired boy said. 'Washing walls.'

'Who loves ya, baby?' Billo replied.

Mrs Malby closed the kitchen door on them, hoping they wouldn't take too long because the noise of the transistor was so loud. She listened to it for a quarter of an hour and then she decided to go out and do her shopping.

In Len Skipps' she said that four children from the Tite Comprehensive had arrived in her house and were at present washing her kitchen walls. She said it again to the man in the fish shop and the man was surprised. It suddenly occurred to her that of course they couldn't have done any painting because she hadn't discussed colours with the teacher. She thought it odd that the teacher hadn't mentioned colours and wondered what colour the paint tins contained. It worried her a little that all that hadn't occurred to her before.

'Hi, Mrs Wheeler,' the boy called Billo said to her in her hall. He was standing there combing his hair, looking at himself in the mirror of the hall-stand. Music was coming from upstairs.

There were yellowish smears on the stair-carpet, which upset Mrs Malby very much. There were similar smears on the landing carpet. 'Oh, but please,' Mrs Malby cried, standing in the kitchen doorway. 'Oh, please, no!' she cried.

Yellow emulsion paint partially covered the shell-pink of one wall. Some had spilt from the tin on to the black-and-white vinyl of the floor and had been walked through. The boy with fuzzy hair was standing on a draining-board applying the same paint to the ceiling. He was the only person in the kitchen.

He smiled at Mrs Malby, looking down at her. 'Hi, Mrs Wheeler,' he said.

'But I said only to wash them,' she cried.

She felt tired, saying that. The upset of finding the smears on the carpets and of seeing the hideous yellow plastered over the quiet shell-pink had already taken a toll. Her emotional outburst had caused her face and neck to become warm. She felt she'd like to lie down.

'Eh, Mrs Wheeler?' The boy smiled at her again, continuing to slap paint on to the ceiling. A lot of it dripped back on top of him, on to the draining-board and on to cups and saucers and cutlery, and on to the floor. 'D'you fancy the colour, Mrs Wheeler?' he asked her.

All the time the transistor continued to blare, a voice inexpertly singing, a tuneless twanging. The boy referred to this sound, pointing at the transistor with his paint-brush, saying it was great. Unsteadily she crossed the kitchen and turned the transistor off. 'Hey, sod it, missus,' the boy protested angrily.

'I said to wash the walls. I didn't even choose that colour.'

The boy, still annoyed because she'd turned off the radio, was gesturing crossly with the brush. There was paint in the fuzz of his hair and on his T-shirt and his face. Every time he moved the brush about paint flew off it. It speckled the windows, and the small dresser, and the electric stove and the taps and the sink.

'Where's the sound gone?' the boy called Billo demanded, coming into the kitchen and going straight to the transistor.

'I didn't want the kitchen painted,' Mrs Malby said again. 'I told you.'

The singing from the transistor recommenced, louder than before. On the draining-board the fuzzy-haired boy began to sway, throwing his body and his head about.

'Please stop him painting,' Mrs Malby shouted as shrilly as she could.

'Here,' the boy called Billo said, bundling her out on to the landing and closing the kitchen door. 'Can't hear myself think in there.'

'I don't want it painted.'

'What's that, Mrs Wheeler?'

'My name isn't Wheeler. I don't want my kitchen painted. I told you.'

'Are we in the wrong house? Only we was told – '

'Will you please wash that paint off?'

'If we come to the wrong house – '

'You haven't come to the wrong house. Please tell that boy to wash off the paint he's put on.'

'Did a bloke from the Comp come in to see you, Mrs Wheeler? Fat bloke?'

'Yes, yes, he did.'

'Only he give instructions – '

'Please would you tell that boy?'

'Whatever you say, Mrs Wheeler.'

'And wipe up the paint where it's spilt on the floor. It's been trampled out, all over my carpets.'

'No problem, Mrs Wheeler.'

Not wishing to return to the kitchen herself, she ran the hot tap in the bathroom on to the sponge-cloth she kept for cleaning the bath. She found that if she rubbed hard enough at the paint on the stair-carpet and on the landing carpet it began to disappear. But the rubbing tired her. As she put away the sponge-cloth, Mrs Malby had a feeling of not quite knowing what was what. Everything that had happened in the last few hours felt like a dream; it also had the feeling of plays she had seen on television; the one thing it wasn't like was reality. As she paused in her bathroom, having placed the sponge-cloth on a ledge under the hand-basin, Mrs Malby saw herself standing there, as she often did in a dream: she saw her body hunched within the same blue dress she'd been wearing when the teacher called, and two touches of red in her pale face, and her white hair tidy on her head, and her fingers seeming fragile. In a dream anything could happen next: she might suddenly find herself forty years younger, Eric and Roy might be alive. She might be even younger; Dr Ramsey might be telling her she was pregnant. In a television play it would be different: the children who had come to her house might kill her. What she hoped for from reality was that order would be restored in her kitchen, that all the paint would be washed away from her walls as she had wiped it from her carpets, that the misunderstanding would be over. For an instant she saw herself in her kitchen, making tea for the children, saying it didn't matter. She even heard herself adding that in a life as long as hers you became used to everything.

She left the bathroom; the blare of the transistor still persisted. She didn't want to sit in her sitting-room, having to listen to it. She climbed the stairs to her bedroom, imagining the coolness there, and the quietness.

'Hey,' the girl protested when Mrs Malby opened her bedroom door.

'Sod off, you guys,' the boy with the red hair ordered.

They were in her bed. Their clothes were all over the floor. Her two budgerigars were flying about the room. Protruding from sheets and blankets she could see the boy's naked shoulders and the back of his head. The girl poked her face up from under him. She gazed at Mrs Malby. 'It's not them,' she whispered to the boy. 'It's the woman.'

'Hi there, missus.' The boy twisted his head round. From the kitchen, still loudly, came the noise of the transistor.

'Sorry,' the girl said.

'Why are they up here? Why have you let my birds out? You've no right to behave like this.'

'We needed sex,' the girl explained.

The budgerigars were perched on the looking-glass on the dressing-table, beadily surveying the scene.

'They're really great, them budgies,' the boy said.

Mrs Malby stepped through their garments. The budgerigars remained where they were. They fluttered when she seized them but they didn't offer any resistance. She returned with them to the door.

'You had no right,' she began to say to the two in her bed, but her voice had become weak. It quivered into a useless whisper, and once more she thought that what was happening couldn't be happening. She saw herself again, standing unhappily with the budgerigars.

In her sitting-room she wept. She returned the budgerigars to their cage and sat in an armchair by the window that looked out over Agnes Street. She sat in sunshine, feeling its warmth but not, as she might have done, delighting in it. She wept because she had intensely disliked finding the boy and girl in her bed. Images from the bedroom remained vivid in her mind. On the floor the boy's boots were heavy and black, composed of leather that did not shine. The girl's shoes were green, with huge heels and soles. The girl's underclothes were purple, the boy's dirty. There'd been an unpleasant smell of sweat in her bedroom.

Mrs Malby waited, her head beginning to ache. She dried away her tears, wiping at her eyes and cheeks with a handkerchief. In Agnes Street people passed by on bicycles, girls from the polish factory returning home to lunch, men from the brickworks. People came out of the greengrocer's with leeks and cabbages in baskets, some carrying paper bags. Watching these people in Agnes Street made her feel better, even though her headache was becoming worse. She felt more composed, and more in control of herself.

'We're sorry,' the girl said again, suddenly appearing, teetering on her clumsy shoes. 'We didn't think you'd come up to the bedroom.'

She tried to smile at the girl, but found it hard to do so. She nodded instead.

'The others put the birds in,' the girl said. 'Meant to be a joke, that was.'

She nodded again. She couldn't see how it could be a joke to take two budgerigars from their cage, but she didn't say that.

'We're getting on with the painting now,' the girl said. 'Sorry about that.'

She went away and Mrs Malby continued to watch the people in Agnes Street. The girl had made a mistake when she'd said they were getting on with the painting: what she'd meant was that they were getting on with washing it off. The girl had come straight downstairs to say she was sorry; she hadn't been told by the boys in the kitchen that the paint had been applied in error. When they'd gone, Mrs Malby said to herself, she'd open her bedroom window wide in order to get rid of the odour of sweat. She'd put clean sheets on her bed.

From the kitchen, above the noise of the transistor, came the clatter of raised voices. There was laughter and a crash, and then louder laughter. Singing began, attaching itself to the singing from the transistor.

She sat for twenty minutes and then she went and knocked on the kitchen door, not wishing to push the door open in case it knocked someone off a chair. There was no reply. She opened the door gingerly.

More yellow paint had been applied. The whole wall around the window was covered with it, and most of the wall behind the sink. Half of the ceiling had it on it; the woodwork that had been white was now a glossy dark blue. All four of the children were working with brushes. A tin of paint had been upset on the floor.

She wept again, standing there watching them, unable to prevent her tears. She felt them running warmly on her cheeks and then becoming cold. It was in this kitchen that she had cried first of all when the two telegrams had come in

1942, believing when the second one arrived that she would never cease to cry. It would have seemed ridiculous at the time, to cry just because her kitchen was all yellow.

They didn't see her standing there. They went on singing, slapping the paint-brushes back and forth. There'd been neat straight lines where the shell-pink met the white of the woodwork, but now the lines were any old how. The boy with the red hair was applying the dark-blue gloss.

Again the feeling that it wasn't happening possessed Mrs Malby. She'd had a dream a week ago, a particularly vivid dream in which the Prime Minister had stated on television that the Germans had been invited to invade England since England couldn't manage to look after herself any more. That dream had been most troublesome because when she'd woken up in the morning she'd thought it was something she'd seen on television, that she'd actually been sitting in her sitting-room the night before listening to the Prime Minister saying that he and the Leader of the Opposition had decided the best for Britain was invasion. After thinking about it, she'd established that of course it hadn't been true; but even so she'd glanced at the headlines of newspapers when she went out shopping.

'How d'you fancy it?' the boy called Billo called out to her, smiling across the kitchen at her, not noticing that she was upset. 'Neat, Mrs Wheeler?'

She didn't answer. She went downstairs and walked out of her hall-door, into Agnes Street and into the greengrocer's that had been her husband's. It never closed in the middle of the day; it never had. She waited and Mr King appeared, wiping his mouth. 'Well then, Mrs Malby?' he said.

He was a big man with a well-kept black moustache and Jewish eyes. He didn't smile much because smiling wasn't his way, but he was in no way morose, rather the opposite.

'So what can I do for you?' he said.

She told him. He shook his head and repeatedly frowned as he listened. His expressive eyes widened. He called his wife.

While the three of them hurried along the pavement to Mrs Malby's open hall-door it seemed to her that the Kings doubted her. She could feel them thinking that she must have got it all wrong, that she'd somehow imagined all this stuff about yellow paint and pop music on a radio, and her birds flying around her bedroom while two children were lying in her bed. She didn't blame them; she knew exactly how they felt. But when they entered her house the noise from the transistor could at once be heard.

The carpet of the landing was smeared again with the paint. Yellow footprints led to her sitting-room and out again, back to the kitchen.

'You bloody young hooligans,' Mr King shouted at them. He snapped the switch on the transistor. He told them to stop applying the paint immediately. 'What the hell d'you think you're up to?' he demanded furiously.

'We come to paint out the old ma's kitchen,' the boy called Billo explained, unruffled by Mr King's tone. 'We was carrying out instructions, mister.'

'So it was instructions to spill the blooming paint all over the floor? So it was instructions to cover the windows with it and every knife and fork in the place? So it was instructions to frighten the life out of a poor woman by messing about in her bedroom?'

'No one frightens her, mister.'

'You know what I mean, son.'

Mrs Malby returned with Mrs King and sat in the cubbyhole behind the shop, leaving Mr King to do his best. At three o'clock he arrived back, saying that the children had gone. He telephoned the school and after a delay was put in touch with the teacher who'd been to see Mrs Malby. He made this telephone call in the shop but Mrs Malby could hear him saying that what had happened was a disgrace. 'A woman of eighty-seven,' Mr King protested, 'thrown into a state of misery. There'll be something to pay on this, you know.'

There was some further discussion on the telephone, and then Mr King replaced the receiver. He put his head into the cubbyhole and announced that the teacher was coming round immediately to inspect the damage. 'What can I entice you to?' Mrs Malby heard him asking a customer, and a woman's voice replied that she needed tomatoes, a cauliflower, potatoes and Bramleys. She heard Mr King telling the woman what had happened, saying that it had wasted two hours of his time.

She drank the sweet milky tea which Mrs King had poured her. She tried not to think of the yellow paint and the dark-blue gloss. She tried not to remember the scene in the bed-room and the smell there'd been, and the new marks that had appeared on her carpets after she'd wiped off the original ones. She wanted to ask Mr King if these marks had been washed out before the paint had had a chance to dry, but she didn't like to ask this because Mr King had been so kind and it might seem like pressing him.

'Kids nowadays,' Mrs King said. 'I just don't know.'

'Birched they should be,' Mr King said, coming into the cubbyhole and picking up a mug of the milky tea. 'I'd birch the bottoms off them.'

Someone arrived in the shop, Mr King hastened from the cubbyhole. 'What can I entice you to, sir?' Mrs Malby heard him politely enquiring and the voice of the teacher who'd been to see her replied. He said who he was and Mr King wasn't polite any more. An experience like that, Mr King declared thunderously, could have killed an eighty-seven-year-old stone dead.

Mrs Malby stood up and Mrs King came promptly forward

to place a hand under her elbow. They went into the shop like that. 'Three and a half p,' Mr King was saying to a woman who'd asked the price of oranges. 'The larger ones at four.'

Mr King gave the woman four of the smaller size and accepted her money. He called out to a youth who was passing by on a bicycle, about to start an afternoon paper round. He was a youth who occasionally assisted him on Saturday mornings: Mr King asked him now if he would mind the shop for ten minutes since an emergency had arisen. Just for once, Mr King argued, it wouldn't matter if the evening papers were a little late.

'Well, you can't say they haven't brightened the place up, Mrs Malby,' the teacher said in her kitchen. He regarded her from beneath his grey fringe. He touched one of the walls with the tip of a finger. He nodded to himself, appearing to be satisfied.

The painting had been completed, the yellow and the dark-blue gloss. Where the colours met there were untidily jagged lines. All the paint that had been spilt on the floor had been wiped away, but the black-and-white vinyl had become dull and grubby in the process. The paint had also been wiped from the windows and from other surfaces, leaving them smeared. The dresser had been wiped down and was smeary also. The cutlery and the taps and the cups and saucers had all been washed or wiped.

'Well, you wouldn't believe it!' Mrs King exclaimed. She turned to her husband. However had he managed it all? she asked him. 'You should have seen the place!' she said to the teacher.

'It's just the carpets,' Mr King said. He led the way from the kitchen to the sitting-room, pointing at the yellow on the landing carpet and on the sitting-room one. 'The blooming stuff dried,' he explained, 'before we could get to it. That's where compensation comes in.' He spoke sternly, addressing the teacher. 'I'd say she has a bob or two owing.'

Mrs King nudged Mrs Malby, drawing attention to the fact that Mr King was doing his best for her. The nudge suggested that all would be well because a sum of money would be paid, possibly even a larger sum than was merited. It suggested also that Mrs Malby in the end might find herself doing rather well.

'Compensation?' the teacher said, bending down and scratching at the paint on the sitting-room carpet. 'I'm afraid compensation's out of the question.'

'She's had her carpets ruined,' Mr King snapped quickly. 'This woman's been put about, you know.'

'She got her kitchen done free,' the teacher snapped back at him.

'They released her pets. They got up to tricks in a bed. You'd no damn right – '

'These kids come from broken homes, sir. I'll do my best with your carpets, Mrs Malby.'

'But what about my kitchen?' she whispered. She cleared her throat because her whispering could hardly be heard. 'My kitchen?' she whispered again.

'What about it, Mrs Malby?'

'I didn't want it painted.'

'Oh, don't be silly now.'

The teacher took his jacket off and threw it impatiently on to a chair. He left the sitting-room. Mrs Malby heard him running a tap in the kitchen.

'It was best to finish the painting, Mrs Malby,' Mr King said. 'Otherwise the kitchen would have driven you mad, half done like that. I stood over them till they finished it.'

'You can't take paint off, dear,' Mrs King said, 'once it's on. You've done wonders, Leo,' she said to her husband. 'Young devils.'

'We'd best be getting back,' Mr King said.

'It's quite nice, you know,' his wife added. 'Your kitchen's quite cheerful, dear.'

The Kings went away and the teacher rubbed at the yellow on the carpets with her washing-up brush. The landing carpet was marked anyway, he pointed out, poking a finger at the stains left behind by the paint she'd removed herself with the sponge-cloth from the bathroom. She must be delighted with the kitchen, he said.

She knew she mustn't speak. She'd known she mustn't when the Kings had been there; she knew she mustn't now. She might have reminded the Kings that she'd chosen the original colours in the kitchen herself. She might have complained to the man as he rubbed at her carpets that the carpets would never be the same again. She watched him, not saying anything, not wishing to be regarded as a nuisance. The Kings would have considered her a nuisance too, agreeing to let children into her kitchen to paint it and then making a fuss. If she became a nuisance the teacher and the Kings would drift on to the same side, and the Reverend Bush would somehow be on that side also, and Miss Tingle, and even Mrs Grove and Mrs Halbert. They would agree among themselves that what had happened had to do with her elderliness, with her not understanding that children who brought paint into a kitchen were naturally going to use it.

'I defy anyone to notice that,' the teacher said, standing up, gesturing at the yellow blurs that remained on her carpets. He put his jacket on. He left the washing-up brush and the bowl of water he'd been using on the floor of her sitting-room. 'All's well that ends well,' he said. 'Thanks for your co-operation, Mrs Malby.'

She thought of her two sons, Eric and Roy, not knowing quite why she thought of them now. She descended the stairs with the teacher, who was cheerfully talking about

25

community relations. You had to make allowances, he said, for kids like that; you had to try and understand; you couldn't just walk away.

Quite suddenly she wanted to tell him about Eric and Roy. In the desire to talk about them she imagined their bodies, as she used to in the past, soon after they'd been killed. They lay on desert sand, desert birds swooped down on them. Their four eyes were gone. She wanted to explain to the teacher that they'd been happy, a contented family in Agnes Street, until the war came and smashed everything to pieces. Nothing had been the same afterwards. It hadn't been easy to continue with nothing to continue for. Each room in the house had contained different memories of the two boys growing up. Cooking and cleaning had seemed pointless. The shop which would have been theirs would have to pass to someone else.

And yet time had soothed the awful double wound. The horror of the emptiness had been lived with, and if having the Kings in the shop now wasn't the same as having your sons there at least the Kings were kind. Thirty-four years after the destruction of your family you were happy in your elderliness because time had been merciful. She wanted to tell the teacher that also, she didn't know why, except that in some way it seemed relevant. But she didn't tell him because it would have been difficult to begin, because in the effort there'd be the danger of seeming senile. Instead she said goodbye, concentrating on that. She said she was sorry, saying it just to show she was aware that she hadn't made herself clear to the children. Conversation had broken down between the children and herself, she wanted him to know she knew it had.

He nodded vaguely, not listening to her. He was trying to make the world a better place, he said. 'For kids like that, Mrs Malby. Victims of broken homes.'

Another Christmas

You always looked back, she thought. You looked back at other years, other Christmas cards arriving, the children younger. There was the year Patrick had cried, disliking the holly she was decorating the living-room with. There was the year Bridget had got a speck of coke in her eye on Christmas Eve and had to be taken to the hospital at Hammersmith in the middle of the night. There was the first year of their marriage, when she and Dermot were still in Waterford. And ever since they'd come to London there was the presence on Christmas Day of their landlord, Mr Joyce, a man whom they had watched becoming elderly.

She was middle-aged now, with touches of grey in her fluffy jet-black hair, a woman known for her cheerfulness, running a bit to fat. Her husband was the opposite: thin and seeming ascetic, with more than a hint of the priest in him, a good man. 'Will we get married, Norah?' he'd said one night in the Tara Ballroom in Waterford, November 6th, 1953. The proposal had astonished her: it was his brother Ned, bulky and fresh-faced, a different kettle of fish altogether, whom she'd been expecting to make it.

Patiently he held a chair for her while she strung paper-chains across the room, from one picture-rail to another. He warned her to be careful about attaching anything to the electric light. He still held the chair while she put sprigs of holly behind the pictures. He was cautious by nature and alarmed by little things, particularly anxious in case she fell off chairs. He'd never mount a chair himself, to put up decorations or anything else: he'd be useless at it in his opinion and it was his opinion that mattered. He'd never been able to do a thing about the house but it didn't matter because since the boys had grown up they'd attended to whatever she couldn't manage herself. You wouldn't dream of re-marking on it: he was the way he was, considerate and thoughtful in what he did do, teetotal, clever, full of fondness for herself and for the family they'd reared, full of respect for her also.

'Isn't it remarkable how quick it comes round, Norah?' he said while he held the chair. 'Isn't it no time since last year?'

'No time at all.'

'Though a lot happened in the year, Norah.'

'An awful lot happened.'

Two of the pictures she decorated were scenes of Water-ford: the quays and a man driving sheep past the Bank of Ireland. Her mother had given them to her, taking them down from the hall of the farm-house.

There was a picture of the Virgin and Child, and other, smaller pictures. She placed her last sprig of holly, a piece with berries on it, above the Virgin's halo.

'I'll make a cup of tea,' she said, descending from the chair and smiling at him.

'A cup of tea'd be great, Norah.'

The living-room, containing three brown armchairs and a table with upright chairs around it, and a sideboard with a television set on it, was crowded by this furniture and seemed even smaller than it was because of the decorations that had been added. On the mantelpiece, above a built-in gas fire, Christmas cards were arrayed on either side of an ornate green clock.

The house was in a terrace in Fulham. It had always been too small for the family, but now that Patrick and Brendan no longer lived there things were easier. Patrick had married a girl called Pearl six months ago, almost as soon as his period

28

of training with the Midland Bank had ended. Brendan was training in Liverpool, with a firm of computer manufacturers. The three remaining children were still at school, Bridget at the nearby convent, Cathal and Tom at the Sacred Heart Primary. When Patrick and Brendan had moved out the room they'd always shared had become Bridget's. Until then Bridget had slept in her parents' room and she'd have to return there this Christmas because Brendan would be back for three nights. Patrick and Pearl would just come for Christmas Day. They'd be going to Pearl's people, in Croydon, on Boxing Day – St Stephen's Day, as Norah and Dermot always called it, in the Irish manner.

'It'll be great, having them all,' he said. 'A family again, Norah.'

'And Pearl.'

'She's part of us now, Norah.'

'Will you have biscuits with your tea? I have a packet of Nice.'

He said he would, thanking her. He was a meter-reader with North Thames Gas, a position he had held for twenty-one years, ever since he'd emigrated. In Waterford he'd worked as a clerk in the Customs, not earning very much and not much caring for the stuffy, smoke-laden office he shared with half-a-dozen other clerks. He had come to England because Norah had thought it was a good idea, because she'd always wanted to work in a London shop. She'd been given a job in Dickins & Jones, in the household linens department, and he'd been taken on as a meter-reader, cycling from door to door, remembering the different houses and where the meters were situated in each, being agreeable to householders: all of it suited him from the start. He devoted time to thought while he rode about, and in particular to religious matters.

In her small kitchen she made the tea and carried it on a tray into the living-room. She'd been late this year with the decorations. She always liked to get them up a week in advance because they set the mood, making everyone feel right for Christmas. She'd been busy with stuff for a stall Father Malley had asked her to run for his Christmas Sale. A fashion stall he'd called it, but not quite knowing what he meant she'd just asked people for any old clothes they had, jumble really. Because of the time it had taken she hadn't had a minute to see to the decorations until this afternoon, two days before Christmas Eve. But that, as it turned out, had been all for the best. Bridget and Cathal and Tom had gone up to Putney to the pictures, Dermot didn't work on a Monday afternoon: it was convenient that they'd have an hour or two alone together because there was the matter of Mr Joyce to bring up. Not that she wanted to bring it up, but it couldn't be just left there.

'The cup that cheers,' he said, breaking a biscuit in half. Deliberately she put off raising the subject she had in mind. She watched him nibbling the biscuit and then dropping three heaped spoons of sugar into his tea and stirring it. He loved tea. The first time he'd taken her out, to the Savoy Cinema in Waterford, they'd had tea afterwards in the cinema café and they'd talked about the film and about people they knew. He'd come to live in Waterford from the country, from the farm his brother had inherited, quite close to her father's farm. He reckoned he'd settled, he told her that night: Waterford wasn't sensational, but it suited him in a lot of ways. If he hadn't married her he'd still be there, working eight hours a day in the Customs and not caring for it, yet managing to get by because he had his religion to assist him.

'Did we get a card from Father Jack yet?' he enquired, referring to a distant cousin, a priest in Chicago.

'Not yet. But it's always on the late side, Father Jack's. It was February last year.'

She sipped her tea, sitting in one of the other brown

armchairs, on the other side of the gas fire. It was pleasant being there alone with him in the decorated room, the green clock ticking on the mantelpiece, the Christmas cards, dusk gathering outside. She smiled and laughed, taking another biscuit while he lit a cigarette. 'Isn't this great?' she said. 'A bit of peace for ourselves?'

Solemnly he nodded.

"Peace comes dropping slow," he said, and she knew he was quoting from some book or other. Quite often he said things she didn't understand. 'Peace and goodwill,' he added, and she understood that all right.

He tapped the ash from his cigarette into an ashtray which was kept for his use, beside the gas fire. All his movements were slow. He was a slow thinker, even though he was clever. He arrived at a conclusion, having thought long and carefully; he balanced everything in his mind. 'We must think about that, Norah,' he said that day, twenty-two years ago, when she'd suggested that they should move to England. A week later he'd said that if she really wanted to he'd agree.

They talked about Bridget and Cathal and Tom. When they came in from the cinema they'd only just have time to change their clothes before setting out again for the Christmas party at Bridget's convent.

'It's a big day for them. Let them lie in in the morning, Norah.'

'They could lie in for ever,' she said, laughing in case there might seem to be harshness in this recommendation. With Christmas excitement running high, the less she heard from them the better.

'Did you get Cathal the gadgets he wanted?'

'Chemistry stuff. A set in a box.'

'You're great the way you manage, Norah.'

She denied that. She poured more tea for both of them. She said, as casually as she could:

'Mr Joyce won't come. I'm not counting him in for Christmas Day.'

'He hasn't failed us yet, Norah.'

'He won't come this year.' She smiled through the gloom at him. 'I think we'd best warn the children about it.'

'Where would he go if he didn't come here? Where'd he get his dinner?'

'Lyons used to be open in the old days.'

'He'd never do that.'

'The Bulrush Café has a turkey dinner advertised. There's a lot of people go in for that now. If you have a mother doing a job she maybe hasn't the time for the cooking. They go out to a hotel or a café, three or four pounds a head – '

'Mr Joyce wouldn't go to a café. No one could go into a café on their own on Christmas Day.'

'He won't come here, dear.'

It had to be said: it was no good just pretending, laying a place for the old man on an assumption that had no basis to it. Mr Joyce would not come because Mr Joyce, last August, had ceased to visit them. Every Friday night he used to come, for a cup of tea and a chat, to watch the nine o'clock news with them. Every Christmas Day he'd brought carefully chosen presents for the children, and chocolates and nuts and cigarettes. He'd given Patrick and Pearl a radio as a wedding present.

'I think he'll come all right. I think maybe he hasn't been too well. God help him, it's a great age, Norah.'

'He hasn't been ill, Dermot.'

Every Friday Mr Joyce had sat there in the third of the brown armchairs, watching the television, his bald head inclined so that his good ear was closer to the screen. He was tallish, rather bent now, frail and bony, with a modest white moustache. In his time he'd been a builder, which was how he had come to own property in Fulham, a self-made man

32

who'd never married. That evening in August he had been quite as usual. Bridget had kissed him good-night because for as long as she could remember she'd always done that when he came on Friday evenings. He'd asked Cathal how he was getting on with his afternoon paper round.

There had never been any difficulties over the house. They considered that he was fair in his dealings with them; they were his tenants and his friends. When the Irish bombed English people to death in Birmingham and Guildford he did not cease to arrive every Friday evening and on Christmas Day. The bombings were discussed after the News, the Tower of London bomb, the bomb in the bus, and all the others. 'Maniacs,' Mr Joyce said and nobody contradicted him.

'He would never forget the children, Norah. Not at Christmastime.'

His voice addressed her from the shadows. She felt the warmth of the gas fire reflected in her face and knew if she looked in a mirror she'd see that she was quite flushed. Dermot's face never reddened. Even though he was nervy, he never displayed emotion. On all occasions his face retained its paleness, his eyes acquired no glimmer of passion. No wife could have a better husband, yet in the matter of Mr Joyce he was so wrong it almost frightened her.

'Is it tomorrow I call in for the turkey?' he said.

She nodded, hoping he'd ask her if anything was the matter because as a rule she never just nodded in reply to a question. But he didn't say anything. He stubbed his cigarette out. He asked if there was another cup of tea in the pot.

'Dermot, would you take something round to Mr Joyce?'
'A message, is it?'
'I have a tartan tie for him.'
'Wouldn't you give it to him on the day, Norah? Like you always do.' He spoke softly, still insisting. She shook her head.

It was all her fault. If she hadn't said they should go to England, if she hadn't wanted to work in a London shop, they wouldn't be caught in the trap they'd made for themselves. Their children spoke with London accents. Patrick and Brendan worked for English firms and would make their homes in England. Patrick had married an English girl. They were Catholics and they had Irish names, yet home for them was not Waterford.

'Could you make it up with Mr Joyce, Dermot? Could you go round with the tie and say you were sorry?'

'Sorry?'

'You know what I mean.' In spite of herself her voice had acquired a trace of impatience, an edginess that was unusual in it. She did not ever speak to him like that. It was the way she occasionally spoke to the children.

'What would I say I was sorry for, Norah?'

'For what you said that night.' She smiled, calming her agitation. He lit another cigarette, the flame of the match briefly illuminating his face. Nothing had changed in his face. He said:

'I don't think Mr Joyce and I had any disagreement, Norah.'

'I know, Dermot. You didn't mean anything – '

'There was no disagreement, girl.'

There had been no disagreement, but on that evening in August something else had happened. On the nine o'clock news there had been a report of another outrage and afterwards, when Dermot had turned the television off, there'd been the familiar comment on it. He couldn't understand the mentality of people like that, Mr Joyce said yet again, killing just anyone, destroying life for no reason. Dermot had shaken his head over it, she herself had said it was uncivilised. Then Dermot had added that they mustn't of course forget what the Catholics in the North had suffered. The bombs

34

were a crime but it didn't do to forget that the crime would not be there if generations of Catholics in the North had not been treated as animals. There'd been a silence then, a difficult kind of silence which she'd broken herself. All that was in the past, she'd said hastily, in a rush, nothing in the past or the present or anywhere else could justify the killing of innocent people. Even so, Dermot had added, it didn't do to avoid the truth. Mr Joyce had not said anything.

'I'd say there was no need to go round with the tie, Norah. I'd say he'd make the effort on Christmas Day.'

'Of course he won't.' Her voice was raised, with more than impatience in it now. But her anger was controlled. 'Of course he won't come.'

'It's a time for goodwill, Norah. Another Christmas: to remind us.'

He spoke slowly, the words prompted by some interpretation of God's voice in answer to a prayer. She recognised that in his deliberate tone.

'It isn't just another Christmas. It's an awful kind of Christmas. It's a Christmas to be ashamed, and you're making it worse, Dermot.' Her lips were trembling in a way that was uncomfortable. If she tried to calm herself she'd become jittery instead, she might even begin to cry. Mr Joyce had been generous and tactful, she said loudly. It made no difference to Mr Joyce that they were Irish people, that their children went to school with the children of I.R.A. men. Yet his generosity and his tact had been thrown back in his face. Everyone knew that the Catholics in the North had suffered, that generations of injustice had been twisted into the shape of a cause. But you couldn't say it to an old man who had hardly been outside Fulham in his life. You couldn't say it because when you did it sounded like an excuse for murder.

'You have to state the truth, Norah. It's there to be told.'

'I never yet cared for a North of Ireland person, Catholic or Protestant. Let them fight it out and not bother us.'

'You shouldn't say that, Norah.'

'It's more of your truth for you.'

He didn't reply. There was the gleam of his face for a moment as he drew on his cigarette. In all their married life they had never had a quarrel that was in any way serious, yet she felt herself now in the presence of a seriousness that was too much for her. She had told him that whenever a new bombing took place she prayed it might be the work of the Angry Brigade, or any group that wasn't Irish. She'd told him that in shops she'd begun to feel embarrassed because of her Waterford accent. He'd said she must have courage, and she realised now that he had drawn on courage himself when he'd made the remark to Mr Joyce. He would have prayed and considered before making it. He would have seen it in the end as his Catholic duty.

'He thinks you don't condemn people being killed.' She spoke quietly even though she felt a wildness inside her. She felt she should be out on the streets, shouting in her Waterford accent, violently stating that the bombers were more despicable with every breath they drew, that hatred and death were all they deserved. She saw herself on Fulham Broadway, haranguing the passers-by, her greying hair blown in the wind, her voice more passionate than it had ever been before. But none of it was the kind of thing she could do because she was not that kind of woman. She hadn't the courage, any more than she had the courage to urge her anger to explode in their living-room. For all the years of her marriage there had never been the need of such courage before: she was aware of that, but found no consolation in it.

'I think he's maybe seen it by now,' he said. 'How one thing leads to another.'

She felt insulted by the words. She willed herself the

strength to shout, to pour out a torrent of fury at him, but the strength did not come. Standing up, she stumbled in the gloom and felt a piece of holly under the sole of her shoe. She turned the light on.

'I'll pray that Mr Joyce will come,' he said.

She looked at him, pale and thin, with his priestly face. For the first time since he had asked her to marry him in the Tara Ballroom she did not love him. He was cleverer than she was, yet he seemed half blind. He was good, yet he seemed hard in his goodness, as though he'd be better without it. Up to the very last moment on Christmas Day there would be the pretence that their landlord might arrive, that God would answer a prayer because His truth had been honoured. She considered it hypocrisy, unable to help herself in that opinion.

He talked but she did not listen. He spoke of keeping faith with their own, of being a Catholic. Crime begot crime, he said, God wanted it to be known that one evil led to another. She continued to look at him while he spoke, pretending to listen but wondering instead if in twelve months' time, when another Christmas came, he would still be cycling from house to house to read gas meters. Or would people have objected, requesting a meter-reader who was not Irish? An objection to a man with an Irish accent was down-to-earth and ordinary. It didn't belong in the same grand category as crime begetting crime or God wanting something to be known, or in the category of truth and conscience. In the present circumstances the objection would be understandable and fair. It seemed even right that it should be made, for it was a man with an Irish accent in whom the worst had been brought out by the troubles that had come, who was guilty of a cruelty no one would have believed him capable of. Their harmless elderly landlord might die in the course of that same year, a friendship he had valued lost, his last Christmas lonely. Grand though it might seem in one way, all of it was petty.

Once, as a girl, she might have cried, but her contented marriage had caused her to lose that habit. She cleared up the tea things, reflecting that the bombers would be pleased if they could note the victory they'd scored in a living-room in Fulham. And on Christmas Day, when a family sat down to a conventional meal, the victory would be greater. There would be crackers and chatter and excitement, the Queen and the Pope would deliver speeches. Dermot would discuss these Christmas messages with Patrick and Brendan, as he'd discussed them in the past with Mr Joyce. He would be as kind as ever. He would console Bridget and Cathal and Tom by saying that Mr Joyce hadn't been up to the journey. And whenever she looked at him she would remember the Christmases of the past. She would feel ashamed of him, and of herself.

Matilda's England

1. The Tennis Court

Old Mrs Ashburton used to drive about the lanes in a governess cart drawn by a donkey she called Trot. We often met her as we cycled home from school, when my brother and my sister were at the Grammar School and I was still at Miss Pritchard's Primary. Of the three of us I was Mrs Ashburton's favourite, and I don't know why that was except that I was the youngest. 'Hullo, my Matilda,' Mrs Ashburton would whisper in her throaty, crazy-sounding way. 'Matilda,' she'd repeat, lingering over the name I so disliked, drawing each syllable away from the next. 'Dear Matilda.' She was excessively thin, rather tall, and frail-looking. We made allowances for her because she was eighty-one.

Usually when we met her she was looking for wild flowers, or if it was winter or autumn just sitting in her governess cart in some farmer's gateway, letting the donkey graze the farmer's grass. In spring she used to root out plants from the hedges with a little trowel. Most of them were weeds, my brother said; and looking back on it now, I realise that it wasn't for wild flowers, or weeds, or grazing for her donkey that she drove about the lanes. It was in order to meet us cycling back from school.

'There's a tennis court at Challacombe Manor,' she said one day in May, 1939. 'Any time you ever wanted to play, Dick.' She stared at my brother with piercing black eyes that were the colour of quality coal. She was eccentric, standing there in a long, very old and bald fur coat, stroking the ears of her donkey while he nibbled a hedge. Her hat was attached to her grey hair by a number of brass hat-pins. The hat was of

41

faded green felt, the hat-pins had quite large knobs at the ends of them, inlaid with pieces of green glass. Green, Mrs Ashburton often remarked, was her favourite colour, and she used to remove these hat-pins to show us the glass additions, emphasising that they were valueless. Her bald fur coat was valueless also, she assured us, and not even in its heyday would it have fetched more than five pounds. In the same manner she remarked upon her summer hats and dresses, and her shoes, and the governess cart, and the donkey.

'I mean, Dick,' she said that day in 1939, 'it's not much of a tennis court, but it was once, of course. And there's a net stacked away in one of the out-houses. And a roller, and a marker. There's a lawnmower, too, because naturally you'll need that.'

'You mean, we could play on your court, Mrs Ashburton?' my sister Betty said.

'Of course I mean that, my dear. That's just what I mean. You know, before the war we really did have marvellous tennis parties at Challacombe. Everyone came.'

'Oh, how lovely!' Betty was fourteen and Dick was a year older, and I was nine. Betty was fair-haired like the rest of us, but much prettier than me. She had very blue eyes and a wide smiling mouth that boys at the Grammar School were always trying to kiss, and a small nose, and freckles. Her hair was smooth and long, the colour of hay. It looked quite start-ling sometimes, shining in the sunlight. I used to feel proud of Betty and Dick when they came to collect me every afternoon at the Primary School. Dick was to leave the Grammar School in July, and on the afternoons of that warm May, as Betty and I cycled home with him, we felt sorry that he wouldn't be there next term. But Dick said he was glad. He was big, as tall as my father, and very shy. He'd begun to smoke, a habit not approved of by my father. On the way home from school we had to stop and go into a ruined cottage so that he could have a Woodbine. He was going to work on the farm; one day the farm would be his.

'It would be lovely to play tennis,' Betty said.

'Then you must, my dear. But if you want to play this summer you'll have to get the court into trim.' Mrs Ashburton smiled at Betty in a way that made her thin, elderly face seem beautiful. Then she smiled at Dick. 'I was passing the tennis court the other day, Dick, and I suddenly thought of it. Now why shouldn't those children get it into trim? I thought. Why shouldn't they come and play, and bring their friends?'

'Yes,' Dick said.

'Why ever don't you come over to Challacombe on Saturday? Matilda, too, of course. Come for tea, all three of you.'

Mrs Ashburton smiled at each of us in turn. She nodded at us and climbed into the governess cart. 'Saturday,' she repeated.

'Honestly, Betty!' Dick glared crossly at my sister, as though she were responsible for the invitation. 'I'm not going, you know.'

He cycled off, along the narrow, dusty lane, big and red-faced and muttering. We followed him more slowly, talking about Mrs Ashburton. 'Poor old thing!' Betty said, which was what people round about often said when Mrs Ashburton was mentioned, or when she was seen in her governess cart.

*

The first thing I remember in all my life was my father breaking a fountain-pen. It was a large black-and-white pen, like tortoiseshell or marble. That was the fashion for fountain-pens then: two or three colours marbled together, green and black, blue and white, red and black-and-white. Conway

43

Stewart, Waterman's, Blackbird. Propelling pencils were called Eversharp.

The day my father broke his pen I didn't know all that: I learnt it afterwards at Miss Pritchard's Primary. I was three the day he broke the pen. 'It's just a waste of blooming money!' he shouted. He smashed the pen across his knee while my mother anxiously watched. Waste of money or not, she said, it wouldn't help matters to break the thing. She fetched him the ink and a dip-pen from a drawer of the dresser. He was still angry, but after a minute or two he began to laugh. He kissed my mother, pulling her down on to the knee he'd broken the pen over. Dick, who must have been nine then, didn't even look up from his homework. Betty was there too, but I can't remember what she was doing.

The kitchen hasn't changed much. The old range has gone, but the big light-oak dresser is still there, with the same brass handles on its doors and drawers and the same Wedgwood-blue dinner-set on its shelves, and cups and jugs hanging on hooks. The ceiling is low, the kitchen itself large and rectangular, with the back stairs rising from the far end of it, and a door at the bottom of them. There are doors to the pantry and the scullery, and to the passage that leads to the rest of the house, and to the yard. There's a long narrow light-oak table, with brass handles on its drawers, like the dresser ones, and oak chairs that aren't as light as all the other oak because chairs darken with use. But the table isn't scrubbed once a week any more, and the brass does't gleam. I know, because now and again I visit the farm-house.

I remember the kitchen with oil-lamps, and the time, the day after my fifth birthday, when the men came to wire the house for electricity. My mother used to talk about an Aga, and often when she took us shopping with her she'd bring us to Archers', the builders' merchants, to look at big cream-coloured Agas. After a time, Mr Gray of the

Aga department didn't even bother to bustle up to her when he saw her coming. She'd stand there, plump and pink-cheeked, her reddish hair neat beneath the brim of her hat, touching the display models, opening the oven doors and lifting up the two big hot-plate covers. When we returned to the farm-house my father would tease her, knowing she'd been to Archers' again. She'd blush, cutting ham at tea-time or offering round salad. My father would then forget about it. 'Well, I'm damned,' he'd say, and he'd read out an item from the weekly paper, about some neighbouring farmer or new County Council plans. My mother would listen and then both of them would nod. They were very good friends, even though my father teased her. She blushed like a rose, he said: he teased her to see it.

Once, before the electricity came, I had a nightmare. It was probably only a few months before, because when I came crying down to the kitchen my father kept comforting me with the reminder that it would soon be my fifth birthday. 'You'll never cry then, Matilda,' he whispered to me, cuddling me to him. 'Big girls of five don't cry.' I fell asleep, but it's not that that I remember now, not the fear from the nightmare going away, or the tears stopping, or my father's caressing: it's the image of my parents in the kitchen as I stumbled down the back stairs. There were two oil-lamps lit and the fire in the range was glowing red-hot behind its curved bars, and the heavy black kettle wasn't quite singing. My father was asleep with last Saturday's weekly paper on his knees, my mother was reading one of the books from the bookcase in the dining-room we never used, probably *The Garden of Allah*, which was her favourite. The two sheepdogs were asleep under the table, and when I opened the door at the top of the stairs they both barked because they knew that at that particular time no one should be opening that door. 'Oh, now, now,' my mother said, coming to me, listening to me when I said that there were cows on my bedroom wall. I remember the image of the two of them because they looked so happy sitting there, even though my mother hadn't got her Aga, even though my father was sometimes worried about the farm.

Looking back on it now, there was a lot of happiness, although perhaps not more than many families experience. Everything seems either dismal or happy in retrospect, and the happiness in the farm-house is what I think of first whenever I think now of that particular past. I remember my mother baking in the kitchen, flour all over her plump arms, and tiny beads of sweat on her forehead, because the kitchen was always hot. I remember my father's leathery skin and his smile, and the way he used to shout at the sheepdogs, and the men, Joe and Arthur, sitting on yellow stubble, drinking tea out of a bottle, on a day hay had been cut.

Our farm had once been the home-farm of Challacombe Manor, even though our farm-house was two miles away from the manor house. There'd been servants and gardeners at Challacombe Manor then, and horses in the stables, and carriages coming and going. But the estate had fallen into rack and ruin after the First World War because Mr Ashburton hadn't been able to keep it going and in the end, in 1924, he'd taken out various mortgages. When he died, in 1929, the extent of his debts was so great that Mrs Ashburton had been obliged to let Lloyd's Bank foreclose on the mortgages, which is how it came about that my father bought Challacombe Farm. It was a tragedy, people round about used to say, and the real tragedy was that Mr Ashburton had come back from the war in such a strange state that he hadn't minded about everywhere falling into rack and ruin. According to my father, Lloyd's Bank owned Callacombe Manor itself and had granted Mrs Ashburton permission to live there in her lifetime. It wouldn't surprise him, my father said, if it turned out that Lloyd's Bank owned Mrs Ashburton as well. 'He drank himself to death,' people used to say about Mr Ashburton. 'She watched him and didn't have the heart to stop him.' Yet before the First World War Mr Ashburton had been a different kind of man, energetic and sharp. The Challacombe estate had been a showpiece.

To me in particular Mrs Ashburton talked about her husband. She was lucky that he'd come back from the war, even if he hadn't been able to manage very well. His mind had been affected, she explained, but that was better than being dead. She told me about the men who'd died, gardeners at Challacombe Manor, and farm workers on the estate, and men she and her husband had known in the town. 'I thanked God,' Mrs Ashburton said, 'when he came safely back here all in one piece. Everything fell to bits around us, but it didn't matter because at least he was still alive. You understand, Matilda?'

I always nodded, although I didn't really understand. And then she'd go on about the estate as it had been, and then about her husband and the conversations they used to have. Sometimes she didn't address me directly. She smiled and just talked, always returning to the men who had been killed and how lucky she was that her husband had at least come back. She'd prayed, she said, that he'd come back, and every time another man from the estate or from the neighbourhood had been reported dead she'd felt that there was a better chance that her husband wouldn't die also. 'By the law of averages,' she explained, 'some had to come back. Some men have always come back from wars, you convince yourself.'

At this point I would always nod again, and Mrs Ashburton would say that looking back on it now she felt ashamed that she had ever applied the law of averages to the survival or death of men. Doing so was as horrible as war itself: the women who were left at home became cruel in their fear and their selfishness. Cruelty was natural in war, Mrs Ashburton said.

At the time she'd hated the Germans and she was ashamed of that too, because the Germans were just people like other people. But when she talked about them the remains of the hatred were still in her voice, and I imagined the Germans from what she told me about them: people who ate black bread and didn't laugh much, who ate raw bacon, who were dour, grey and steely. She described the helmets they wore in wartime. She told me what a bayonet was, and I used to feel sick when I thought of one going into a man's stomach and being twisted in there to make sure the man would die. She told me about poison gas, and the trenches, and soldiers being buried alive. The way she spoke I knew she was repeating, word for word, the things her husband had told her, things that had maybe been the cause of his affected mind. Even her voice sounded unusual when she talked about the war, as though she was trying to imitate her husband's voice, and the terror that had been in it. He used to cry, she said, as he walked about the gardens, unable to stop the tears once they'd begun.

Dick didn't say anything while we rode the two miles over to Challacombe Manor that Saturday. He didn't even say anything when he suddenly dismounted and leaned his bicycle against a black gate, and climbed over the gate to have a smoke behind the hedge. If my father had come by he'd have known what was happening because he would have seen Betty and myself waiting in the lane, surrounded by the cloud of smoke that Dick always managed to make with his Woodbine. Our job was to warn him if we saw my father coming, but my father didn't come that afternoon and when Dick had finished we continued on our way.

We'd often been to tea at Challacombe Manor before. Mrs Ashburton said we were the only visitors she had because most of her friends were dead, which was something that happened, she explained, if you were eighty-one. We always had tea in the kitchen, a huge room that smelt of oil, with armchairs in it and a wireless, and an oil-stove on which Mrs Ashburton cooked, not wishing to have to keep the range going. There were oatcakes for tea, and buttered white and brown bread, and pots of jam that Mrs Ashburton bought in the town, and a cake she bought also, usually a fruitcake. Afterwards we'd walk through the house with her, while she pointed out the places where the roof had given way, and the dry rot, and windows that were broken. She hadn't lived in most of the house since the war, and had lived in even less of it since her husband had died in 1929. We knew these details by heart because she'd told us so many times. In one of the out-houses there was an old motor-car with flat tyres, and the gardens were now all overgrown with grass and weeds. Rhododendrons were choked, and buddleia and kerria and hydrangeas.

The house was grey and square with two small wings, a stone Georgian house with wide stone steps leading to a front door that had pillars on either side of it and a fan-light above it. The gravel expanse in front of it was grassy now, and slippery in wet weather because of moss that had accumulated. French windows opened on to it on either side of the hall-door, from the rooms that had been the drawing-room and the dining-room. Lawns stretched around the house, with grass like a meadow on them now. The tennis court, which we'd never known about until Mrs Ashburton mentioned it, was hidden away, beyond the jungle of shrubbery.

'You see?' she said. 'You see, Dick?' She was wearing a long, old-fashioned dress and a wide-brimmed white hat, and sunglasses because the afternoon was fiercely bright.

The grass on the tennis court was a yard high, as high as the rusty iron posts that were there to support the net. 'Look,' Mrs Ashburton said.

She led us to the stable-yard, past the out-house where the motor-car was, and into a smaller out-house. There was a lawnmower there, as rusty as the tennis posts, and a marker in the same condition, and an iron roller. Tucked into the beams above our heads was a rolled-up tennis net. 'He adored tennis,' she said. 'He really loved it.'

She turned and we followed her across the stable-yard, into the kitchen by the back door. She talked about her husband while she made tea.

We ate the bought fruitcake, listening to her. We'd heard it all before, but we always considered it was worth it because of the cake and the biscuits and the buttered bread and the pots of jam. And always before we left she gave us ginger beer and pieces of chocolate broken up on a saucer. She told us about the child which might have been born to her husband and herself, six months after the beginning of the war, but which had miscarried. 'Everything went wrong,' she said. She told us about the parties there'd been at Challacombe Manor. Champagne and strawberries and cream, and parties with games that she described, and fancy dress.

'No reason at all,' she said, 'why we shouldn't have a tennis party.'

Dick made a sighing sound, a soft, slight noise that Mrs Ashburton didn't hear.

'Tennis party?' Betty murmured.

'No reason, dear.'

That morning Dick and Betty had had an argument. Betty had said that of course he must go to tea with Mrs Ashburton, since he'd always gone in the past. And Dick had said that Mrs Ashburton had been cunning: all these years, he said, she'd been inviting us to tea so that when the time was ripe she could get us to clean up her old tennis court. 'Oh, don't be silly!' Betty had cried, and then had said that it would be the cruellest thing that Dick had ever done if he didn't go to tea with an old woman just because she'd mentioned her tennis court. I'd been cross with Dick myself, and none of us felt very happy because the matter of the tennis court had unattractively brought into the open the motive behind our putting up with Mrs Ashburton. I didn't like it when she called me her Matilda and put her arms around me, and said she was sure her child would have been a little girl, and that she was almost as sure that she'd have called her Matilda. I didn't like it when she went on and on about the war and her husband coming back a wreck, or about the champagne and the strawberries and cream. 'Poor Mrs Ashburton!' we'd always said, but it wasn't because she was poor Mrs Ashburton that we'd filled the emptiness of Saturday afternoons by cycling over to Challacombe Manor.

'Shall we go and have another look at it?' she said when we'd eaten all the food that was on the table. She smiled in her frail, almost beautiful way, and for a moment I wondered if Dick wasn't perhaps right about her cunning. She led the way back to the overgrown tennis court and we all four stood looking at it.

'It's quite all right to smoke, Dick,' Mrs Ashburton said, 'if you want to.'

Dick laughed because he didn't know how else to react. He'd gone as red as a sunset. He kicked at the rusty iron tennis post, and then as casually as he could he took a packet of squashed Woodbines from his pocket and began to fiddle with a box of matches. Betty poked him with her elbow, suggesting that he should offer Mrs Ashburton a cigarette.

'Would you like one, Mrs Ashburton?' Dick said, proffering the squashed packet.

'Well, you know, I think I would, Dick.' She laughed and took the cigarette, saying she hadn't smoked a cigarette since 1915. Dick lit it for her. Some of the matches fell from the matchbox on the the long grass. He picked them up and replaced them, his own cigarette cocked out of the corner of his mouth. They looked rather funny, the two of them, Mrs Ashburton in her big white hat and sunglasses.

'You'd need a scythe,' Dick said.

*

That was the beginning of the tennis party. When Dick walked over the next Saturday with a scythe, Mrs Ashburton had a packet of twenty Craven A waiting for him. He scythed the grass and got the old hand-mower going. The stubble was coarse and by the time he'd cut it short there were quite large patches of naked earth, but Betty and Mrs Ashburton said they didn't matter. The court would do as it was for this summer, but in the spring, Dick said, he'd put down fresh grass-seed. It rained heavily a fortnight later, which was fortunate, because Dick was able to even out some of the bumps with the roller. Betty helped him, and later on she helped him mark the court out. Mrs Ashburton and I watched, Mrs Ashburton holding my hand and often seeming to imagine that I was the child which hadn't been born to her.

We took to going to Challacombe Manor on Sunday mornings as well as Saturdays. There were always packets of Craven A, and ginger beer and pieces of chocolate. 'Of course, it's not her property,' my father said whenever anyone mentioned the tennis court, or the net that Mrs Ashburton had found rolled up in an out-house. At dinnertime on Sundays, when we all sat around the long table in the kitchen, my father would ask Dick how he'd got on with the court. He'd then point out that the tennis court and everything that went with it was the property of Lloyd's Bank. Every Sunday dinnertime we had the same: roast beef and roast potatoes and

Yorkshire pudding, and carrots or brussels sprouts according to the seasonal variation, and apple-pie and cream.

Dick didn't ever say much when my father asked him about the tennis court. 'You want to be careful, lad,' my father used to say, squashing roast potatoes into gravy. 'Lloyd's is strict, you know.' My father would go on for ages, talking about Lloyd's Bank or the Aga cooker my mother wanted, and you never quite knew whether he was being serious or not. He would sit there with his jacket on the back of his chair, not smiling as he ate and talked. Farmers were like that, my mother once told Betty when Betty was upset by him. Farmers were cautious and watchful and canny. He didn't at all disapprove of what Betty and Dick and Mrs Ashburton were doing with the tennis court, my mother explained, rather the opposite; but he was right when he reminded them that everything, including the house itself, was the property of Lloyd's Bank.

Mrs Ashburton found six tennis racquets in presses, which were doubtless the property of Lloyd's Bank also. Dick examined them and said they weren't too bad. They had an antiquated look, and the varnish had worn off the frames, but only two of them had broken strings. Even those two, so Dick said, could be played with. He and Mrs Ashburton handed the racquets to one another, blowing at the dust that had accumulated on the presses and the strings. They lit up Craven A cigarettes, and Mrs Ashburton insisted on giving Dick ten shillings to buy tennis balls with.

I sat with Mrs Ashburton watching Dick and Betty playing their first game on the court. The balls bounced in a peculiar way because in spite of all the rolling there were still hollows and bumps on the surface. The grass wasn't green. It was a brownish yellow, except for the bare patches, which were ochre-coloured. Mrs Ashburton clapped every time there was a rally, and when Dick had beaten Betty 6-1, 6-4, he taught me how to hit the ball over the net, and how to volley it and keep it going. 'Marvellous, Matilda!' Mrs Ashburton cried, in her throaty voice, applauding again. 'Marvellous!'

We played all that summer, every Saturday and Sunday until the end of term, and almost every evening when the holidays came. We had to play in the evenings because at the end of term Dick began to work on the farm. 'Smoke your cigarettes if you want to,' my father said the first morning of the holidays, at breakfast. 'No point in hiding it, boy.' Friends of Dick's and Betty's used to come to Challacombe Manor to play also, because that was what Mrs Ashburton wanted: Colin Gregg and Barbara Hosell and Peggy Goss and Simon Turner and Willie Beach.

Sometimes friends of mine came, and I'd show them how to do it, standing close to the net, holding the racquet handle in the middle of the shaft. Thursday, August 31st, was the day Mrs Ashburton set for the tennis party: Thursday because it was half-day in the town.

Looking back on it now, it really does seem that for years and years she'd been working towards her tennis party. She'd hung about the lanes in her governess cart waiting for us because we were the children from the farm, the nearest children to Challacombe Manor. And when Dick looked big and strong enough and Betty of an age to be interested, she'd made her bid, easing matters along with fruitcake and Craven A. I can imagine her now, on her own in that ruin of a house, watching the grass grow on her tennis court and watching Dick and Betty growing up and dreaming of one more tennis party at Challacombe, a party like there used to be before her husband was affected in the head by the Kaiser's War.

'August 31st,' Betty reminded my parents one Sunday at dinnertime. 'You'll both come,' she said fiercely, blushing when they laughed at her.

'I hear Lloyd's is on the rampage,' my father said laboriously. 'Short of funds. Calling everything in.'

Dick and Betty didn't say anything. They ate their roast beef, pretending to concentrate on it.

'Course they're not,' my mother said.

'They'll sell Challacombe to some building fellow, now that it's all improved with tennis courts.'

'Daddy, don't be silly,' Betty said, blushing even more. All three of us used to blush. We got it from my mother. If my father blushed you wouldn't notice.

'True as I'm sitting here, my dear. Nothing like tennis courts for adding a bit of style to a place.'

Neither my mother nor my father had ever seen the tennis court. My father wouldn't have considered it the thing, to go walking over to Challacombe Manor to examine a tennis court. My mother was always busy, cooking and polishing brass. Neither my father nor my mother knew the rules of tennis. When we first began to play Betty used to draw a tennis court on a piece of paper and explain.

'Of course we'll come to the tennis party,' my mother said quietly. 'Of course, Betty.'

In the middle of the tennis party, my father persisted, a man in a hard black hat from Lloyd's Bank would walk on to the court and tell everyone to go home.

'Oh, Giles, don't be silly now,' my mother said quite sharply, and added that there was such a thing as going on too much. My father laughed and winked at her.

*

Mrs Ashburton asked everyone she could think of to the tennis party, people from the farms round about and shop-keepers from the town. Dick and Betty asked their friends and their friends' parents, and I asked Belle Frye and the Gorrys and the Seatons. My mother and Betty made meringues and brandy-snaps and fruitcakes and Victoria sponge cakes and scones and buns and shortbread. They made sardine sandwiches and tomato sandwiches and egg sandwiches and ham sandwiches. I buttered the bread and whipped up cream and wrapped the plates of sandwiches in damp tea-cloths. Dick cleared a place in the shrubbery beside the tennis court and built a fire to boil kettles on. Milk was poured into bottles and left to keep cool in the larder. August 31st was a fine, hot day.

At dinnertime my father pretended that the truck which was to convey all the food, and all of us too, to the tennis court had a broken carburettor. He and Joe had been working on it all morning, he said, but utterly without success. No one took any notice of him.

I remember, most of all, what they looked like. Mrs Ashburton thin as a rake in a long white dress and her wide-brimmed white hat and her sunglasses. My father in his Sunday clothes, a dark blue suit, his hair combed and his leathery brown face shining because he had shaved it and washed it specially. My mother had powder on her cheeks and her nose, and a touch of lipstick on her lips, although she didn't usually wear lipstick and must have borrowed Betty's. She was wearing a pale blue dress speckled with tiny white flowers. She'd spent a fortnight making it herself, for the occasion. Her reddish hair was soft and a little unruly, being freshly washed. My father was awkward in his Sunday suit, as he always was in it. His freckled hands lolled uneasily by his sides, or awkwardly held tea things, cup and saucer and plate. My mother blushed beneath her powder, and sometimes stammered, which she did when she was nervous.

Betty was beautiful that afternoon, in a white tennis dress that my mother had made her. Dick wore long white flannels that he'd been given by old Mr Bowe, a solicitor in the town who'd been to other tennis parties at Challacombe Manor but had no further use for white flannel trousers, being seventy-two now and too large for the trousers he'd kept for more than fifty years. My mother had made me a tennis dress, too, but I felt shy that day and didn't want to do anything except hand round plates of meringues and cake. I certainly didn't want to play, for the tennis was serious: mixed doubles, Betty and Colin Gregg against Dick and Peggy Goss, and Simon Turner and Edie Turner against Barbara Hosell and Willie Beach.

People were there whom my father said he hadn't seen for years, people who had no intention of playing tennis, any more than he had. Between them, Dick and Betty and Mrs Ashburton had cast a wide net, and my father's protests at the mounds of food that had been prepared met with their answer as car after car drew up, and dog-carts and pony-and-traps. Belle Frye and I passed around the plates of meringues, and people broke off in their conversations to ask us who we were. Mrs Ashburton had spread rugs on the grass around the court, and four white ornamental seats had been re-painted by Dick the week before. 'Just like the old days,' a man called Mr Race said, a corn merchant from the town. My mother nervously fidgeted, and I could feel her thinking that perhaps my father's laborious joke would come true, that any moment now the man from Lloyd's Bank would arrive and ask people what on earth they thought they were doing, playing tennis without the Bank's permission.

But that didn't happen. The balls zipped to and fro across the net, pinging off the strings, throwing up dust towards the end of the afternoon. Voices called out in exasperation at missed shots, laughter came and went. The sun continued to shine warmly, the tennis players wiped their foreheads with increasing regularity, the rugs on the grass were in the shade. Belle Frye and I collected the balls and threw them back to the servers. Mr Bowe said that Dick had the makings of a fine player.

Mrs Ashburton walked among the guests with a packet of Craven A in her hand, talking to everyone. She kept going up to my mother and thanking her for everything she'd done. Whenever she saw me she kissed me on the hair. Mr Race said she shook hands like a duchess. The rector, Mr Throataway, laughed jollily.

At six o'clock, just as people were thinking of going, my father surprised everyone by announcing that he had a barrel of beer and a barrel of cider in the truck. I went with him and there they were, two barrels keeping cool beneath a tarpaulin, and two wooden butter-boxes full of glasses that he'd borrowed from the Heart of Oak. He drove the truck out from beneath the shade of the trees and backed it close to the tennis court. He and Dick set the barrels up and other men handed round the beer and cider, whichever anyone wanted. 'Just like him,' I heard a woman called Mrs Garland saying. 'Now, that's just like him.'

It was a quarter to ten that evening before they stopped playing tennis. You could hardly see the ball as it swayed about from racquet to racquet, looping over the net, driven out of court. My father and Mr Race went on drinking beer, and Joe and Arthur, who'd arrived after milking, stood some distance away from them, drinking beer also. Mrs Garland and my mother and Miss Sweet and Mrs Tissard made more tea, and the remains of the sandwiches and cakes were passed around by Belle Frye and myself. Joe said he reckoned it was the greatest day in Mrs Ashburton's life. 'Don't go drinking that cider now,' Joe said to Belle Frye and myself.

We all sat around in the end, smacking at midges and finishing the sandwiches and cakes. Betty and Colin Gregg had cider, and you could see from the way Colin Gregg kept looking at Betty that he was in love with her. He was holding her left hand as they sat there, thinking that no one could see because of the gloom, but Belle Frye and I saw, all right. Just before we all went home, Belle Frye and I were playing at being ghosts round at the front of the house and we came across Betty and Colin Gregg kissing behind a rhododendron bush. They were lying on the grass with their arms tightly encircling one another, kissing and kissing as though they were never going to stop. They didn't even know Belle Frye and I were there. 'Oh, Colin!' Betty kept saying. 'Oh, Colin, Colin!'

We wanted to say goodbye to Mrs Ashburton, but we couldn't find her. We ran around looking everywhere, and then Belle Frye suggested that she was probably in the house.

'Mrs Ashburton!' I called, opening the door that led from the stable-yard to the kitchen. 'Mrs Ashburton!'

It was darker in the kitchen than it was outside, almost pitch-dark because the windows were so dirty that even in daytime it was gloomy.

'Matilda,' Mrs Ashburton said. She was sitting in an arm-chair by the oil-stove. I knew she was because that was where her voice came from. We couldn't see her.

'We came to say goodbye, Mrs Ashburton.'

She told us to wait. She had a saucer of chocolate for us, she said, and we heard her rooting about on the table beside her. We heard the glass being removed from a lamp and then she struck a match. She lit the wick and put the glass back. In the glow of lamplight she looked exhausted. Her eyes seemed to have receded, the thinness of her face was almost sinister.

We ate our chocolate in the kitchen that smelt of oil, and Mrs Ashburton didn't speak. We said goodbye again, but she didn't say anything. She didn't even nod or shake her head. She didn't kiss me like she usually did, so I went and kissed her instead. The skin of her face felt like crinkled paper.

'I've had a very happy day,' she said when Belle Frye and I had reached the kitchen door. 'I've had a lovely day,' she said, not seeming to be talking to us but to herself. She was crying, and she smiled in the lamplight, looking straight ahead of her. 'It's all over,' she said. 'Yet again.'

We didn't know what she was talking about and presumed she meant the tennis party. 'Yet again,' Belle Frye repeated as we crossed the stable-yard. She spoke in a soppy voice because she was given to soppiness. 'Poor Mrs Ashburton!' she said, beginning to cry herself, or pretending to. 'Imagine being eighty-one,' she said. 'Imagine sitting in a kitchen and remembering all the other tennis parties, knowing you'd have to die soon. Race you,' Belle Frye said, forgetting to be soppy any more.

Going home, Joe and Arthur sat in the back of the truck with Dick and Betty. Colin Gregg had ridden off on his bicycle, and Mr Bowe had driven away with Mrs Tissard beside him and Mr Tissard and Miss Sweet in the dickey of his Morris Cowley. My mother, my father and myself were all squashed into the front of the truck, and there was so little room that my father couldn't change gear and had to drive all the way to the farm in first. In the back of the truck Joe and Arthur and Dick were singing, but Betty wasn't, and I could imagine Betty just sitting there, staring, thinking about Colin Gregg. In Betty's bedroom there were photographs of Clark Gable and Ronald Colman, and Claudette Colbert and the little Princesses. Betty was going to marry Colin, I kept saying to myself in the truck. There'd be other tennis parties and Betty would be older and would know her own mind, and Colin Gregg would ask her and she'd say yes. It was very beautiful, I thought, as the truck shuddered over the uneven back avenue of Challacombe Manor. It was as beautiful as the tennis party itself, the white dresses and Betty's long hair, and everyone sitting and watching in the sunshine, and evening slowly descending. 'Well, that's the end of that,' my father said, and he didn't seem to be talking about the tennis party because his voice was too serious for that. He repeated a conversation he'd had with Mr Bowe and one he'd had with Mr Race, but I didn't listen because his voice was so lugubrious, not at all like it had been at the tennis party. I was huddled on my mother's knees, falling asleep. I imagined my father was talking about Lloyd's Bank again, and I could hear my mother agreeing with him.

I woke up when my mother was taking off my dress in my bedroom.

'What is it?' I said. 'Is it because the tennis party's over? Why's everyone so sad?'

My mother shook her head, but I kept asking her because she was looking sorrowful herself and I wasn't sleepy any more. In the end she sat on the edge of my bed and said that people thought there was going to be another war against the Germans.

'Germans?' I said, thinking of the grey, steely people that Mrs Ashburton had so often told me about, the people who ate black bread.

It would be all right, my mother said, trying to smile. She told me that we'd have to make special curtains for the windows so that the German aeroplanes wouldn't see the lights at night. She told me there'd probably be sugar rationing.

I lay there listening to her, knowing now why Mrs Ashburton had said that yet again it was all over, and knowing what would happen next. I didn't want to think about it, but I couldn't help thinking about it: my father would go away, and Dick would go also, and Joe and Arthur and Betty's Colin Gregg. I would continue to attend Miss Pritchard's Primary and then I'd go on to the Grammar, and my father would be killed. A soldier would rush at my father with a bayonet and twist the bayonet in my father's stomach, and Dick would do the same to another soldier, and Joe and

Arthur would be missing in the trenches, and Colin Gregg would be shot.

My mother kissed me and told me to say my prayers before I went to sleep. She told me to pray for the peace to continue, as she intended to do herself. There was just a chance, she said, that it might.

She went away and I lay awake, beginning to hate the Germans and not feeling ashamed of it, like Mrs Ashburton was. No German would ever have played tennis that day, I thought, no German would have stood around having tea and sandwiches and meringues, smacking away the midges when night came. No German would ever have tried to re-capture the past, or would have helped an old woman to do so, like my mother and my father had done, and Mr Race and Mr Bowe and Mr Throataway and Mrs Garland and Betty and Dick and Colin Gregg. The Germans weren't like that. The Germans wouldn't see the joke when my father said that for all he knew Lloyd's Bank owned Mrs Ashburton.

I didn't pray for the peace to continue, but prayed instead that my father and Dick might come back when the war was over. I didn't pray that Joe and Arthur and Colin Gregg should come back since that would be asking too much, because some men had to be killed, according to Mrs Ashburton's law of averages. I hadn't understood her when Mrs Ashburton had said that cruelty was natural in wartime, but I understood now. I understood her law of averages and her sitting alone in her dark kitchen, crying over the past. I cried myself, thinking of the grass growing on her tennis court, and the cruelty that was natural.

2. The Summer-house

My father came back twice to the farm, unexpectedly, without warning. He walked into the kitchen, the first time one Thursday morning when there was nobody there, the second time on a Thursday afternoon.

My mother told us how on the first occasion she'd been crossing the yard with four eggs, all that the hens had laid, and how she'd sensed that something was different. The sheepdogs weren't in the yard, where they usually were at this time. Vaguely she'd thought that that was unusual. Hours later, when Betty and Dick and I came in from school, our parents were sitting at the kitchen table, talking. He was still in his army uniform. The big brown tea-pot was on the table, and two cups with the dregs of tea in them, and bread on the bread-board, and butter and blackberry jam. There was a plate he'd eaten a fry from, with the marks of egg-yolk on it. Even now it seems like yesterday. He smiled a slow, teasing smile at us, as though mocking the emotion we felt at seeing him there, making a joke even of that. Then Betty ran over to him and hugged him. I hugged him too. Dick stood awkwardly.

The second time he returned he walked into the kitchen at half-past four, just after I'd come in from school. I was alone, having my tea.

'Hullo, Matilda,' he said.

I was nearly eleven then. Betty was sixteen and Dick was seventeen. Dick wasn't there that second time: he'd gone into the army himself. Betty had left the Grammar School and was helping my mother to keep the farm going. I was still at Miss Pritchard's Primary.

I was going to be pretty, people used to say, although I couldn't see it myself. My hair had a reddish tinge, like my mother's, but it was straight and uninteresting. I had freckles, which I hated, and my eyes were a shade of blue I didn't much care for either. I detested being called Matilda. Betty and Dick, I considered, were much nicer names, and Betty was beautiful now. My friend Belle Frye was getting to be beautiful also. She claimed to have Spanish blood in her, though it was never clear where it came from. Her hair was jet-black and her skin, even in the middle of winter, was almost as deeply brown as her eyes. I'd have loved to look like her and to be called Belle Frye, which I thought was a marvellous name.

I made my father tea that Thursday afternoon and I felt a bit shy because I hadn't seen him for so long. He didn't comment on my making the tea, although he might have said that I hadn't been able to before. Instead he said he hadn't had a decent cup of tea since he'd been home the last time. 'It's great to be home, Matilda,' he said.

A few weeks later my mother told me he was dead. She told me at that same time of day and on a Thursday also: a warm June afternoon that had been tiring to trudge home from school through.

'Belle Frye had to stay in for two hours,' I was saying as I came into the kitchen. My mother told me to sit down.

The repetition was extraordinary, the three Thursday afternoons. That night in bed I was aware of it, lying awake thinking about him, wondering if he'd actually been killed on a Thursday also.

All the days of the week had a special thing about them: they had different characters and even different colours. Monday was light-brown, Tuesday black, Wednesday grey, Thursday orange, Friday yellow, Saturday purplish, Sunday white. Tuesday was a day I liked because we had double

History, Friday was cosy, Saturday I liked best of all. Thursday would be special now: I thought that, marking the day with my grief, unable to cry any more. And then I remembered that it had been a Thursday afternoon when old Mrs Ashburton had invited everyone for miles round to her tennis party, when I had realised for the first time that there was going to be a war against the Germans: Thursday, August 31st, 1939.

I would have liked there to be a funeral, and I kept thinking about one. I never mentioned it to my mother or to Betty, or asked them if my father had had a funeral in France. I knew he hadn't. I'd heard him saying they just had to leave you there. My mother would cry if I said anything about it.

Then Dick came back, the first time home since he'd joined the army. He'd been informed too, and time had passed, several months, so that we were all used to it by now. It was even quite like the two occasions when my father had returned, Dick telling stories about the army. We sat in the kitchen listening to him, huddled round the range, with the sheepdogs under the table, and when the time came for him to go away I felt as I'd felt when my father had gone back. I knew that Betty and my mother were thinking about Dick in that way, too: I could feel it, standing in the yard holding my mother's hand.

Colin Gregg, who'd kissed Betty at Mrs Ashburton's tennis party, came to the farm when he was home on leave. Joe and Arthur, who'd worked for my father on the farm, came also. At one time or another they all said they were sorry about my father's death, trying not to say it when I was listening, lowering their voices, speaking to my mother.

*

Two years went by like that. Dick still came back, and Colin Gregg and Joe and Arthur. I left Miss Pritchard's Primary and went to the Grammar School. I heard Betty confiding to my mother that she was in love with Colin Gregg, and you could see that it was Colin Gregg being in the war she thought about now, not Dick. Belle Frye's father had had his left arm amputated because of a wound, and had to stay at home after that. A boy who'd been at the Grammar School, Roger Laze, had an accident with a gun when he was shooting rabbits, losing half his left foot. People said it was a lie about the rabbit-shooting. They said his mother had shot his foot off so that he wouldn't have to go into the army.

At church on Sundays the Reverend Throataway used to pray for victory and peace, and at school there was talk about the Russians, and jokes about Hitler and Göring and most of all about Goebbels. I remembered how old Mrs Ashburton used to talk about the previous war, from which her husband had come back with some kind of shell-shock. She'd made me think of Germans as being grey and steely, and I hated them now, just as she had. Whenever I thought about them I could see their helmets, different from the helmets of English soldiers, protecting their necks as well as their heads. Whenever I thought of the time before the war I thought of Mrs Ashburton, who had died soon after she'd given her tennis party. On the way home from school I'd sometimes go into the garden of Challacombe Manor and stand there looking at the tall grass on the tennis court, remembering all the people who'd come that afternoon, and how they'd said it was just like my father to say the tennis party was a lot of nonsense and then to bring on beer and cider at the end of the day. The tennis party had been all mixed up with our family. It felt like the last thing that had happened before the war had begun. It was the end of our being as we had been in our farm-house, just as in the past, after the previous war, there must have been another end: when the farm had ceased to be the home-farm of Challacombe Manor, when the estate had been divided up after Mrs Ashburton's husband hadn't been able to run it any more.

When I wandered about the overgrown garden of Challacombe Manor I wondered what Mr Ashburton had been like before the war had affected him, but I couldn't quite see him in my mind's eye: all I could see was the person Mrs Ashburton had told me about, the silent man who'd come back, who hadn't noticed that everything was falling into rack and ruin around him. And then that image would disappear and I'd see my father instead, as he'd been in the farm-house. I remembered without an effort the brown skin of his arms and his brown, wide forehead and the way crinkles formed at the sides of his eyes. I remembered his hands on the kitchen table at mealtimes, or holding a newspaper. I remembered his voice saying there'd been frost. 'Jack Frost's been,' he used to say.

When I was twelve I began to pray a lot. I prayed that my father should be safe in Heaven and not worried about us. I prayed that Dick should be safe in the war, and that the war would soon end. In Divinity lessons the Reverend Throataway used to explain to us that God was in the weeds and the insects, not just in butterflies and flowers. God was involved in the worst things we did as well as our virtues, he said, and we drove another thorn into His beloved son's head when we were wicked. I found that difficult to understand. I looked at weeds and insects, endeavouring to imagine God's presence in them but not succeeding. I asked Belle Frye if she could, but she giggled and said God was a carpenter called Joseph, the father of Jesus Christ. Belle Frye was silly and the Reverend Throataway so vague and complicated that his arguments about the nature of God seemed to me like foolish chatter. God was neither a carpenter nor a presence in weeds and insects. God was a figure in robes, with a beard and shreds of cloud around Him. The Paradise that was mentioned in the

Bible was a garden with tropical plants in it, through which people walked, Noah and Moses and Jesus Christ and old Mrs Ashburton. I could never help thinking that soon the Reverend Throataway would be there too: he was so old and frail, with chalk on the black material of his clothes, sometimes not properly shaved, as if he hadn't the energy for it. I found it was a consolation to imagine the Paradise he told us about, with my own God in it, and to imagine Hitler and Göring and Goebbels, with flames all around them, in Hell. The more I thought about it all and prayed, the closer I felt to my father. I didn't cry when I thought about him any more, and my mother's face wasn't all pulled down any more. His death was just a fact now, but I didn't ever want not to feel close to him. It was as if being close to him was being close to God also, and I wanted that so that God could answer my prayer about keeping Dick safe in the war. I remembered how Mrs Ashburton had worked it out that by the law of averages some men have to come back from a war, and I suggested to the robed figure in charge of the tropical Paradise that in all fairness our family did not deserve another tragedy. With my eyes tightly closed, in bed at night or suddenly stopping on the journey to school, I repetitiously prayed that Dick would be alive to come back when the war was over. That was all I asked for in the end because I could feel that my father was safe in the eternal life that the Reverend Throataway spoke of, and I didn't ask any more that the war should be over soon in case I was asking too much. I never told anyone about my prayers and I was never caught standing still with my eyes closed on the way to school. My father used to smile at me when I did that and I could faintly hear his voice teasing Dick about his smoking or teasing my mother about the Aga cooker she wanted, or Betty about almost anything. I felt it was all right when he smiled like that and his voice came back. I felt he was explaining to me that God had agreed to look after us now, provided I prayed properly and often and did not for a single instant doubt that God existed and was in charge. Mrs Ashburton had been doubtful about that last point and had told me so a few times, quite frightening me. But Mrs Ashburton would be in possession of the truth now, and would be forgiven.

My thoughts and my prayers seemed like a kind of world to me, a world full of God, with my father and Mrs Ashburton in their eternal lives, and the happiness that was waiting for the Reverend Throataway in his. It was a world that gradually became as important as the reality around me. It affected everything. It made me different. Belle Frye was still my friend, but I didn't like her the way I once had.

One wet afternoon she and I clambered into Challacombe Manor through a window that someone had smashed. We hadn't been there since the night of the tennis party, when we'd found Mrs Ashburton crying and she'd given us pieces of chocolate. We'd run out into the night, whispering excitedly about an old woman crying just because a party was over. I wouldn't have believed it then if someone had said I'd ever think Belle Frye silly.

'Whoever's going to live here?' she whispered in the dank hall after we'd climbed through the window. 'D'you think it'll just fall down?'

'There's a mortgage on it. Lloyd's Bank have it.'

'What's that mean then?'

'When the war's finished they'll sell the house off to someone else.'

All the furniture in the drawing-room had been taken away, stored in the cellars until someone, some day, had time to attend to it. People had pulled off pieces of the striped red wallpaper, boys from the Grammar School probably. There were names and initials and dates scrawled on the plaster. Hearts with arrows through them had been drawn.

'Anyone could come and live here,' Belle Frye said.

'Nobody'd want to.'

We walked from room to room. The dining-room still had a sideboard in it. There was blue wallpaper on the walls: none of that had been torn off, but there were great dark blots of damp on it. There were bundled-up newspapers all over the floor, and empty cardboard boxes that would have been useless for anything because they'd gone soft due to the damp. Upstairs there was a pool of water on a landing and in one of the bedrooms half the ceiling had fallen down. Everywhere there was a musty smell.

'It's haunted,' Belle Frye said.

'Of course it isn't.'

'She died here, didn't she?'

'That doesn't make it haunted.'

'I can feel her ghost.'

I knew she couldn't. I thought she was silly to say it, pretending about ghosts just to set a bit of excitement going. She said it again and I didn't answer.

We crawled out again, through the broken window. We wandered about in the rain, looking in the out-houses and the stables. The old motor-car that used to be in one of them had been taken away. The iron roller that Dick had rolled the tennis court with was still there, beside the tennis court itself.

'Let's try in here,' Belle Frye said, opening the door of the summer-house.

All the times I'd come into the garden on my own I'd never gone into the summer-house. I'd never even looked through a window of Challacombe Manor itself, or poked about the out-houses. I'd have been a bit frightened, for even though I thought it was silly of Belle Frye to talk about ghosts it wouldn't have surprised me to see a figure moving in the empty house or to hear something in one of the stables, a tramp maybe or a prisoner escaped from the Italian prisoner-of-war camp five miles away. The Italians were small black-haired men whom we often met being marched along a road to work in the fields. They always waved and were given to laughing and singing. But even so I wouldn't have cared to meet one on his own.

In the centre of the summer-house was the table that had been covered with a white cloth, with sandwiches and cakes and the tea-urn on it, for the tennis party. The tennis marker was in a corner, placed there by Dick, I supposed, after he'd marked the court. The net was beside it, and underneath it, almost hidden by it, were two rugs, one of them brown and white, a kind of Scottish tartan pattern, the other grey. Both of these rugs belonged in our farm-house. Could they have been lying in the summer-house since the tennis party? I wondered. I couldn't remember when I'd seen them last.

Facing one another across the table were two chairs which I remembered being there on the day of the party. They were dining-room chairs with red plush seats, brought from the house with a dozen or so others and arrayed on one side of the tennis court so that people could watch the games in comfort. These two must have been left behind when the others had been returned. I was thinking that when I remembered my father hurriedly putting them into the summer-house at the end of the day. 'It'll maybe rain,' he'd said.

'Hey, look,' Belle Frye said. She was pointing at an ashtray on the table, with cigarette-butts and burnt-out matches in it. 'There's people using this place,' she said, giggling. 'Maybe an escaped prisoner,' she suggested, giggling again.

'Maybe.' I said it quickly, not wanting to pursue the subject. I knew the summer-house wasn't being used by an escaped prisoner. Our rugs hadn't been there since the day of the tennis party. They were part of something else, together with the cigarette-butts and the burnt-out matches.

71

And then, quite abruptly, it occurred to me that the summer-house was where Betty and Colin Gregg came when Colin Gregg was on leave: they came to kiss, to cuddle one another like they'd been cuddling in the rhododendrons after the tennis party. Betty had brought the rugs specially, so that they could be warm and comfortable.

'I bet you it's an Eye-tie,' Belle Frye said. 'I bet you there's one living here.'

'Could be.'

'I'm getting out of it.'

We ran away. We ran through the overgrown garden on that wet afternoon and along the lane that led to the Fryes' farm. I should have turned in the opposite direction after we'd left the garden, but I didn't: I went with her because I didn't want her silliness to spoil everything. I thought it was romantic, Betty and Colin Gregg going to the summer-house. I remembered a film called *First Love,* which Betty had gone on about. It had Deanna Durbin in it.

'I'm going to tell,' Belle Frye said, stopping for breath before we came to the Fryes' farmyard. Her eyes jangled with excitement. There were drops of moisture in her smooth black hair.

'Let's have it a secret, Belle.'

'He could murder you, a blooming Eye-tie.'

'It's where my sister and Colin Gregg go.' I had to say it because I knew she'd never be able to keep a secret that involved an Italian prisoner of war. I knew that even if no prisoner had escaped people would go to the summer-house to see for themselves. I knew for a fact, I said, that it was where Betty and Colin Gregg went, and if she mentioned it to anyone I'd tell about going into Challacombe Manor through a broken window. She'd said as we'd clambered through it that her father would murder her if he knew. He'd specifically told her that she mustn't go anywhere near the empty house because the floor-boards were rotten and the ceilings falling down.

'But why would you tell?' she cried, furious with me. 'What d'you want to tell for?'

'It's private about the summer-house. It's a private thing of Betty's.'

She began to giggle. We could watch, she whispered. We could watch through the window to see what they got up to. She went on giggling and whispering and I listened to her, not liking her. In the last year or so she'd become like that, repeating the stories she heard from the boys at school, all to do with undressing and peeping. There were rhymes and riddles and jokes that she repeated also, none of them funny. She'd have loved peeping through the summer-house window.

'No,' I said. 'No.'

'But we could. We could wait till he was home on leave. We needn't make a sound.' Her voice had become shrill. She was cross with me again, not giggling any more. Her eyes glared at me. She said I was stupid, and then she turned and ran off. I knew she'd never peep through the summer-house window on her own because it wasn't something you could giggle over when you were alone. And I knew she wouldn't try and persuade anyone to go with her because she believed me when I said I'd tell about breaking into Challacombe Manor. Her father was a severe man; she was, fortunately, terrified of him.

*

I thought about the summer-house that evening when I was meant to be learning a verse of *The Lady of Shalott* and writing a composition, *The Worst Nightmare I Ever Had*. I imagined Betty and Colin Gregg walking hand in hand through the overgrown garden and then slipping into the summer-house when it became dusky. A summer's evening it was, with pink in the sky, and the garden was scented with the blossoms of its shrubs. I imagined them sitting on the two dining-chairs at the table, Colin telling her about the war while he smoked his cigarettes, and Betty crying because he would be gone in twelve hours' time and Colin comforting her, and both of them lying down on the rugs so that they could be close enough to put their arms around each other.

In the kitchen while I tried to record the details of a nightmare all I could think about was the much pleasanter subject of my sister's romance. She was in the kitchen also. She'd changed from her farm-working clothes into a navy-blue skirt and a matching jersey. I thought she was more beautiful than usual. She and my mother were sitting on either side of the range, both of them knitting, my mother reading a book by A. J. Cronin at the same time, my sister occasionally becoming lost in a reverie. I knew what she was thinking about. She was wondering if Colin Gregg was still alive.

Months went by and neither he nor Dick came back. There were letters, but there were also periods when no letters arrived and you could feel the worry, for one of them or the other. The war was going to be longer than everyone had thought. People looked gloomy sometimes, and when I caught their gloom I imagined bodies lying unburied and men in aeroplanes, with goggles on, the aeroplanes on fire and the men in goggles burning to death. Ages ago France had been beaten, and I remembered that in a casual moment in a Divinity class the Reverend Throataway had said that that could never happen, that the French would never give in. We would never give in either, Winston Churchill said, but I imagined the Germans marching on the lanes and the roads and through the fields, not like the cheerful Italians. The Germans were cruel in their helmets and their grey steeliness. They never smiled. They knew you hated them.

Belle Frye would have thought I was mad if I'd told her any of that, just like she'd have thought I was mad if I'd mentioned about praying and keeping my father vivid in my mind. She was the first friend I'd ever had, but the declining of our friendship seemed almost natural now. We still sat next to one another in class, but we didn't always walk home together. Doing that had always meant that one of us had to go the long way round and avoiding this extra journey now became an excuse. Not having had Dick and Betty to walk home with for so long, I'd enjoyed Belle Frye's company, but now I found myself pretending to be in a hurry or just slipping away when she wasn't looking. She didn't seem to mind, and we still spent days together, at the weekends or in the holidays. We'd have tea in each other's kitchen, formally invited by our mothers, who didn't realise that we weren't such friends. And that was still quite nice.

Sometimes in the evenings my mother used to go to see a woman called Mrs Latham because Mrs Latham was all alone in the Burrow Farm, three miles away. On these occasions I always hoped Betty would talk to me about Colin Gregg, that she'd even mention the summer-house. But she never did. She'd sit there knitting, or else writing a letter to him. She'd hear me say any homework I had to learn by heart, a theorem or poetry or spelling. She'd make me go to bed, just like my mother did, and then she'd turn on the wireless and listen to *Monday Night at Eight* or *Waterlogged Spa* or *Itma*. She'd become very quiet, less impatient with me than she'd been when we were younger, more grown-up, I suppose. I often used to think about her on those nights when my mother was out, when she was left alone in the kitchen listening to the wireless. I used to feel sorry for her.

And then, in that familiar sudden way, Colin Gregg came back on leave.

*

That was the beginning of everything. The evening after he came back was a Saturday, an evening in May. I'd been at the Fryes' all afternoon and when we'd finished tea we played cards for an hour or so and then Mrs Frye said it was time for me to go home. Belle wanted to walk with me, even though we'd probably have walked in silence. I was glad when her father said no. It was too late and in any case he had to go out himself, to set his rabbit snares: he'd walk with me back to our farm. I said goodbye, remembering to thank Mrs Frye, and with his remaining arm Mr Frye pushed his bicycle on the road beside me. He didn't talk at all. He was completely different from my father, never making jokes or teasing. I was quite afraid of him because of his severity.

The sheepdogs barked as I ran across our yard and into the kitchen. My mother had said earlier that she intended to go over to see Mrs Latham that evening. By eight o'clock Betty and Colin Gregg were to be back from the half-past four show at the pictures, so that I wouldn't be in the house alone. It was twenty-past eight now, and they weren't there.

I ran back into the yard, wanting to tell Mr Frye, but already he'd cycled out of sight. I didn't at all like the idea of going to bed in the empty house.

I played with the dogs for a while and then I went to look at the hens, and then I decided that I'd walk along the road to meet Betty and Colin Gregg. I kept listening because at night you could always hear the voices of people cycling in the lanes. I kept saying to myself that my mother wouldn't want me to go to bed when there was no one in the farm-house. It was very still, with bits of red in the sky. I took the short cut through the garden of Challacombe Manor and I wasn't even

thinking about Betty and Colin Gregg when I saw two
bicycles in the shrubbery at the back of the summer-house. I
didn't notice them at first because they were almost entirely
hidden by rhododendron bushes. They reminded me of the
rugs half hidden beneath the tennis net.

Colin Gregg was going away again on Monday. He was
being sent somewhere dangerous, he didn't know where, but
I'd heard Betty saying to my mother that she could feel in her
bones it was dangerous. When my mother had revealed that
she intended to visit Mrs Latham that evening I'd said to
myself that she'd arranged the visit so that Colin Gregg and
Betty could spend the evening on their own in our kitchen.
But on the way back from the pictures they'd gone into the
summer-house, their special place.

Even now I can't think why I behaved like Belle Frye,
unable to resist something. It was silly curiosity, and yet at
the time I think it may have seemed more than just that. In
some vague way I wanted to have something nice to think
about, not just my imagining the war, and my prayers for
Dick's safety and my concern with people's eternal lives. I
wanted to see Betty and Colin Gregg together. I wanted to
feel their happiness, and to see it.

It was then, while I was actually thinking that, that I
realised something was the matter. I realised I'd been stupid
to assume they could take the short cut through the garden:
you couldn't take the short cut if you were coming from the
town on a bicycle because you had to go through fields. You'd
come by the lanes, and if you wanted to go to the summer-
house you'd have to turn back and go there specially. It
seemed all wrong that they should do that when they were
meant to be back in the farm-house by eight o'clock.

I should have turned and gone away. In the evening light I
was unable to see the bicycles clearly, but even so I was aware
that neither of them was Betty's. They passed out of my sight

as I approached one of the summer-house's two small windows.

I could see nothing. Voices murmured in the summer-house, not saying anything, just quietly making sounds. Then a man's voice spoke more loudly, but I still couldn't hear what was being said. A match was struck and in a sudden vividness I saw a man's hand and a packet of Player's cigarettes on the table, and then I saw my mother's face. Her reddish hair was untidy and she was smiling. The hand that had been on the table put a cigarette between her lips and another hand held the match to it. I had never in my life seen my mother smoking a cigarette before.

The match went out and when another one was struck it lit up the face of a man who worked in Blow's drapery. My mother and he were sitting facing one another at the table, in the two chairs with the red plush seats.

*

Betty was frying eggs at the range when I returned to the kitchen. Colin Gregg had had a puncture in his back tyre. They hadn't even looked yet to see if I was upstairs. I said we'd all forgotten the time at the Fryes', playing cards.

In bed I kept remembering that my mother's eyes had been different, not like they'd been for a long time, two dark-blue sparks. I kept saying to myself that I should have recognised her bicycle in the bushes because its mudguards were shaped like a V, not rounded like the mudguards of modern bicycles.

I heard Colin and Betty whispering in the yard and then the sound of his bicycle as he rode away and then, almost immediately, the sound of my mother's bicycle and Betty saying something quietly and my mother quietly replying. I heard them coming to bed, Betty first and my mother twenty minutes later. I didn't sleep, and for the first time in my life I watched the sky becoming brighter when morning began to come. I heard my mother getting up and going out to do the milking.

At breakfast-time it was as though none of it had happened, as though she had never sat on the red plush chair in the summer-house, smoking cigarettes and smiling at a man from a shop. She ate porridge and brown bread, reading a book: *Victoria Four-Twenty* by Cecil Roberts. She reminded me to feed the hens and she asked Betty what time Colin Gregg was coming over. Betty said any minute now and began to do the washing up. When Colin Gregg came he mended one of the cow-house doors.

That day was horrible. Betty tried to be cheerful, upset because Colin Gregg was being sent to somewhere dangerous. But you could feel the effort of her trying and when she thought no one was looking, when my mother and Colin were talking to one another, her face became unhappy. I couldn't stop thinking about my father. Colin Gregg went back to the war.

*

A month went by. My mother continued to say she was going to see Mrs Latham and would leave Betty and me in the kitchen about once a week.

'Whatever's the matter with Matilda?' I heard Betty saying to her once, and later my mother asked me if I had a stomach ache. I used to sit there at the table trying to understand simultaneous equations, imagining my mother in the summer-house, the two bicycles half hidden in the bushes, the cigarettes and the ashtray.

'The capital of India,' I would say. 'Don't tell me; I know it.'

'Begins with a "D",' Betty would prompt.

He came to the kitchen one evening. He ate cabbage and

baked potatoes and fish pie, chewing the cabbage so carefully you couldn't help noticing. He was thin, with one eye that was funny, dead or crooked or something, and a bony nose. His teeth were narrowly crowded, his whole face pulled out to an edge, like the head of a hatchet. His hair was jet-black, parted in the middle and oiled. His hands were clean, with tapering fingers. I was told his name but I didn't listen, not wishing to know it.

'Where'd you get the fish?' he asked my mother in a casual way. His head was cocked a little to one side. He was smiling with his narrow teeth, making my mother flustered as she used to get in the past, when my father was alive. She was even beginning to blush, not that I could see a cause for it. She said:

'Betty, where did you get the cod?'

'Timpson's,' Betty said.

Betty smiled at him and my mother said quickly that Timpson's were always worth trying in case they'd got any fish in, although of course you could never tell. It sounded silly the way she said it.

'I like fish,' he said.

'We must remember that.'

'They say it's good for you,' Betty said.

'I always liked fish,' the man said. 'From a child I've enjoyed it.'

'Eat it up now,' my mother ordered me.

'Don't you like fish, Matilda?' he said.

Betty laughed. 'Matilda doesn't like lots of things. Fish, carrots, eggs. Semolina. Ground rice. Custard. Baked apples, gravy, cabbage.'

He laughed, and my mother laughed. I bent my head over the plate I was eating from. My face had gone as hot as a fire.

'Unfortunately there's a war on,' he said. 'Hard times, Matilda.'

I considered that rude. It was rude the way he'd asked where the fish had come from. He was stupid, as well. Who wanted to hear that he liked fish? He was a fool, like Stupid Miller, who'd been at Miss Pritchard's Primary. He was ridiculous-looking and ugly, with his pointed face and crushed-together teeth. He'd no right to say there was a war on since he wasn't fighting in it.

They listened to the news on the wireless and afterwards they listened to the national anthem of the countries which were fighting against Germany. He offered my mother and Betty cigarettes and they both took one. I'd never seen Betty smoking a cigarette before. He'd brought a bottle of some kind of drink with him. They drank it sitting by the range, still listening to the national anthems.

'Good-night, Matilda,' he said, standing up when my mother told me it was time to go to bed. He kissed me on the cheek and I could feel his damp teeth. I didn't move for a moment after he'd done that, standing quite close to him. I thought I was going to bring up the fish pie and if I did I wanted to cover his clothes with it. I wouldn't have cared. I wouldn't have been embarrassed.

I heard Betty coming to bed and then I lay for hours, waiting for the sound of his bicycle going away. I couldn't hear their voices downstairs, the way I'd been able to hear voices when Betty had been there. Betty's had become quite loud and she'd laugh repeatedly. I guessed they'd been playing cards, finishing off the bottle of drink he'd brought. When I'd been there Betty had suggested rummy and he'd said that not a drop of the drink must be left. He'd kept filling up Betty's and my mother's glasses, saying the stuff was good for you.

I crossed the landing to the top of the stairs that led straight down into the kitchen. I thought they must have fallen asleep by the range because when a board creaked beneath my feet no one called out. I stood at the turn of the narrow staircase, peering through the shadows at them.

Betty had taken one of the two lamps with her as she always did. The kitchen was dim, with only the glow from the other. On the table, close to the lamp, was the bottle and one of the glasses they'd drunk from. The two dogs were stretched in front of the range. My mother was huddled on the man's knee. I could see his tapering fingers, one hand on the black material of her dress, the other stroking her hair. While I watched he kissed her, bending his damp mouth down to her lips and keeping it there. Her eyes were closed but his were open, and when he finished kissing her he stared at her face.

I went on down the stairs, shuffling my bare feet to make a noise. The dogs growled, pricking up their ears. My mother was halfway across the kitchen, tidying her hair with both hands, murmuring at me.

'Can't you sleep, love?' she said. 'Have you had a dream?'

I shook my head. I wanted to walk forward, past her to the table. I wanted to pick up the bottle he'd brought and throw it on to the flags of the floor. I wanted to shout at him that he was ugly, no more than a half-wit, no better than Stupid Miller, who hadn't been allowed in the Grammar School. I wanted to say no one was interested in his preference for fish.

My mother put her arms around me. She felt warm from sitting by the range, but I hated the warmth because it had to do with him. I pushed by her and went to the sink. I drank some water even though I wasn't thirsty. Then I turned and went upstairs again.

'She's sleepy,' I heard my mother say. 'She often gets up for a drink when she's sleepy. You'd better go, dear.'

He muttered something else and my mother said that they must have patience.

'One day,' she said. 'After it's all over.'

'It'll never end.' He spoke loudly, not muttering any more. 'This bloody thing could last for ever.'

'No, no, my dear.'

'It's all I want, to be here with you.'

'It's what I want too. But there's a lot in the way.'

'I don't care what's in the way.'

'We have to care, dear.'

'I love you,' he said.

'My own darling,' my mother said.

*

She was the same as usual the next day, presumably imagining that being half-asleep I hadn't noticed her sitting on the man's knees and being kissed by his mouth. In the afternoon I went into the summer-house. I looked at the two plush-seated chairs, imagining the figures of my mother and the man on them. I carried the chairs, one by one, to an out-house and up a ladder to a loft. I put the tennis net underneath some seed-boxes. I carried the two rugs to the well in the cobbled yard and dropped them down it. I returned to the summer-house, thinking of doing something else, I wasn't sure what. There was a smell of stale tobacco, coming from butts in the ashtray. On the floor I found a tie-pin with a greyhound's head on it and I thought the treacherous, ugly-looking dog suited him. I threw it into the rhododendron shrubbery.

'Poor chap,' I heard Betty saying that evening. 'It's a horrid thing to have.' She'd always noticed that he looked delicate, she added.

'He doesn't get enough to eat,' my mother said.

In spite of her sympathy, you could see that Betty wasn't much interested in the man: she was knitting and trying to

listen to *Bandwagon*. As far as Betty was concerned he was
just some half-sick man whom my mother felt sorry for, the
way she was supposed to feel sorry for Mrs Latham of
Burrow Farm. But my mother wanted to go on talking about
him, with a pretended casualness. It wasn't the right work for
a person who was tubercular, she said, serving in a shop.

I imagined him in Blow's, selling pins and knitting-needles
and satin by the yard. I thought the work suited him like the
greyhound's head tie-pin did.

'What's it mean, tubercular?' I asked Belle Frye, and she
said it meant you suffered from a disease in your lungs.

'I expect you could fake it.'

'What'd you want to do that for?'

'To get out of the war. Like Mrs Laze shot off Roger
Laze's foot.'

'Who's faking it then?'

'That man in Blow's.'

I couldn't help myself: I wanted it to be known that he was
faking a disease in his lungs. I wanted Belle Frye to tell
people, giggling at him in Blow's, pointing him out. But in
fact she wasn't much interested. She nodded, and then
shrugged in a jerky way she had, which meant she was
impatient to be talking about something else. You could tell
she didn't know the man in Blow's had become a friend of my
mother's. She hadn't seen them on their bicycles; she wouldn't
have wanted to change the subject if she'd looked through the
summer-house window and seen them with their cigarettes.
Before that I hadn't thought about her finding out, but now
I wondered if perhaps she would some time, and if other
people would. I imagined the giggling and the jokes made up
by the boys in the Grammar School, and the severity of
Mr Frye, and the astonishment of people who had liked my
father.

I prayed that none of that would happen. I prayed that the

man would go away, or die. I prayed that my mother would be upset again because my father had been killed in the war, that she would remember the time when he had been in the farm-house with us. I prayed that whatever happened she would never discredit him by allowing the man from Blow's to be there in the farm-house, wearing my father's clothes.

Every day I prayed in the summer-house, standing close to the table with my eyes closed, holding on to the edge of it. I went there specially, and more vividly than ever I could see my father in the tropical garden of his eternal life. I could see old Mrs Ashburton walking among the plants with her husband, happy to be with him again. I could see the bearded face of the Almighty I prayed to, not smiling but seeming kind.

*

'Oh, my God,' was all my mother could say, whispering it between her bursts of tears. 'Oh, my God.'

Betty was crying too, but crying would do no good. I stood there between them in the kitchen, feeling I would never cry again. The telegram was still on the table, its torn envelope beside it. It might have said that Dick was coming home on leave, or that Colin Gregg was. It looked sinister on the table because Dick was dead.

I might have said to my mother that it was my fault as well as hers. I might have said that I'd known I should pray only for Dick to be safe and yet hadn't been able to prevent myself praying for the other too: that she'd be as she used to be, that she wouldn't ever marry the man from Blow's.

But I didn't say that. I didn't say I'd prayed about the man, I just said it was a Thursday again.

'Thursday?' my mother whispered, and when I explained she didn't understand. She hadn't even noticed that the two times my father had come home it had been a Thursday and that the tennis party had been on a Thursday and that the other telegram had come on a Thursday too. She shook her head, as if denying all this repetition, and I wanted to hurt her when she did that because the denial seemed all part and parcel of the summer-house and the man from Blow's. More deliberately than a moment ago I again didn't confess that I had ceased to concentrate on Dick's safety in my prayers. Instead I said that in a war against the Germans you couldn't afford to take chances, you couldn't go kissing a man when your husband had been killed.

'Oh, my God,' my mother said again.

Betty was staring at her, tears still coming from her eyes, bewildered because she'd never guessed about my mother and the man.

'It has nothing to do with this,' my mother whispered. 'Nothing.'

I thought Betty was going to attack my mother, maybe hammer at her face with her fists, or scratch her cheeks. But she only cried out, shrieking like some animal caught in a trap. The man was even married, she shrieked, his wife was away in the Women's Army. It was horrible, worse than ever when you thought of that. She pointed at me and said I was right: Dick's death was a judgement, things happened like that.

My mother didn't say anything. She stood there, white-faced, and then she said the fact that the man was married didn't make anything worse.

She spoke to Betty, looking at her, not at me. Her voice was quiet. She said the man intended to divorce his wife when the war came to an end. Of course what had happened wasn't a judgement.

'You won't marry him now,' Betty said, speaking as quietly.

My mother didn't reply. She stood there by the table and there was a silence. Then she said again that Dick's death and

86

the man were two different things. It was terrible, she said, to talk as we were talking at a time like this. Dick was dead: that was the only thing that mattered.

'They used to go to the summer-house,' I said. 'They had two of our rugs there.'

My mother turned her head away, and I wanted Betty to remember as I was remembering and I believe she did. I could sense her thinking of the days when my father was alive, when Dick used to smoke cigarettes on the way home from school, when we were all together in the farm-house, not knowing we were happy. That time seemed to haunt the kitchen just then, as if my mother was thinking about it too, as if our remembering had willed it back.

'He could never come here now,' Betty said to my mother. 'You couldn't do it to Matilda.'

I didn't know why she should have particularly mentioned me since it concerned us all, and anyway I felt it was too late to bother about me. Too much had happened. I felt I'd been blown to pieces, as if I'd been in the war myself, as if I'd been defeated by it, as old Mrs Ashburton had been defeated by her war. The man would come to live in the farm-house. He would wear my father's clothes. He would sit by the range, reading the newspaper. He would eat at the table, and smile at me with his narrow teeth.

My mother left the kitchen. She went upstairs and after a few minutes we heard her sobbing in her bedroom. Sobbing would do no good, I thought, any more than crying would.

*

I walked by myself through the fields. Dick's death wasn't the same as my father's. There was the same emptiness and the same feeling that I never wanted to eat anything again or to drink anything again, but it was different because this was the second time. Dick was dead and we'd get used to it: that was something I knew now.

I didn't cry and I didn't pray. Praying seemed nonsense as I walked through the fields; praying was as silly as Belle Frye's thinking that God was a carpenter or the Reverend Throataway saying God was in weeds. God wasn't like that in the least. He wasn't there to listen to what you prayed for. God was something else, something harder and more awful and more frightening.

I should have known that the man from Blow's would be married, that he'd have a wife who was helping in the war while he was going on about a disease. It was somehow all of a piece with Betty wanting to hit my mother, and Mrs Laze shooting off her son's foot so that he could stay alive, and God being frightening. Facts and images rattled in my mind, senselessly jumbled, without rhyme or reason. Dick was there too, dead and unburied in his uniform, something ordinary to get used to.

I sat in the sunshine on a bank that had primroses on it. I could have returned to the farm-house and let my mother put her arms around me, but I continued to sit there, still not crying, remembering Mrs Ashburton saying that cruelty in wartime was natural. At the time I hadn't understood what she'd meant, but I could feel the cruelty she'd spoken of now. I could feel it in myself, in my wanting my mother to be more unhappy than I was. Dick's death was more bearable because she could be blamed, as Betty had blamed her in speaking of a judgement.

3. The Drawing-room

I am writing this in the drawing-room, in fact at Mrs Ash-burton's writing-desk. I don't think of it as a story – and certainly not as a letter, for she can never read it – but as a record of what happened in her house after the war. If she hadn't talked to me so much when I was nine there would not be this record to keep, and I would not still feel her presence. I do not understand what has happened, but as I slowly move towards the age she was when she talked to me I slowly understand a little more. What she said has haunted me for thirty-nine years. It has made me old before my time, and for this I am glad. I feel like a woman of sixty; I'm only forty-eight.

*

In 1951 the house was bought by people called Gregary. 'Filthy rich,' my stepfather said.

My stepfather had just been made manager at Blow's drapery in the town. He used to drive off every day in a blue pre-war baby Ford, and I was always glad to see him go. I worked on the farm with Joe and Arthur, like my father had, like my brother Dick would have if he hadn't been killed in the desert offensive.

I thought it was typical of my stepfather to know that the Gregarys were rich. It was the kind of information he picked up in Blow's, conversing across his counter, the gossip enlivening his hatchet face and his funny eye. He said Mr Gregary was a businessman involved in the manufacture of motor-car components.

He'd made a killing during the war: my stepfather called him a post-war tycoon.

On my twenty-first birthday my mother insisted on giving a kind of party. We had it in the farm-house kitchen. We cooked a turkey and a ham and my mother made a great fuss about the vegetables that had been my favourites when I was small: celery and parsnips and carrots, and roast potatoes. The carrots were to be in a parsley sauce, the parsnips roasted with the potatoes. We made trifle because trifle had been a childhood favourite also, and brandy-snaps. It was impossible not to recall the preparations for Mrs Ashburton's tennis party on the Thursday before the war, but of course I didn't mention that. My mother believed that I didn't want to live in the present. I often felt her looking at me and when I turned my head I could see for a moment, before she changed her expression, that she believed I dwelt far too much on times that were not our own.

Fifteen people came to my birthday party, not counting my mother and my stepfather and myself. My sister Betty, who had married Colin Gregg, came with her two children. Belle Frye had married Martin Draper, who'd inherited the mill at Bennett's Cross: they brought the baby that had made the marriage necessary. Mr and Mrs Frye were there, and Miss Pritchard, who'd taught us all at the Primary School. Joe and Arthur, and Joe's wife, Maudie, came; and Mrs Laze and her son Roger. The idea was, I believe, that I might one day marry Roger, but it wasn't a prospect I relished. He limped because of his foot, and he hardly ever spoke, being shy like his mother. I didn't dislike him, I just didn't want to marry him.

All the time I kept wishing my mother hadn't given this party. It made me think of my other birthdays. Not that there was any reason to avoid doing that, except that naturally the past seemed better, especially the distant past, before the war. Miss Pritchard was the only person I ever talked to about things like that. 'Come and talk to me whenever you want to, Matilda,' she'd said one day in 1944, and ever since I'd been visiting her in her tiny sitting-room, knowing she was lonely because she was retired now. In a way our conversations reminded me of my conversations with Mrs Ashburton, except that it was Mrs Ashburton, not I, who used to do the talking and half the time I hadn't understood her. It was I who'd suggested that Miss Pritchard should come to my birthday party. I'd heard my mother saying to my stepfather that she couldn't understand it: she thought it extraordinary that I didn't want to invite lots of the boys I'd been at the Grammar School with, that I didn't want to have a gramophone going and tables of whist. My stepfather said he didn't think people played whist like they used to. He stood up for me, the way he always did, even though he didn't know I was listening. He made such efforts and still I couldn't like him.

Seventeen of us sat down at the kitchen table at half-past six and my stepfather poured out cider for us, and Kia-Ora for Betty's children. Belle Frye's baby was put to sleep upstairs. I couldn't think of her as Belle Draper, and haven't ever been able to since. Martin Draper had been a silly kind of boy at school and he still was silly now.

My stepfather carved the turkey and my mother the ham. Everyone was talking about Challacombe Manor having been sold to the people called Gregory.

'The son's going to run the place,' my stepfather said. 'Tax fiddle, I dare say.'

You could see that Miss Pritchard didn't know what he was talking about, and you could see that she suspected he didn't know what he was talking about himself. In his gossipy way he was always referring to tax fiddles and how people had made a fortune and what price such and such a shop in the town would fetch. The fact that he'd mentioned income tax evasion in connection with the Gregarys didn't mean that there was any truth in the suggestion. Even so, the reference, coupled with the information that Mr Gregary was in the motor-components industry, established the Gregarys as people of a certain kind. Carving the turkey, my stepfather said that in his opinion Challacombe would be restored to its former splendour.

'They haven't the land,' Mr Frye pointed out, for he himself farmed eighty acres of what had once been the Challacombe estate.

'It couldn't never be the same,' Joe added.

Plates of turkey and ham were passed from hand to hand until everyone present was attended to. My mother said that people must take vegetables and start, else the food would get cold. A more lively chatter about the new people at Challacombe broke out as the cider was consumed. Two of the Gregary daughters were married and living in some other part of the country, a third one was at a university. The son was the apple of his parents' eye. The father owned a grey Daimler.

The old range which had been in our kitchen all during my childhood had only the week before been replaced by a cream-coloured Aga. The acquisition of an Aga had been my mother's dream for almost as long as I could remember. I think she'd grown to hate the range, lighting it every morning with sticks and paper, the struggles she'd had with it during the war, trying to burn wood instead of coal. But I'd been sorry to see it go. I tried to stop myself being like that about things, but I couldn't help it.

'To the birthday girl,' my stepfather said, raising his glass of cider. 'Many happy returns, my best.'

It was that that I didn't care for in him: I wasn't his best, my mother was. Yet he'd say it casually, wanting to pay a compliment but overdoing it so that you didn't believe him, so that you distrusted him.

'Matilda,' other people said, holding up their glasses also. 'To Matilda.'

'Oh, my love!' my mother cried out, getting up and running round the table to kiss me. 'Oh, little Matilda!' I could feel the warm dampness of tears as her cheek came into contact with mine, and the touch of her mouth, reminding me of childhood. It was a long time since my mother had kissed me.

Everyone made a fuss then, even Martin Draper and Joe and Arthur. I can still see the sunburnt face of Colin Gregg, and his pale smooth hair, his eyes seeming to laugh at me as he wished me many happy returns. For a split second he reminded me of my father.

Betty said the turkey was delicious because she could see I was embarrassed by all the attention. Belle Frye said the next thing after a twenty-first was getting married. She reminded us that she'd been married herself within a fortnight of becoming twenty-one. She giggled and Martin Draper went red because everyone knew they'd got married in a hurry. She'd been terrified at the time of what her father would say, but to her surprise he'd taken the whole thing calmly, pointing out that there were worse than Martin Draper, reminding her that he'd just inherited the Bennett's Cross mill. It was Mrs Frye who'd been upset, unable to find consolation in her son-in-law's inheritance of a mill. Belle deserved better, she'd said.

'There's that chap on the haberdashery counter,' my step-father said, winking his good eye all round the table, resting it for a moment on Roger Laze in order to stir up rivalry. 'Keen as mustard, that chap is.'

I knew he'd say that. As soon as Belle Frye had mentioned that the next thing after a twenty-first was a wedding I knew he'd refer to the chap on the haberdashery counter, a pimpled youth with no roof to his mouth. It was typical of my stepfather that he'd notice a counter-hand's interest in me. He'd repeatedly mentioned it before. It was typical that he'd mention it now, in public, assuming I'd be pleased that everyone should know I had an admirer, not thinking to himself that no girl would want even remotely to be associated with an unattractive shop-boy. It wasn't teasing, even though he winked: it was an attempt to be kind. My father would just have teased. He'd have made me blush and I'd have been angry and would have complained to my mother afterwards. It seemed silly now that I'd ever minded.

'Delicious, this stuffing is,' Betty said. 'Eat every scrap of your ham,' she warned one of her children, with a threat in her voice.

'Tip-top ham,' my stepfather said.

'I'll always remember the day Matilda was born,' Joe said. 'I nearly got sacked for letting a heifer wander.'

'A beautiful autumn,' Miss Pritchard said quietly, '1930.'

I was six weeks early, my mother said, a fact she'd told me before. She'd been over to Bennett's Cross in the trap and had had to pull hard on the reins when the pony had taken fright at a piece of newspaper on the road. It was that that had brought me on.

'Old Ashburton's funeral the day before,' Arthur said.

'I never knew that.' I looked at him, interested at last in the conversation, for it wasn't important that I'd been six weeks early or that the autumn had been beautiful. But it did seem strange that in all my conversations with Mrs Ashburton it had never become established that the man she talked so much about had been buried the day before my birth.

'Big old funeral,' Arthur said.

Miss Pritchard nodded and I could see the memory of it in

her face. She wouldn't of course have attended it because the Ashburtons and she wouldn't have been on any kind of terms, there being nothing to connect them. She'd told me that when I'd asked her once; she'd explained that to people like the Ashburtons she'd been just a schoolteacher, adding that she'd only been invited to Mrs Ashburton's tennis party because everyone else had. But she'd have drawn the blinds of the school-house and would have waited in the gloom until the funeral had gone by.

I watched her as she ate her turkey and ham. I watched her thinking and remembering, not taking part in the conversations around her. She was slight and fragile-looking, wearing a brown suit with a necklace of beads falling on to a brown jersey. She'd retired about eighteen months ago; it was impossible to believe that we'd ever considered her unfair.

'You're looking lovely, dear,' Mrs Laze whispered across the table at me, leaning and poking her head out so that no one else would hear, for she was a woman who rarely spoke. The story was still told that she'd shot off Roger's foot during the war so that he wouldn't be called up, but now that the war was over it was increasingly difficult to visualise the scene and I began to think the rumour wasn't true. They both still said that an accident had happened when he was setting out to shoot rabbits.

'Thank you, Mrs Laze.'

I wasn't looking lovely, just ordinary in a lavender-coloured dress, my hair straight and reddish, freckles everywhere. Betty and Belle Frye were far prettier than I was, as they'd always been. And Betty's girls were prettier than I'd been at their age. My face was uninteresting, not quite plain, but too round, too lacking in special characteristics. I greatly disliked my hair and always had.

'D'you remember the day you kept us all in, Miss

Pritchard?' Colin Gregg said, laughing. 'The entire top class?'

'*Long fields of barley and of rye,*' Martin Draper said, laughing also. '*An abbot on an ambling pad.*'

Miss Pritchard laughed herself. She'd taught Joe and Arthur too. Roger Laze had been a favourite of hers, she'd never liked Belle Frye. She used to shout at Martin Draper because he couldn't understand things.

'Who's else for ham?' my stepfather cried out, on his feet again, waving a carving knife about. 'Ham? Turkey? Orders taken now please. Pass up the plates, young Martin.'

'The builders moved in today,' I heard Roger Laze saying in his quiet voice, answering a question Miss Pritchard had asked him. He was referring to Challacombe Manor, and I imagined the builders shaking their heads over the place, over the broken windows and the leaking roof and the floorboards that gave way when you walked on them. 'D'you remember that day?' Belle Frye shouted down the table at me, and I smiled at her and said yes, knowing she meant the day we'd climbed in through a window.

'Go round with the cider, love,' my stepfather murmured at me because my mother and Betty were busy seeing to the vegetables.

'Oh, I'm sorry,' I whispered back at him apologetically, feeling I should have noticed that no one was attending to people's glasses.

'No matter,' he said.

I don't know what I wanted then. I don't know what birthday present I'd have awarded myself if I'd been able to, October 2nd, 1951. When I'd left the Grammar School it seemed natural to work on the farm, and I preferred it to the other occupations people suggested to me. My stepfather said he could get me into Blow's and my mother wanted me to try for a position in the accounting department of the

Electricity Board because she said I was good at figures, which I wasn't. She used also to say it might be nice to be a receptionist in the Hogarth Arms Hotel. Miss Pritchard said I should become a teacher.

But I liked our farm. I liked it all the year round, the cold dairy on icy mornings, the clatter of cans and churns, driving in the cattle on a warm afternoon, working the sheepdogs. I didn't mind when the yard was thick with muck. I didn't object to the smell of silage. I even liked the hens.

Joe did all the rough work, clearing drains and the hedging and muck-spreading. My mother helped, especially at hay-making. Everyone helped then, even my stepfather; Colin Gregg and Betty came over, and the Fryes and the Lazes. More than anything else, hay-making reminded me of the past. Belle Frye and I used to run about when we were children, trying to be useful but really being a nuisance. I remembered dinnertimes, pasties and meat sandwiches in the fields, and cider and tea. My father used to eye the sky, but it always seemed to be fine then, for just long enough. 'We can laugh at it now,' he used to say when rain came and the hay was safely in.

On my twenty-first birthday I kept thinking of my mother and my stepfather becoming older in the farm-house, my stepfather retiring from Blow's and being around all during the day. It was the same resentment I'd had of him when I was a child, before he married my mother, but of course it wasn't so intense now and it wasn't so violent. Yet it felt all wrong when I contemplated remaining with them in the farm-house. It felt as if I'd married him too.

I opened my presents when we'd had our trifle, and I felt that everyone had been generous. Miss Pritchard had given me a cameo brooch which she used to wear herself and which I'd often admired. There were even little things from Betty's children. My mother and stepfather had bought me a sewing-machine and Betty a little clock for beside my bed, and Belle Frye a framed photograph of Trevor Howard, which was a joke really and typical of Belle Frye. Joe and Maudie had brought honeycombs and Mrs Laze and Roger a set of make-up and scent. There was another parcel, wrapped in red tissue paper and tied with a bow. It contained an eggcup and a matching saucer, and my stepfather said they came from the youth in Blow's. I didn't believe they did. I believed my stepfather had wrapped up the eggcup and saucer, thinking I'd be pleased if he pretended the boy had sent them. I felt awkward and embarrassed; I'd no idea what to say.

We played games with Betty's children afterwards, snap and Snakes and Ladders. Roger Laze sat next to me, too shy to say a word; I often wondered if he was in pain from his foot. At a quarter-past nine Betty and Colin Gregg had to go because it was long past their children's bedtime, and Joe and Maudie said they must be getting along also.

'So must I,' Miss Pritchard said.

She refused a lift with Colin and Betty and I said I'd like to walk with her because the night was beautiful, glaring with moonlight. I could see my mother thought I was silly to want to walk a mile and a half with an old schoolteacher who was being silly herself not to accept a lift when a lift was going. It was typical of me, my mother was thinking, like not having a more suitable twenty-first birthday party. Yet that walk through the moonlit lanes was the nicest part of it.

'Well, Matilda?' Miss Pritchard asked.

I knew what she was talking about. I said I didn't know; just stay on at the farm, I supposed.

'You'd be quite good with children, you know.'

'No.'

'Oh, well, perhaps you'll become a farmer's wife. You could do worse, I suppose.'

'I don't want to marry anyone.' The square face of Roger
Laze came into my mind, and the face of the youth in Blow's.
'I really don't.'

'People often don't until someone comes along. Mr Right
he's called.' Miss Pritchard laughed, and then we talked about
other things, in particular about the new people at Challacombe Manor and what a difference it would make having
that big old house occupied again.

*

Mr Gregary was a stout man and his wife was exceedingly
thin. Their son was much older than I'd thought he'd be,
thirty-seven as it turned out. They called him Ralphie. His
brown hair was balding, and as if to make up for that he had a
moustache. It was neat and not very big, like a trimmed
brown hedge in the pinkness of his face. He was bulky and
quite tall, rather clumsy in his movements.

All three of them came over to the farm one morning.
They'd driven down from London to see how the builders
were getting on and they came over to introduce themselves.
Neither my mother nor I liked them.

'Cooee!' Mrs Gregary called out in our yard, standing there
in unsuitable shoes and clothes. Her husband and her son
were poking about the out-houses, pointing things out to one
another as if they owned the place. They were dressed in
tweed suits which you could see had been put on specially for
the occasion; Mr Gregary carried a shooting-stick.

'Forgive the intrusion!' Mrs Gregary shouted at me when I
came out of the byre. Her voice was shrill, like a bird's. A
smile broke her bony face in half. Her hair was very smart;
her lipstick matched the red of the suit she was wearing.

'We're the Gregarys,' her husband said. 'Challacombe
Manor.'

'This was the home-farm, wasn't it?' his son asked, more modestly than his parents might have, less casually.

I said it had been and brought them into the kitchen, not knowing what on earth else to do with them. I was wearing fawn corduroy trousers and a fawn jersey that was darned and dirty. My mother was covered in flour, making a cake at the kitchen table. She became as flustered as I'd ever seen her when I walked in with the three Gregarys.

They were totally unlike their predecessor at Challacombe Manor, seeming a different species from her. As my mother cleared away her cake-making stuff I kept imagining Mrs Ashburton frowning over the Gregarys, bewildered by them and their conversation. In a humble way that annoyed me my mother apologised because the sitting-room wasn't warm, giving the Gregarys to believe it just happened to be that on this one particular morning a fire hadn't been lit there. I don't ever remember a fire being lit in the sitting-room, which was a room that smelt of must. The only time I remember anyone sitting down in it was when my father entertained a man from the taxation authorities, going through papers with him and giving him whisky.

'Now please don't put yourselves out!' Mrs Gregary shrilled. 'Anything does for the Gregarys.'

'We've been pigging it up in the house all morning,' her husband added, and he and his wife laughed over this, finding it amusing. The son laughed less.

'You could do with tea, I'm sure,' my mother said. She was cross with me for bringing them into the kitchen to find her all red-faced and floury, but what could I have done? Her hair was untidy and she was wearing a pair of slippers. 'Put out the cups, Matilda,' she ordered, finding it hard to keep the displeasure out of her voice, worried in case the Gregarys thought it was directed at them.

'So you're a Matilda?' the woman said, smiling her bony smile. 'What an enchanting name!'

She'd sat down at the table. The two men were poking about the place, trying to work out what the kitchen had been like when the house had first been built. They murmured about an open fire and an oven in the wall. They glanced up the steep back stairs that led straight out of a corner of the kitchen. They even opened cupboards.

'There'd have been a wheel there,' the son said, pointing at the Aga, 'which you turned to operate the bellows.'

His father wasn't listening to him. 'Structurally in splendid nick,' he was saying. 'Not a dodgy wall, I'd say.'

'More than you could claim for the manor!' the woman cried, her sudden shrillness making my mother jump. 'My God, the damage!'

'It's been a long time empty,' my mother said.

'Dry rot, wet rot, you name it!' cried the woman. She had four rings on the fingers of her left hand and two on her right. It seemed a mistake of some kind that she was coming to live in Challacombe Manor, like an absurdity in a dream.

'We'll be interested in buying land,' Mr Gregary revealed. His head was very neat, with strands of hair brushed into its baldness. His face had a polished look, like faintly pink marble. The flesh of his chins didn't wobble, but was firm and polished too. His eyes had a flicker of amusement in them.

'It's Ralphie's venture really,' Mrs Gregary said. 'We'll only ever come on visits.'

'Oh no, no,' the son protested.

'Longish visits, darling.'

'We're all in love with Challacombe Manor actually,' Mr Gregary said. 'We can't resist it.'

I wanted to say I loved it too, just to make the statement and by making it to imply that my love was different from theirs. I wanted it to be clear that I had loved Challacombe

Manor all my life, that I loved our farm, and the gardens of Challacombe and the lanes around it, and the meadow we used to walk through on the way home from school, a journey which had been boring at the time. I wanted to say that I loved the memory of the past, of the Challacombe Mrs Ashburton had told me about, as it had been before the first of the two wars, and the memory of our family as it had been before the second. I wanted to say all that to show them how silly it was to stand there in a tweed suit and to state you were in love with a house and couldn't resist it. I wanted to belittle what wasn't real.

Politely I offered them milk and sugar, not saying anything. My mother told me to get some biscuits and Mrs Gregary said not to bother, but I got them anyway. I put some on to a plate and handed them around while my mother talked about the farm-house and the farm. The Gregarys' son smiled at me when I held the plate out to him, and all of a sudden I was aware of a pattern of events. It seemed right that Challacombe Manor had stood there empty for so long, and Mrs Ashburton's voice echoed in my mind, telling me something when I was nine. I didn't know what it was, but all the same I felt that sense was being woven into the confusion. An event had occurred that morning in the kitchen, and it seemed extraordinary that I hadn't guessed it might, that I hadn't known that this was how things were meant to be.

'They think we're peasants, finding us like this,' my mother said crossly when they'd gone.

'It doesn't matter what they think.'

*

A long time went by, more than a year. Challacombe Manor was put to rights. The garden was cleared of the brambles that choked it; for the second time in my memory the tennis court became a tennis court again; the masonry of the summer-house was repointed. I watched it all happening. I stood in the garden and sometimes Ralphie Gregary stood beside me, as if seeking my approval for what he was doing. I walked with him through the fields; I showed him the short cut we'd taken every day from school, the walk through the meadow and then through the garden; I told him about the tennis party Mrs Ashburton had given on the Thursday afternoon before the second of the two wars.

One day we had a picnic, one Sunday morning. We had it in the garden, near a magnolia tree; there was white wine and chicken and tomatoes and chives, and then French cheese and grapes. He told me about the boarding-school he'd been to. When he left it he went into his father's motor-components business and then he had fought in the war. During the war he had slowly come to the conclusion that what he wanted to do when it was over was to live a quiet life. He had tried to return to his father's business but he hadn't cared for it in the least. 'This is what I like,' he said. I felt quite heady after the wine, wanting to lie down in the warmth of the afternoon sun. I told him how Dick and Betty and I had collected ladybirds for Mrs Ashburton so that they could eat the aphids that attacked the roses. I showed him the table in the summer-house which had been laden with food on the day of the tennis party. I smiled at him and he smiled back at me, understanding my love of the past.

'You can't make it come back, you know,' Miss Pritchard pointed out to me that same day, in her tiny sitting-room.

'I hate the present.'

We ate the macaroons she'd made, and drank tea from flowered porcelain. It was all right for Miss Pritchard. Miss Pritchard was too old to belong in the present, she didn't have to worry about it.

'You mustn't hate it.' Her pale eyes were like ice, looking

into mine. For a moment she was frightening, as she used to be when you didn't know something at school. But I knew she didn't mean to frighten me. 'You should love the man you marry, Matilda.'

She didn't know, she couldn't be expected to understand. Mrs Ashburton would have known at once what was in my mind.

'He says he loves me,' I said.

'That isn't the same.'

'Mrs Ashburton – '

'Oh, for heaven's sake forget her!'

I shook my head. 'It'll be all right, Miss Pritchard.' He wasn't like his parents, I tried to explain to her; he was thoughtful and much quieter than either his father or his mother. In all sorts of ways he had been kind to me; he considered me beautiful even though I was not; there was a goodness about him.

'You're doing something wrong,' Miss Pritchard said.

I shook my head again and smiled at her. Already I had persuaded Ralphie to have the drawing-room of Challacombe Manor redecorated as it had been in Mrs Ashburton's time, with the same striped red wallpaper, and brass lamps on the walls, connected now to the electricity he'd had put in. A lot of the furniture from the drawing-room was still there, stored in the cellars, locked in after Mrs Ashburton's death so that it wouldn't be stolen. It was the kind of thing that had happened in the war, a temporary measure until everyone had time to think again. No one knew who'd put it there, and some of it had suffered so much from damp that it had to be abandoned. But there were four upright armchairs, delicately inlaid, which needed only to be re-upholstered. I had them done as I remembered them, in crimson and pink stripes that matched the walls. There were the two small round mahogany tables I'd admired, and the pictures of local landscapes

in heavy gilt frames, and the brass fire-irons, and Mrs Ashburton's writing-desk and the writing-desk that had been her
husband's. The pale patterned carpet came from Persia, she
had told me. A corner of it had been nibbled by rats, but
Ralphie said we could put a piece of furniture over the
damage.

He told me he'd loved me the moment he'd seen me in our
farmyard. He had closed his eyes in that moment; he had
thought he was going to faint. There was no girl in England
who was loved as much as I was, he said shyly, and I wondered if it would sound any different if Roger Laze had said
it, or the counter-hand in Blow's. When I'd handed him the
biscuits, I said I'd felt the same because there didn't seem
any harm in saying that, in telling a minor lie in order to be
kind. His parents didn't like what was happening, and my
mother and stepfather didn't either. But none of that
mattered because Ralphie and I were both grown-up, because
Ralphie was getting on for forty and had a right to make a
choice. And I intended to be good to him, to cook nice food
for him and listen to his worries.

*

The wedding reception took place in the Hogarth Arms,
although the Gregarys suggested the Bower House Hotel,
twelve miles away, because there was more room there. They
wanted to pay for everything, but my mother wouldn't agree
to that. I suppose, in a way, it was all a bit awkward. You could
feel the Gregarys thinking that my stepfather worked in a
shop, that it was ridiculous of Ralphie to imagine he could
take a girl from a farmyard and put her into Challacombe
Manor.

Miss Pritchard came to the service and to the Hogarth
Arms afterwards. Betty and Belle Frye were my matrons of

honour and someone I'd never seen before was best man. I asked all sorts of people, the Fryes of course and Mrs Laze and Roger, and other people I'd been at school with, and Mrs Latham from Burrow Farm. I asked people from the shops in the town, and the people from the Hare and Hounds at Bennett's Cross, and the man from the artificial insemination centre, and Joe and Maudie, and Arthur. The Gregarys asked lots of people also, people like themselves.

I kept wanting to close my eyes as I stood in the lounge of the Hogarth Arms. I wanted to float away on the bubbles of the champagne I'd drunk. I couldn't understand why Miss Pritchard didn't see that everything was all right, that strictly speaking everything was perfect: I was there in my wedding-dress, married to Ralphie, who wasn't unkind; Challacombe Manor was as it used to be in its heyday, it was as Mrs Ashburton had known it as a bride also. Going to live there and watching over it seemed to make up for everything, for all the bad things that had happened, my father's death, and Dick's, and the arm that Mr Frye had had blown off, and Roger Laze's foot. The Fryes had sold their land to Ralphie because farming hadn't been easy since the losing of the arm. They'd be tenants in their farm-house now for the rest of their lives, with a couple of acres they rented back from Ralphie: the arrangement suited them because there was no son to leave the farm to and they could enter old age in comfort. With the passing of time our own farm would revert to being the home-farm again, when it became too much for my mother. I couldn't help feeling that Ralphie knew it was what I wanted, and in his thoughtful kindliness had quietly brought it all about.

'Bless you, child,' my stepfather said.

I smiled at him because it was the thing to do on my wedding-day, but when he drew away his narrow face from mine after he'd kissed me I could see in it a reflection of what

Miss Pritchard had said: he believed I shouldn't have married a man I didn't love, not even Ralphie, who was good and kind. It was in my mother's face too when she kissed me, and in my sister's and Belle Frye's, but not in the Gregarys' because none of them knew me.

'I'm happy,' I kept saying, smiling.

*

We went away to a hotel and then we came back to Challacombe. I'd almost imagined there'd be servants waiting, but of course there weren't. Instead there were the people called Stritch, a man and his wife. I'd always known the Stritches. I remembered Belle Frye and myself singing as we went by their cottage, raising our voices in a song about a bad-tempered woman because that was what Mrs Stritch was. I didn't like finding them there when we came back from our honeymoon.

There were small, silly misunderstandings between Ralphie and myself. They didn't matter because Ralphie's goodness lapped over them, and when I think about them I can't even remember very clearly what some of them were. All I can remember was that Ralphie always listened to me: I think he believed he needed to be gentle with me because I was still almost a child. I couldn't understand why he hadn't married someone before. I asked him, but all he ever did was to smile and shake his head. I had the feeling that in his mind there was the house, and the estate, and me; that I was part of the whole; that he had fallen in love with everything. All that, of course, should have been a bond between us, because the house and the estate formed the island of common ground where both of us were happy. Our marriage had Challacombe at its heart, and I was only alarmed when Ralphie spoke about our children because I didn't see that there was a need for them. Children, it seemed to me, would be all wrong. They would distort the pattern I could so precisely sense. They felt particularly alien.

Ralphie was patient with me. 'Yes, I understand,' he had said on the evening of our marriage, standing in front of me in the bedroom of the hotel he'd brought me to. The walls of the room were papered with a pinkish paper; Ralphie was wearing a flannel suit. In the hotel restaurant, called the Elizabethan Room, we had had dinner and wine. I'd had a coupe Jacques and Ralphie some kind of apricot soufflé. 'Yes,' he said again in the pinkish bedroom, and I talked to him for ages, making him sit beside me on one of the two beds in the room, holding his hand and stroking it. 'Yes, I understand,' he said, and I really think he did; I really think he understood that there was no question of children at Challacombe. He kept saying he loved me; he would never not love me, he said.

On the evening when we returned from our honeymoon I brought up the subject of the Stritches straight away. I explained it all to Ralphie when we were having supper, but he replied that he'd told me ages ago the Stritches were going to be at Challacombe. The arrangement apparently was that Mrs Stritch would come to the house every day except Sunday, and her husband would work in the garden. Ralphie repeated most earnestly that he'd told me all this before, that he'd quite often mentioned the Stritches, and had asked my opinion of them. I knew he was mistaken, but I didn't want to say so. Ralphie had a lot on his mind, buying the Fryes' land and negotiating to buy Mrs Laze's, and wondering how to go about buying my mother's. He didn't know much about farming, but he was keenly endeavouring to learn. All of it took time: he couldn't be blamed if he made little mistakes about what he'd said to me and what he hadn't.

'You see, it's awkward, Ralphie,' I explained again one

night at supper, smiling at him. 'Belle Frye and I said terrible things to her.'

'Oh, Mrs Stritch'll have forgotten. Darling, it's donkeys' years ago.'

For some reason I didn't like him using that endearment, especially when he put the word at the beginning of a sentence, as he often for some reason did. I don't know why I objected so much to that. It was how it sounded, I think, a sort of casualness that seemed out of place in the house. There was another thing: he had a way of turning the pages of a newspaper, one page and then another, until finally he pored over the obituaries and the little advertisements. I didn't like the way he did that. And I didn't like the way he sometimes drummed the surface of a table with one hand when he was thinking, as if playing the piano. Another thing was, he wore leather gaiters.

'It's just that it's embarrassing for me,' I said, still smiling. 'Having her around.'

He ate beetroot and a sardine salad I had prepared because he'd told me he liked sardines. I'd made him wait that morning in the car while I went into a shop and bought several tins. I wouldn't let him see what they were, wanting it to be a surprise. He said:

'Actually, Mrs Stritch is very nice. And he's doing wonders with the garden.'

'We called her terrible names. She'd be hanging out her washing or something and we'd deliberately raise our voices. "Worst temper in Dorset," Belle would say and then we'd giggle. "Driven her husband to drink," I'd say. "Mrs Stritch is a – very nice lady," we used to call out in sing-song voices.'

'All children call people names.'

'Oh, Betty would never have let me do that. Going home from school with Betty and Dick was different. But then they left, you see. They left the Grammar when Belle and I were

just finishing at Miss Pritchard's Primary, the same time
that – '

'Darling, the Stritches have to be here. We have to have
help.'

'I wish you wouldn't do that, Ralphie.'

'Do what?'

'I wish you wouldn't begin a sentence like that.'

He frowned at my smile, not understanding what was in my
mind even though he was an understanding person. He didn't
understand when I explained that I could manage the house
on my own, that I didn't need Mrs Stritch in the way. I
explained to him that Mrs Stritch had once taken a pair of
gloves from Blow's. 'Please let's try it,' he said, and of course
I didn't want to be difficult. I wanted him to see that I was
prepared to try what he wished to try.

'Yes,' I said, smiling at him.

*

Like a black shadow she was in the drawing-room. She leaned
back in her chair, one hand stretched out to the round table
in front of her. It was just a memory, not the ghost of Mrs
Ashburton, nothing like that. But the memory would have
been better if Mrs Stritch hadn't always been around when
Ralphie wasn't. Ralphie would go off every morning in his
gaiters, and then Mrs Stritch would arrive. She would dust
and clean and carry buckets of soapy water about the house.
Her husband would come to the kitchen to have lunch with
her, and Ralphie and I would have lunch in the dining-room.
All afternoon I'd continue to be aware of her in the house,
making little noises as she did her work. When it was time
for her to go Ralphie would be back again.

'We're buying the Lazes' land,' he said one evening, crossing the drawing-room and pouring some whisky for himself

from a decanter. I could see that he was delighted. 'I think your mother'll want to sell too,' he said.

I knew she would. Joe and Arthur were getting old, my stepfather was always saying the day would come. He'd no interest in the farm himself, and my mother would be glad not to have the responsibility.

'But you'll let the Lazes stay on in the farm-house?' I said, because it worried me that they should have to move away.

He shook his head. He said they didn't want to. They wanted to go and live nearer the town, like the Fryes did.

'The Fryes? But the Fryes don't want to move away. You said they were going to farm a couple of acres – '

'They've changed their minds.'

I didn't smile at him any more because I didn't like what he was saying. He'd explained quite clearly that the Fryes would stay in the farm-house, and that the Lazes could if they wanted to. He had reassured me about that. Yet he said now:

'You wanted the estate to be all together again, Matilda.'

'I didn't want people driven off, Ralphie. Not the Fryes and the Lazes. And what about my mother? Will she go also?'

'It'll be your mother's choice, Matilda. As it was theirs.'

'You've bought them all out. You promised me one thing and – '

'We need the housing for our own men.'

I felt deceived. I imagined a discussion between Ralphie and the man he'd hired to look after the estate, a cold-faced man called Epstone. I imagined Epstone saying that if you were going to do the thing, do it properly, offer them enough and they'll go. I imagined a discussion between Ralphie and his father, Ralphie asking if he could have another loan in order to plan his estate correctly and his father agreeing.

'Well, I dare say,' I said to Ralphie, smiling at him again, determined not to be cross.

'In the old days on the Challacombe estate,' he said, 'it would have happened less humanely.'

I didn't want to hear him going on about that so I didn't ask him what he meant. Even though he was considerate, I had begun to feel I was his property. It was an odd feeling, and I think it came from the other feeling I had, that he'd married me because I was part of an idea he'd fallen in love with. I used to look at the china vases on the drawing-room mantelpiece and feel like one of them, or like the carpets and the new wallpaper. I was part of something his money had created, and I don't think he noticed that the rattling of his newspaper or the clink of the decanter against his glass had a way of interrupting my thoughts. These noises, and his footsteps in the hall or in a room, were like the noises Mrs Stritch made with her buckets and the Electrolux, but of course I never told him that.

I have forgotten a little about all that time in the house with Ralphie. He didn't always tell me what was happening on the estate; in a way he talked more readily to Mrs Stritch, for I often heard him. He also talked to himself. He would pace up and down the lawns Mr Stritch had restored, wagging his head or nodding, while I watched him from a window of the house. As time went by, it was clear that he had done what he'd wanted. As he said, the estate was all of a piece again. He had bought our farm and the farm-house, offering so much for both that it couldn't be resisted. Joe and Arthur worked for him now.

Years were passing. Sometimes I walked over to see Miss Pritchard, going by the meadow we'd gone through on our way to school. I can't quite recall what we talked about as we had tea; only bits from our conversations come back to me. There is my own cheerfulness, my smiling at Miss Pritchard, and Miss Pritchard's glumness. Now and again I walked down to our farm and sat for a while with my mother, getting up to go before my stepfather returned. I went to see Betty and Belle, but I did that less and less. I began to think that they were all a little jealous of me. I thought that because I sensed an atmosphere when I went on these visits. 'You're cruel, Matilda,' Miss Pritchard said once, seeming to be unable to control the ill-temper that had caused the remark to surface. She turned her head away from me when she'd spoken. 'Cruel,' she said again, and I laughed because of course that was nonsensical. I remember thinking it was extraordinary that Miss Pritchard should be jealous.

Ralphie, I believe, must have begun to live some kind of life of his own. He often went out in the evenings, all dressed up. He came back jovial and would come to my room to kiss me good-night, until eventually I asked him not to. When I enquired at breakfast about where he'd been the night before his answer was always the same, that he had been to a house in the neighbourhood for dinner. He always seemed surprised that I should ask the question, claiming on each occasion that he had told me these details beforehand and that I had, in fact, refused to accompany him. In all this I really do not think he can have been right.

I welcomed the occasions when Ralphie went out in the evenings. I drew the curtains in the drawing-room and sat by the fire, just happy to be there. I thought of the time when we were all together in the farm-house, my father teasing Betty about Colin Gregg, Dick going as red as a sunset because my father mentioned an empty Woodbine packet he'd found. Every Sunday morning Ralphie went to church and, since Mrs Stritch didn't come on Sundays, that was another good time. Ralphie would return and sit opposite me in the dining-room, carving the beef I'd cooked him, looking at me now and again from his pink face, his teeth like chalk beneath the trim brown hedge of his moustache. I wanted to explain to him that I was happy in the house when Mrs Stritch wasn't there and when he wasn't there. I wanted to make him understand that old Mrs Ashburton had wanted me to be in her house, that that was why she had told me so much when I was a child, that everything had to do with the two wars there'd been. He didn't know as much about war as Mrs Ashburton had, even though he'd fought in one: I wanted to explain that to him, too. But I never did because his eyes would have begun to goggle, which they had a way of doing if something he couldn't comprehend was put to him. It was easier just to cook his meals and smile at him.

There was another thing Ralphie said I had forgotten: a conversation about a party he gave. When I asked him afterwards he repeatedly assured me we'd had a conversation about it, and in all honesty I believe it must have been his own memory that was at fault. Not that it matters in the least which way round it was. What mattered at the time was that the house was suddenly full of people. I was embroidering in the drawing-room, slowly stitching the eye of a peacock, and the next thing was that Ralphie's parents were embracing me, pretending they liked me. It seemed they had come for the weekend, so that they could be at the party, which was to be on the following night. They brought other people with them in their grey Daimler, people called Absom. Mrs Absom was thin, like Mrs Gregary, but younger than Mrs Gregary. Mr Absom was stout, like Mr Gregary, but not like polished marble, and younger also.

Mrs Stritch's daughter Nellie came to help on the Saturday morning and stayed all day. Apparently Ralphie had given Mrs Stritch money to buy navy-blue overalls for both of them so that they'd stand out from the guests at the party. They bought them in Blow's, Mrs Stritch told me, and it was quite funny to think that my stepfather might have served them, even fitted them with the overalls. Mr Stritch was there on the night of the party also, organising the parking of cars.

It all took place in the drawing-room. People stood around with drinks in their hands. Ralphie introduced them to me, but I found it hard to know what to say to them. It was his mother, really, who gave the party, moving about the drawing-room as if she owned it. I realised then why she'd come for the weekend.

'So how you like Challacombe Manor, Mrs Gregary?' a man with very short hair asked me.

Politely I replied that I was fond of the house.

'Ralphie!' the man said, gesturing around him. 'Fantastic!' He added that he enjoyed life in the country, and told me the names of his dogs. He said he liked fishing and always had.

There were fifty-two people in the drawing-room, which had begun to smell of cigarette-smoke and alcohol. It was hot because Mrs Gregary had asked Mrs Stritch to make up an enormous fire, and it was becoming noisier because as the party advanced people talked more loudly. A woman, wearing a coffee-coloured dress, appeared to be drunk. She had sleek black hair and kept dropping her cigarette on to Mrs Ashburton's Persian carpet. Once when she bent to pick it up she almost toppled over.

'Hullo,' a man said. 'You're Mrs Ralphie.'

He was younger than the short-haired man. He stood very close to me, pressing me into a corner. He told me his name but I didn't listen because listening was an effort in the noisy room.

'Ever been there?' this man shouted at me. 'Ferns magnificent, this time of year.'

He smiled at me, revealing jagged teeth. 'Ferns,' he shouted, and then he said that he, or someone, had a collection of stuffed birds. I could feel one of his knees pressing into the side of my leg. He asked me something and I shook my head again. Then he went away.

Mrs Stritch and her daughter had covered the dining-room table with food. All kinds of cold meats there were, and various salads, and tarts of different kinds, and huge bowls of whipped cream, and cheeses. They'd done it all at the direction of Mrs Gregary: just by looking at the table you could see Mrs Gregary's hand in it, Mrs Stritch wouldn't have known a thing about it. The sideboard was entirely taken up with bottles of wine and glasses. The electric light wasn't turned on: there were slender red candles everywhere, another touch of Mrs Gregary's, or even Mrs Absom's. I had crossed the hall to the dining-room in order to get away from the noise for a moment. I thought I'd sit there quietly for a little; I was surprised to see all the food and the candles.

I was alone in the dining-room, as I'd guessed I would be. But it wasn't any longer a room you could be quiet in. Everything seemed garish, the red glitter of the wine bottles, the red candles, dish after dish of different food, the cheeses. It made me angry that Mrs Gregary and Mrs Absom should have come to Challacombe Manor in order to instruct Mrs Stritch, that Mrs Gregary should strut about in the drawing-room, telling people who she was.

I jumbled the food about, dropping pieces of meat into the bowls of cream, covering the tarts with salad. I emptied two wine bottles over everything, watching the red stain spreading on the table-cloth and on the cheeses. They had no right to be in the house, their Daimler had no right to be in the garage. I had asked years ago that Mrs Stritch should not be here.

In the drawing-room someone said to me:

'I enjoy to get out after pheasants, to tramp with my dogs.'

It was the short-haired man. I hadn't noticed that he was a foreigner. I knew before he told me that he was German.

'You have dogs, Mrs Gregary?'

I smiled at him and shook my head. It seemed extraordinary that there should be a German in this drawing-
room. I remembered when Mrs Ashburton used to talk to me
about the First World War that I'd imagined the Germans as
grey and steel-like, endlessly consuming black bread. This
man didn't seem in the least like that.

'Hasenfuss,' he said. 'The name, you know.'

For a moment the room was different. People were dancing
there at some other party. A man was standing near the door,
waiting for someone to arrive, seeming a little anxious. It was
all just a flash, as if I had fallen asleep and for a moment had
had a dream.

'We are enemies and then we are friends. I advise on
British beer, I enjoy your British countryside. It is my pro-
fession to advise on British beer. I would not enjoy to live in
Germany today, Mrs Gregary.'

'You are the first German I have ever met.'

'Oh, I hope not the last.'

Again the drawing-room was different. There was the
music and the dancing and the man by the door. The
girl he was waiting for arrived. It was Mrs Ashburton, as she
was in the photographs she'd showed me when I was nine.
And he was the man she'd married.

'Here I am standing,' said the short-haired German, 'in the
house of the people who put Mr Hitler in his place.' He
laughed loudly when he'd made that remark, displaying more
gold fillings than I had ever before seen in anyone's mouth.
'Your father-in-law, you know, made a lot of difference to
the war.'

I didn't know what he was talking about. I was thinking
of the dining-room and what would happen when everyone
walked into it. It was like something Belle Frye and I might
have done together, only we'd never have had the courage.
It was worse than singing songs outside Mrs Stritch's cottage.

'In that I mean,' the German said, 'the manufacturing of guns.'

I hadn't known that. My stepfather had said that the Gregarys had made a killing, but I hadn't thought about it. Ralphie had never told me that his father's motor-components business had made guns during the war, that the war had made him rich. It was the war that enabled Ralphie now to buy up all the land and set the Challacombe estate to rights again. It was the war that had restored this drawing-room.

'The world is strange,' the German said.

I went upstairs and came down with Ralphie's gaiters. I remember standing at the door of the drawing-room, looking at all the people drinking, and seeing again, for an instant, the dancers of the distant past. Mrs Ashburton and her husband were among them, smiling at one another.

I moved into the room and when I reached the fire-place I threw the gaiters on to the flames. Someone noticed me, Mrs Absom, I think it was. She seemed quite terrified as she watched me.

The German was again alone. He told me he enjoyed alcohol, emphasising this point by reaching his glass out towards Mrs Stritch, who was passing with some mixture in a jug. I told him about Mrs Ashburton's husband, how he had returned from the first of the two wars suffering from shell-shock, how the estate had fallen to bits because of that, how everything had had to be mortgaged. I was telling her story, and I was even aware that my voice was quite like hers, that I felt quite like her as well. Everything had happened all over again, I told the German, the repetition was cloying. I told him about Mrs Ashburton's law of averages, how some men always came back from a war, how you had to pray it would be the men who were closest to you, how it would have been better if her own husband had been killed.

The smell of burning leather was unpleasant in the room.

People noticed it. Ralphie poked at his smouldering gaiters with a poker, wondering why they were there. I saw his mother looking at me while I talked to the German. 'Mrs Ashburton did what she could,' I said. 'There's nothing wrong with living in the past.'

I went around from person to person then, asking them to go. The party had come to an end, I explained, but Mrs Gregory tried to contradict that. 'No, no, no,' she cried. 'We've scarcely started.' She ushered people into the dining-room and then, of course, she saw that I was right.

'I would like you to go as well,' I said to Mr Gregory in the hall, while the visitors were rooting for their coats. 'I would like you to go and take the Absoms with you. I did not invite the Absoms here any more than I invited you.' I said it while smiling at him, so that he could see I wasn't being quarrel-some. 'Oh now, look here, Matilda!' he protested.

In the kitchen I told Mrs Stritch that I'd rather she didn't return to the house. I could easily manage on my own, I explained to her, trying to be kind in how I put it. 'It's just that it's embarrassing,' I said, 'having you here.'

The Gregarys and the Absoms didn't go until the follow-ing day, a Sunday. They didn't say goodbye to me, and I only knew that they had finally departed because Ralphie told me. 'Why are you doing this?' he said, sitting down on the other side of the fire in the drawing-room, where I was embroider-ing my peacocks. 'Why, Matilda?' he said again.

'I don't understand you.'

'Yes, you do.'

He had never spoken like that before. All his considerate-ness had disappeared. His eyes were fiery and yet cold. His large hands looked as though they wanted to commit some act of violence. I shook my head at him. He said:

'You're pretending to be deranged.'

I laughed. I didn't like him sitting opposite me like that,

with his eyes and his hands. Everything about him had been a pretence: all he wanted was his own way, to have his mother giving parties in my drawing-room, to have Mrs Stritch forever vacuuming the stairs, to own me as he owned the land and the farms and the house. It was horrible, making money out of war.

'You don't even cook for me,' he said to my astonishment. 'Half-raw potatoes, half-raw chops – '

'Oh, Ralphie, don't be silly. You know I cook for you.'

'The only food that is edible in this house is made by Mrs Stritch. You can cook if you want to, only you can't be bothered.'

'I do my best. In every way I do my best. I want our marriage to be – '

'It isn't a marriage,' he said. 'It's never been a marriage.'

'We were married in the church.'

'Stop talking like that!' He shouted at me again, suddenly on his feet, looking down at me. His face was red with fury; I thought he might pick something up and hit me with it.

'I'm sorry,' I said.

'You're as sane as I am. For God's sake, Matilda!'

'Of course I'm sane,' I said quietly. 'I could not be sitting here if I were not. I could not live a normal life.'

'You don't live a normal life.' He was shouting again, stamping about the room like an animal. 'Every second of every day is devoted to the impression you wish to give.'

'But, Ralphie, why should I wish to give an impression?'

'To cover up your cruelty.'

I laughed again, gently so as not to anger him further. I remembered Miss Pritchard saying I was cruel, and of course there was the cruelty Mrs Ashburton had spoken of, the cruelty that was natural in wartime. I had felt it in myself when my father had been killed, and when Dick had been killed. I had felt it when I had first seen my mother embracing the man who became my stepfather, too soon after my father had died. God, if He existed, I had thought in the end, was something to be frightened of.

'The war is over,' I said, and he looked at me, startled by that remark.

'It isn't for you,' he said. 'It'll never be for you. It's all we ever hear from you, the war and that foolish old woman – '

'It wasn't over for Mrs Ashburton either. How could it be when she lived to see it all beginning again?'

'Oh, for God's sake, stop talking about her. If it hadn't been for her, if she hadn't taken advantage of a nine-year-old child with her rubbish, you would be a normal human being now.' He stood above my chair again, pushing his red face down at me and speaking slowly. 'She twisted you, she filled you full of hate. Whatever you are now, that dead woman has done to you. Millions have suffered in war,' he suddenly shouted. 'Who's asking you to dwell on it, for God's sake?'

'There are people who find it hard to pick up the pieces. Because they're made like that.'

'You'd have picked them up if she hadn't prevented you. She didn't want you to, because she couldn't herself.' Furiously he added, 'Some kind of bloody monster she was.'

I didn't reply to any of that. He said, with a bitterness in his voice which had never been there before, 'All I know is that she has destroyed Challacombe for me.'

'It was never real for you, Ralphie. I shall never forget the happiness in our farm-house. What memories of Challacombe can you have?'

But Ralphie wasn't interested in the happiness in our farm-house, or in memories he couldn't have. All he wanted to do was wildly to castigate me.

'How can I live here with you?' he demanded in a rough,

hard voice, pouring at the same time a glass of whisky for himself. 'You said you loved me once. Yet everything you do is calculated to let me see your hatred. What have I done,' he shouted at me, 'that you hate me, Matilda?'

I quietly replied that he was mistaken. I protested that I did not hate him, but even as I spoke I realised that that wasn't true. I hated him for being what he was, for walking with his parents into the farmyard that morning, for thinking he had a place in the past. I might have confided in him but I did not want to. I might have said that I remembered, years ago, Miss Pritchard coming to see my mother and what Miss Pritchard had said. I had eavesdropped on the stairs that led to the kitchen, while she said she believed there was something the matter with me. It was before the death of Dick, after I'd discovered about my mother and the man who was now my stepfather. 'She dwells on her father's death,' Miss Pritchard had said and she'd gone on to say that I dwelt as well on the conversations I'd had with old Mrs Ashburton. I remembered the feeling I'd had, standing there listening: the feeling that the shell-shock of Mr Ashburton, carried back to Challacombe from the trenches in 1917, had conveyed itself in some other form to his wife, that she, as much as he, had been a victim of violence. I felt it because Miss Pritchard was saying something like it to my mother. 'There are casualties in wars,' she said, 'thousands of miles from where the fighting is.' She was speaking about me. I'd caught a mood, she said, from old Mrs Ashburton, and when my mother replied that you couldn't catch a mood like you caught the measles Miss Pritchard sharply replied that you could. '*Folie à deux* the French call it,' she insisted, an expression I welcomed and have never since forgotten. There had been *folie à deux* all over this house, and in the garden too, when he came back with his mind in pieces. She had shared the horror with him and later she had shared it with me, as if guessing that I, too, would be a casualty. As long as I lived I would honour that *folie* in their house. I would honour her and her husband, and my father and Dick, and the times they had lived in. It was right that the cruelty was there.

'Of course I don't hate you,' I said again. 'Of course not, Ralphie.'

He did not reply. He stood in the centre of the drawing-room with his glass in his hand, seeming like a beast caught in a snare: he had all the beaten qualities of such an animal. His shoulders slouched, his eyes had lost their fire.

'I don't know what to do,' he said.

'You may stay here,' I said, 'with me.' Again I smiled, wishing to make the invitation seem kind. I could feel no pity for him.

'How could I?' he shouted. 'My God, how could I? I lose count of the years in this house. I look at you every day, I look at your eyes and your hair and your face, I look at your hands and your fingernails, and the arch of your neck. I love you; every single inch of you I love. How can I live here and love you like that, Matilda? I shared a dream with you, Matilda, a dream that no one else but you would have understood. I longed for my quiet life, with you and with our children. I married you out of passion and devotion. You give me back nothing.'

'You married me because I was part of something, part of the house and the estate – '

'That isn't true. That's a rubbishy fantasy; not a word of it is true.'

'I cannot help it if I believe it.' I wasn't smiling now. I let my feelings show in my eyes because there was no point in doing otherwise any more. Not in a million years would he understand. 'Yes, I despise you,' I said. 'I have never felt affection for you.'

I said it calmly and bent my head again over my embroidery.

He poured more whisky and sat down in the chair on the other side of the fire-place. I spoke while still embroidering, magenta thread in a feather of my peacock's tail.

'You must never again touch me,' I said. 'Not even in passing me by in a room. We shall live here just as we are, but do not address me with endearments. I shall cook and clean, but there shall be no parties. Your parents are not welcome. It is discourteous to me to give parties behind my back and to employ people I do not care for.'

'You were told, you know perfectly well you were told – '

'You will fatten and shamble about the rooms of this house. I shall not complain. You will drink more whisky, and perhaps lose heart in your dream. "His wife does not go out," people will say; "they have no children. He married beneath him, but it isn't that that cut him down to size."'

'Matilda, please. Please for a moment listen to me – '

'Why should I? And why should you not lose heart in your dream because isn't your dream ridiculous? If you think that your Challacombe estate is like it was, or that you in your vulgarity could ever make it so, then you're the one who is deranged.'

I had not taken my eyes from the peacock's tail. I imagined a patch of damp developing on the ceiling of an upstairs room. I imagined his lifting the heavy lead-lined hatch in the loft and stepping out on to the roof to find the missing tile. I stood with him on the roof and pointed to the tile, lodged in a gutter. I had removed it myself and slid it down the incline of the roof. He could reach it with an effort, by grasping the edge of the chimney-stack to be safe. I heard the thump of his body as it struck the cobbles below. I heard it in the drawing-room as I worked my stitches, while he drank more whisky and for a while was silent.

'Damn you,' he shouted in the end, once more on his feet and seething above me. 'Damn you to hell, Matilda.'

'No matter what you do,' I said, still sewing the magenta thread, 'I shall not leave this house.'

*

He sold everything he'd bought except the house and garden. He sold the land and the farm-houses, the Fryes' and the Lazes' and what had been ours. He didn't tell me about any of it until he'd done it. 'I'll be gone in a week,' he said one day, six or seven months after we'd had that quarrel, and I did not urge him to stay.

*

It is a long time ago now, that day. I can't quite remember Ralphie's going, even though with such vividness I remember so much else. There are new people in all the farm-houses now, whole families have grown up; again the tennis court is overgrown. Miss Pritchard died of course, and my mother and my stepfather. I never saw much of them after Ralphie went, and I never laid eyes on Ralphie or even had a line from him. But if Ralphie walked in now I would take his hand and say I was sorry for the cruelty that possessed me and would not go away, the cruelty she used to talk about, a natural thing in wartime. It lingered and I'm sorry it did, and perhaps after all this time Ralphie would understand and believe, but Ralphie, I know, will never return.

I sit here now in her drawing-room, and may perhaps become as old as she was. Sometimes I walk up to the meadow where the path to school was, but the meadow isn't there any more. There are rows of coloured caravans, and motor-cars and shacks. In the garden I can hear the voices of people drifting down to me, and the sound of music from their wireless sets. Nothing is like it was.

Torridge

Perhaps nobody ever did wonder what Torridge would be like as a man – or what Wiltshire or Mace-Hamilton or Arrowsmith would be like, come to that. Torridge at thirteen had a face with a pudding look, matching the sound of his name. He had small eyes and short hair like a mouse's. Within the collar of his grey regulation shirt the knot of his House tie was formed with care, a maroon triangle of just the right shape and bulk. His black shoes were always shiny.

Torridge was unique in some way: perhaps only because he was beyond the pale and appeared, irritatingly, to be unaware of it. He wasn't good at games and had difficulty in understanding what was being explained in the classroom. He would sit there frowning, half smiling, his head a little to one side. Occasionally he would ask some question that caused an outburst of groaning. His smile would increase then. He would glance around the classroom, not flustered or embarrassed in the least, seeming to be pleased that he had caused such a response. He was naïve to the point where it was hard to believe he wasn't pretending, but his naïveté was real and was in time universally recognised as such. A master called Buller Yeats reserved his cruellest shafts of scorn for it, sighing whenever his eyes chanced to fall on Torridge, pretending to believe his name was Porridge.

Of the same age as Torridge, but similar in no other way, were Wiltshire, Mace-Hamilton and Arrowsmith. All three of them were blond-haired and thin, with a common sharpness about their features. They wore, untidily, the same clothes as Torridge, their House ties knotted any old how, the laces in their scuffed shoes often tied in several places. They excelled at different games and were quick to sense what was what. Attractive boys, adults had more than once called them.

The friendship among the three of them developed because, in a way, Torridge was what he was. From the first time they were aware of him – on the first night of their first term – he appeared to be special. In the darkness after lights-out someone was trying not to sob and Torridge's voice was piping away, not homesick in the least. His father had a button business was what he was saying: he'd probably be going into the button business himself. In the morning he was identified, a boy in red and blue striped pyjamas, still chattering in the wash-room. 'What's your father do, Torridge?' Arrowsmith asked at breakfast, and that was the beginning. 'Dad's in the button business,' Torridge beamingly replied. 'Torridge's, you know.' But no one did know.

He didn't, as other new boys, make a particular friend. For a while he attached himself to a small gang of homesick boys who had only their malady in common, but after a time this gang broke up and Torridge found himself on his own, though it seemed quite happily so. He was often to be found in the room of the kindly housemaster of Junior House, an ageing white-haired figure called Old Frosty, who listened sympathetically to complaints of injustice at the hands of other masters, always ready to agree that the world was a hard place. 'You should hear Buller Yeats on Torridge, sir,' Wiltshire used to say in Torridge's presence. 'You'd think Torridge had no feelings, sir.' Old Frosty would reply that Buller Yeats was a frightful man. 'Take no notice, Torridge,' he'd add in his kindly voice, and Torridge would smile, making it clear that he didn't mind in the least what Buller Yeats said. 'Torridge knows true happiness,' a new young master, known as Mad Wallace, said in an unguarded moment one day, a remark which caused immediate uproar in a Geography class. It was afterwards much repeated, like 'Dad's in the button business' and 'Torridge's, you know.' The true happiness of Torridge became a joke, the particular property of Wiltshire and Mace-Hamilton and Arrowsmith. Furthering the joke, they claimed that knowing Torridge was a rare experience, that the private realm of his innocence and his happiness was even exotic. Wiltshire insisted that one day the school would be proud of him. The joke was worked to death.

At the school it was the habit of certain senior boys to 'take an interest in' juniors. This varied from glances and smiles across the dining-hall to written invitations to meet in some secluded spot at a stated time. Friendships, taking a variety of forms, were then initiated. It was flattering, and very often a temporary antidote for homesickness, when a new boy received the agreeable but bewildering attentions of an important fifth-former. A meeting behind Chapel led to the negotiating of a barbed-wire fence on a slope of gorse bushes, the older boy solicitous and knowledgeable. There were well-trodden paths and nooks among the gorse where smoking could take place with comparative safety. Farther afield, in the hills, there were crude shelters composed of stones and corrugated iron. Here, too, the emphasis was on smoking and romance.

New boys very soon became aware of the nature of older boys' interest in them. The flattery changed its shape, an adjustment was made – or the new boys retreated in panic from this area of school life. Andrews and Butler, Webb and Mace-Hamilton, Dillon and Pratt, Tothill and Goldfish Stewart, Good and Wiltshire, Sainsbury Major and Arrowsmith, Brewitt and King: the liaisons were renowned, the combinations of names sometimes seeming like a music-hall turn, a soft-shoe shuffle of entangled hearts. There was faithlessness, too: the Honourable Anthony Swain made the rounds of the senior boys, a fickle and tartish *bijou*, desired and yet despised.

Torridge's puddingy appearance did not suggest that he had *bijou* qualities, and glances did not readily come his way in the dining-hall. This was often the fate, or good fortune, of new boys and was not regarded as a sign of qualities lacking. Yet quite regularly an ill-endowed child would mysteriously become the object of fifth- and sixth-form desire. This remained a puzzle to the juniors until they themselves became fifth- or sixth-formers and desire was seen to have to do with something deeper than superficial good looks.

It was the apparent evidence of this truth that caused Torridge, first of all, to be aware of the world of *bijou* and protector. He received a note from a boy in the Upper Fifth who had previously eschewed the sexual life offered by the school. He was a big, black-haired youth with glasses and a protruding forehead, called Fisher.

'Hey, what's this mean?' Torridge enquired, finding the note under his pillow, tucked into his pyjamas. 'Here's a bloke wants to go for a walk.'

He read the invitation out: '*If you would like to come for a walk meet me by the electricity plant behind Chapel. Half-past four Tuesday afternoon. R. A. J. Fisher.*'

'Jesus Christ!' said Armstrong.

'You've got an admirer, Porridge,' Mace-Hamilton said.

'Admirer?'

'He wants you to be his *bijou*,' Wiltshire explained.

'What's it mean, *bijou*?'

'Tart, it means, Porridge.'

'Tart?'

'Friend. He wants to be your protector.'

'What's it mean, protector?'

'He loves you, Porridge.'

'I don't even know the bloke.'

'He's the one with the big forehead. He's a half-wit actually.'

'Half-wit?'

'His mother let him drop on his head. Like yours did, Porridge.'

'My mum never.'

Everyone was crowding around Torridge's bed. The note was passed from hand to hand. 'What's your dad do, Porridge?' Wiltshire suddenly asked, and Torridge automatically replied that he was in the button business.

'You've got to write a note back to Fisher, you know,' Mace-Hamilton pointed out.

'Dear Fisher,' Wiltshire prompted, 'I love you.'

'But I don't even – '

'It doesn't matter not knowing him. You've got to write a letter and put it in his pyjamas.'

Torridge didn't say anything. He placed the note in the top pocket of his jacket and slowly began to undress. The other boys drifted back to their own beds, still amused by the development. In the wash-room the next morning Torridge said:

'I think he's quite nice, that Fisher.'

'Had a dream about him, did you, Porridge?' Mace-Hamilton enquired. 'Got up to tricks, did he?'

'No harm in going for a walk.'

'No harm at all, Porridge.'

In fact, a mistake had been made. Fisher, in his haste or his excitement, had placed the note under the wrong pillow. It was Arrowsmith, still allied with Sainsbury Major, whom he wished to attract.

That this error had occurred was borne in on Torridge when he turned up at the electricity plant on the following Tuesday. He had not considered it necessary to reply to

Fisher's note, but he had, across the dining-hall, essayed a smile or two in the older boy's direction: it had surprised him to meet with no response. It surprised him rather more to meet with no response by the electricity plant. Fisher just looked at him and then turned his back, pretending to whistle.

'Hullo, Fisher,' Torridge said.

'Hop it, look. I'm waiting for someone.'

'I'm Torridge, Fisher.'

'I don't care who you are.'

'You wrote me that letter.' Torridge was still smiling. 'About a walk, Fisher.'

'Walk? What walk?'

'You put the letter under my pillow, Fisher.'

'Jesus!' said Fisher.

The encounter was observed by Arrowsmith, Mace-Hamilton and Wiltshire, who had earlier taken up crouched positions behind one of the chapel buttresses. Torridge heard the familiar hoots of laughter, and because it was his way he joined in. Fisher, white-faced, strode away.

'Poor old Porridge,' Arrowsmith commiserated, gasping and pretending to be contorted with mirth. Mace-Hamilton and Wiltshire were leaning against the buttress, issuing shrill noises.

'Gosh,' Torridge said, '*I* don't care.'

He went away, still laughing a bit, and there the matter of Fisher's attempt at communication might have ended. In fact it didn't, because Fisher wrote a second time and this time he made certain that the right boy received his missive. But Arrowsmith, still firmly the property of Sainsbury Major, wished to have nothing to do with R. A. J. Fisher.

When he was told the details of Fisher's error, Torridge said he'd guessed it had been something like that. But Wiltshire, Mace-Hamilton and Arrowsmith claimed that a new sadness had overcome Torridge. Something beautiful had been going to happen to him, Wiltshire said: just as the petals of friendship were opening the flower had been crudely snatched away. Arrowsmith said Torridge reminded him of one of Picasso's sorrowful harlequins. One way or the other, it was agreed that the experience would be beneficial to Torridge's sensitivity. It was seen as his reason for turning to religion, which recently he had done, joining a band of similarly inclined boys who were inspired by the word of the chaplain, a figure known as God Harvey. God Harvey was ascetic, seeming dangerously thin, his face all edge and as pale as paper, his cassock odorous with incense. He conducted readings in his room, offering coffee and biscuits afterwards, though not himself partaking of these refreshments. 'God Harvey's linnets' his acolytes were called, for often a hymn was sung to round things off. Welcomed into this fold, Torridge regained his happiness.

R. A. J. Fisher, on the other hand, sank into greater gloom. Arrowsmith remained elusive, mockingly faithful to Sainsbury Major, haughty when Fisher glanced pleadingly, ignoring all his letters. Fisher developed a look of introspective misery. The notes that Arrowsmith delightedly showed around were full of longing, increasingly tinged with desperation. The following term, unexpectedly, Fisher did not return to the school.

There was a famous Assembly at the beginning of that term, with much speculation beforehand as to the trouble in the air. Rumour had it that once and for all an attempt was to be made to stamp out the smiles and the glances in the dining-hall, the whole business of *bijous* and protectors, even the faithless behaviour of the Honourable Anthony Swain. The school waited and then the gowned staff arrived in the Assembly Hall and waited also, in grim anticipation on a raised dais. Public beatings for past offenders were scheduled, it was whispered: the Sergeant-major – the school's boxing instructor, who had himself told tales of public beatings in the past – would inflict the punishment at the headmaster's bidding. But that did not happen. Small and bald and red-skinned, the headmaster marched to the dais unaccompanied by the Sergeant-major. Twitching with anger that many afterwards declared had been simulated, he spoke at great length of the school's traditions. He stated that for fourteen years he had been proud to be its headmaster. He spoke of decency, and then of his own dismay. The school had been dishonoured; he would wish certain practices to cease. 'I stand before you ashamed,' he added, and paused for a moment. 'Let all this cease,' he commanded. He marched away, tugging at his gown in a familiar manner.

No one understood why the Assembly had taken place at that particular time, on the first day of a summer term. Only the masters looked knowing, as though labouring beneath some secret, but pressed and pleaded with they refused to reveal anything. Even Old Frosty, usually a most reliable source on such occasions, remained awesomely tight-lipped.

But the pronounced dismay and shame of the headmaster changed nothing. That term progressed and the world of *bijous* and their protectors continued as before, the glances, the meetings, cigarettes and romance in the hillside huts. R. A. J. Fisher was soon forgotten, having never made much of a mark. But the story of his error in placing a note under Torridge's pillow passed into legend, as did the encounter by the electricity plant and Torridge's deprivation of a relationship. The story was repeated as further terms passed by; new boys heard it and viewed Torridge with greater interest, imagining what R. A. J. Fisher had been like. The liaisons of Wiltshire with Good, Mace-Hamilton with Webb, and Arrowsmith with Sainsbury Major continued until the three senior boys left the school. Wiltshire, Mace-Hamilton and

Arrowsmith found fresh protectors then, and later these new liaisons came to an end in a similar manner. Later still, Wiltshire, Mace-Hamilton and Arrowsmith ceased to be *bijous* and became protectors themselves.

Torridge pursued the religious side of things. He continued to be a frequent partaker of God Harvey's biscuits and spiritual uplift, and a useful presence among the chapel pews, where he voluntarily dusted, cleaned brass, and kept the hymn-books in a state of repair with Sellotape. Wiltshire, Mace-Hamilton and Arrowsmith continued to circulate stories about him which were not true: that he was the product of virgin birth, that he possessed the gift of tongues but did not care to employ it, that he had three kidneys. In the end there emanated from them the claim that a liaison existed between Torridge and God Harvey. 'Love and the holy spirit,' Wiltshire pronounced, suggesting an ambience of chapel fustiness and God Harvey's grey boniness. The swish of his cassock took on a new significance, as did his thin, dry fingers. In a holy way the fingers pressed themselves on to Torridge, and then their holiness became a passion that could not be imagined. It was all a joke because Torridge was Torridge, but the laughter it caused wasn't malicious because no one hated him. He was a figure of fun; no one sought his downfall because there was no downfall to seek.

*

The friendship between Wiltshire, Mace-Hamilton and Arrowsmith continued after they left the school, after all three had married and had families. Once a year they received the Old Boys' magazine, which told of the achievements of themselves and the more successful of their school-fellows. There were Old Boys' cocktail parties and Old Boys' Day at the school every June and the Old Boys' cricket match. Some of these occasions, from time to time, they attended. Every so often they received the latest rebuilding programme, with the suggestion that they might like to contribute to the rebuilding fund. Occasionally they did.

As middle age closed in, the three friends met less often. Arrowsmith was an executive with Shell and stationed for longish periods in different countries abroad. Once every two years he brought his family back to England, which provided an opportunity for the three friends to meet. The wives met on these occasions also, and over the years the children. Often the men's distant schooldays were referred to, Buller Yeats and Old Frosty and the Sergeant-major, the little red-skinned headmaster, and above all Torridge. Within the three families, in fact, Torridge had become a myth. The joke that had begun when they were all new boys together continued, as if driven by its own impetus. In the minds of the wives and children the innocence of Torridge, his true happiness in the face of mockery and his fondness for the religious side of life all lived on. With some exactitude a physical image of the boy he'd been took root; his neatly knotted maroon House tie, his polished shoes, the hair that resembled a mouse's fur, the pudding face with two small eyes in it. 'My dad's in the button business,' Arrowsmith had only to say to cause instant laughter. 'Torridge's, you know.' The way Torridge ate, the way he ran, the way he smiled back at Buller Yeats, the rumour that he'd been dropped on his head as a baby, that he had three kidneys, all this was considerably appreciated, because Wiltshire and Mace-Hamilton and Arrowsmith related it well.

What was not related was R. A. J. Fisher's error in placing a note beneath Torridge's pillow, or the story that had laughingly been spread about concerning Torridge's relationship with God Harvey. This would have meant revelations that weren't seemly in family circles, the explanation of the world of *bijou* and protector, the romance and cigarettes in the hillside huts, the entangling of hearts. The subject had been touched upon among the three husbands and their wives in the normal course of private conversation, although not everything had been quite recalled. Listening, the wives had formed the impression that the relationships between older and younger boys at their husbands' school were similar to the platonic admiration a junior girl had so often harboured for a senior girl at their own schools. And so the subject had been left.

One evening in June, 1976, Wiltshire and Mace-Hamilton met in a bar called the Vine, in Piccadilly Place. They hadn't seen one another since the summer of 1974, the last time Arrowsmith and his family had been in England. Tonight they were to meet the Arrowsmiths again, for a family dinner in the Woodlands Hotel, Richmond. On the last occasion the three families had celebrated their reunion at the Wiltshires' house in Cobham and the time before with the Mace-Hamiltons in Ealing. Arrowsmith insisted that it was a question of turn and turn about and every third time he arranged for the family dinner to be held at his expense at the Woodlands. It was convenient because, although the Arrowsmiths spent the greater part of each biennial leave with Mrs Arrowsmith's parents in Somerset, they always stayed for a week at the Woodlands in order to see a bit of London life.

In the Vine in Piccadilly Place Wiltshire and Mace-Hamilton hurried over their second drinks. As always, they were pleased to see one another, and both were excited at the prospect of seeing Arrowsmith and his family again. They still looked faintly alike. Both had balded and run to fat. They wore inconspicuous blue suits with a discreet chalk stripe, Wiltshire's a little smarter than Mace-Hamilton's.

'We'll be late,' Wiltshire said, having just related how he'd made a small killing since the last time they'd met. Wiltshire operated in the import-export world; Mace-Hamilton was a chartered accountant.

They finished their drinks. 'Cheerio,' the barman called out to them as they slipped away. His voice was deferentially low, matching the softly-lit surroundings. 'Cheerio, Gerry,' Wiltshire said.

They drove in Wiltshire's car to Hammersmith, over the bridge and on to Barnes and Richmond. It was a Friday evening; the traffic was heavy.

'He had a bit of trouble, you know,' Mace-Hamilton said.

'Arrows?'

'She took a shine to some guy in Mombasa.'

Wiltshire nodded, poking the car between a cyclist and a taxi. He wasn't surprised. One night six years ago Arrowsmith's wife and he had committed adultery together at her suggestion. A messy business it had been, and afterwards he'd felt terrible.

★

In the Woodlands Hotel Arrowsmith, in a grey flannel suit, was not entirely sober. He, too, had run a bit to fat although, unlike Wiltshire and Mace-Hamilton, he hadn't lost any of his hair. Instead, it had dramatically changed colour: what Old Frosty had once called 'Arrows' blond thatch' was grey now. Beneath it his face was pinker than it had been and he had taken to wearing spectacles, heavy and black-rimmed, making him look even more different from the boy he'd been.

In the bar of the Woodlands he drank whisky on his own, smiling occasionally to himself because tonight he had a surprise for everybody. After five weeks of being cooped up with his in-laws in Somerset he was feeling good. 'Have one yourself, dear,' he invited the barmaid, a girl with an excess of lipstick on a podgy mouth. He pushed his own glass towards her while she was saying she didn't mind if she did.

His wife and his three adolescent children, two boys and a girl, entered the bar with Mrs Mace-Hamilton. 'Hi, hi, hi,' Arrowsmith called out to them in a jocular manner, causing his wife and Mrs Mace-Hamilton to note that he was drunk again. They sat down while he quickly finished the whisky that had just been poured for him. 'Put another in that for a start,' he ordered the barmaid, and crossed the floor of the bar to find out what everyone else wanted.

Mrs Wiltshire and her twins, girls of twelve, arrived while drinks were being decided about. Arrowsmith kissed her, as he had kissed Mrs Mace-Hamilton. The barmaid, deciding that the accurate conveying of such a large order was going to be beyond him, came and stood by the two tables that the party now occupied. The order was given; an animated conversation began.

The three women were different in appearance and in manner. Mrs Arrowsmith was thin as a knife, fashionably dressed in a shade of ash-grey that reflected her ash-grey hair. She smoked perpetually, unable to abandon the habit. Mrs Wiltshire was small. Shyness caused her to coil herself up in the presence of other people so that she often resembled a ball. Tonight she was in pink, a faded shade. Mrs Mace-Hamilton was carelessly plump, a large woman attired in a carelessly chosen dress that had begonias on it. She rather frightened Mrs Wiltshire. Mrs Arrowsmith found her trying.

'Oh, heavenly little drink!' Mrs Arrowsmith said, briefly drooping her blue-tinged eyelids as she sipped her gin and tonic.

'It *is* good to see you,' Mrs Mace-Hamilton gushed, beaming at everyone and vaguely raising her glass. 'And how they've all grown!' Mrs Mace-Hamilton had not had children herself.

'Their boobs have grown, by God,' the older Arrowsmith boy murmured to his brother, a reference to the Wiltshire twins. Neither of the two Arrowsmith boys went to their father's school: one was at a preparatory school in Oxford, the other at Charterhouse. Being of an age to do so, they both drank sherry and intended to drink as much of it as they possibly could. They found these family occasions tedious. Their sister, about to go to university, had determined neither to speak nor to smile for the entire evening. The Wiltshire twins were quite looking forward to the food.

Arrowsmith sat beside Mrs Wiltshire. He didn't say anything but after a moment he stretched a hand over her two knees and squeezed them in what he intended to be a brotherly way. He said without conviction that it was great to see her. He didn't look at her while he spoke. He didn't much care for hanging about with the women and children.

In turn Mrs Wiltshire didn't much care for his hand on her knees and was relieved when he drew it away. 'Hi, hi, hi,' he suddenly called out, causing her to jump. Wiltshire and Mace-Hamilton had appeared.

The physical similarity that had been so pronounced when the three men were boys and had been only faintly noticeable between Wiltshire and Mace-Hamilton in the Vine was clearly there again, as if the addition of Arrowsmith had supplied missing reflections. The men had thickened in the same way; the pinkness of Arrowsmith's countenance was a pinkness that tinged the other faces too. Only Arrowsmith's grey thatch of hair seemed out of place, all wrong beside the baldness of the other two: in their presence it might have been a wig, an impression it did not otherwise give. His grey flannel suit, beside their pinstripes, looked like something put on by mistake. 'Hi, hi, hi,' he shouted, thumping their shoulders.

Further rounds of drinks were bought and consumed. The Arrowsmith boys declared to each other that they were drunk and made further *sotto voce* observations about the forming bodies of the Wiltshire twins. Mrs Wiltshire felt the occasion becoming easier as Cinzano Bianco coursed through her bloodstream. Mrs Arrowsmith was aware of a certain familiar edginess within her body, a desire to be elsewhere, alone with a man she did not know. Mrs Mace-Hamilton spoke loudly of her garden.

In time the party moved from the bar to the dining-room. 'Bring us another round at the table,' Arrowsmith commanded the lipsticked barmaid. 'Quick as you can, dear.'

In the large dim dining-room waiters settled them around a table with little vases of carnations on it, a long table beneath the chandelier in the centre of the room. Celery soup arrived at the table, and smoked salmon and pâté, and the extra round of drinks Arrowsmith had ordered, and bottles of Nuits St Georges, and bottles of Vouvray and Anjou Rosé, and sirloin of beef, chicken à la king and veal escalope. The Arrowsmith boys laughed shrilly, openly staring at the tops of the Wiltshire twins' bodies. Potatoes, peas, spinach and carrots were served. Mrs Arrowsmith waved the vegetables away and smoked between courses. It was after this dinner six years ago that she had made her suggestion to Wiltshire, both of them being the worse for wear and it seeming not to matter because of that. 'Oh, *isn't* this jolly?' the voice of Mrs Mace-Hamilton boomed above the general hubbub.

Over Chantilly trifle and Orange Surprise the name of Torridge was heard. The name was always mentioned just about now, though sometimes sooner. 'Poor old bean,' Wiltshire said, and everybody laughed because it was the one subject they all shared. No one really wanted to hear about the Mace-Hamiltons' garden; the comments of the Arrowsmith boys were only for each other; Mrs Arrowsmith's needs could naturally not be voiced; the shyness of Mrs Wiltshire was private too. But Torridge was different. Torridge in a way was like an old friend now, existing in everyone's mind, a family subject. The Wiltshire twins were quite amused to hear of some freshly remembered evidence of Torridge's naïveté; for the Arrowsmith girl it was better at least than being questioned by Mrs Mace-Hamilton; for her brothers it was an excuse to bellow with simulated mirth. Mrs Mace-Hamilton considered that the boy sounded frightful, Mrs Arrowsmith couldn't have cared less. Only Mrs Wiltshire had doubts: she thought the three men were hard on the memory of the boy, but of course had not ever said so. To-night, after Wiltshire had recalled the time when Torridge had been convinced by Arrowsmith that Buller Yeats had dropped dead in his bath, the younger Arrowsmith boy told of a boy at his own school who'd been convinced that his sister's dog had died.

'Listen,' Arrowsmith suddenly shouted out. 'He's going to joins us. Old Torridge.'

There was laughter, no one believing that Torridge was going to arrive, Mrs Arrowsmith saying to herself that her husband was pitiful when he became as drunk as this.

'I thought it would be a gesture,' Arrowsmith said. 'Honestly. He's looking in for coffee.'

'You bloody devil, Arrows,' Wiltshire said, smacking the table with the palm of his hand.

'He's in the button business,' Arrowsmith shouted. 'Torridge's, you know.'

As far as Wiltshire and Mace-Hamilton could remember, Torridge had never featured in an Old Boys' magazine. No news of his career had been printed, and certainly no obituary. It was typical, somehow, of Arrowsmith to have winkled him out. It was part and parcel of him to want to add another dimension to the joke, to recharge its batteries. For the sight of Torridge in middle age would surely make funnier the reported anecdotes.

'After all, what's wrong,' demanded Arrowsmith noisily, 'with old school pals all meeting up? The more the merrier.'

He was a bully, Mrs Wiltshire thought: all three of them were bullies.

*

Torridge arrived at half-past nine. The hair that had been like a mouse's fur was still like that. It hadn't greyed any more; the scalp hadn't balded. He hadn't run to fat; in middle age he'd thinned down a bit. There was even a lankiness about him now, which was reflected in his movements. At school he had moved slowly, as though with caution. Jauntily attired in a pale linen suit, he crossed the dining-room of the Woodlands Hotel with a step as nimble as a tap dancer's.

No one recognised him. To the three men who'd been at school with him the man who approached their dinner table was a different person, quite unlike the figure that existed in the minds of the wives and children.

'My dear Arrows,' he said, smiling at Arrowsmith. The smile was different too, a brittle snap of a smile that came and went in a matter-of-fact way. The eyes that had been small didn't seem so in his thinner face. They flashed with a gleam of some kind, matching the snap of his smile.

'Good God, it's never old Porridge!' Arrowsmith's voice was slurred. His face had acquired the beginnings of an alcoholic crimson, sweat glistened on his forehead.

'Yes, it's old Porridge,' Torridge said quietly. He held his hand out towards Arrowsmith and then shook hands with Wiltshire and Mace-Hamilton. He was introduced to their wives, with whom he shook hands also. He was introduced to the children, which involved further hand-shaking. His hand was cool and rather bony: they felt it should have been damp.

'You're nicely in time for coffee, Mr Torridge,' Mrs Mace-Hamilton said.

'Brandy more like,' Arrowsmith suggested. 'Brandy, old chap?'

'Well, that's awfully kind of you, Arrows. Chartreuse I'd prefer, really.'

A waiter drew up a chair. Room was made for Torridge between Mrs Mace-Hamilton and the Arrowsmith boys. It was a frightful mistake, Wiltshire was thinking. It was mad of Arrowsmith.

Mace-Hamilton examined Torridge across the dinner table. The old Torridge would have said he'd rather not have anything alcoholic, that a cup of tea and a biscuit were more his line in the evenings. It was impossible to imagine this man saying his dad had a button business. There was a suavity about him that made Mace-Hamilton uneasy. Because of what had been related to his wife and the other wives and their children he felt he'd been caught out in a lie, yet in fact that wasn't the case.

The children stole glances at Torridge, trying to see him as the boy who'd been described to them, and failing to. Mrs Arrowsmith said to herself that all this stuff they'd been told over the years had clearly been rubbish. Mrs Mace-Hamilton was bewildered. Mrs Wiltshire was pleased.

'No one ever guessed,' Torridge said, 'what became of R. A. J. Fisher.' He raised the subject suddenly, without introduction.

'Oh God, Fisher,' Mace-Hamilton said.

'Who's Fisher?' the younger of the Arrowsmith boys enquired.

Torridge turned to flash his quick smile at the boy. 'He left,' he said. 'In unfortunate circumstances.'

'You've changed a lot, you know,' Arrowsmith said. 'Don't you think he's changed?' he asked Wiltshire and Mace-Hamilton.

'Out of recognition,' Wiltshire said.

Torridge laughed easily. 'I've become adventurous. I'm a late developer, I suppose.'

'What kind of unfortunate circumstances?' the younger Arrowsmith boy asked. 'Was Fisher expelled?'

'Oh no, not at all,' Mace-Hamilton said hurriedly.

'Actually,' Torridge said, 'Fisher's trouble all began with the writing of a note. Don't you remember? He put it in my pyjamas. But it wasn't for me at all.'

He smiled again. He turned to Mrs Wiltshire in a way that seemed polite, drawing her into the conversation. 'I was an innocent at school. But innocence eventually slips away. I found my way about eventually.'

'Yes, of course,' she murmured. She didn't like him, even though she was glad he wasn't as he might have been. There was malevolence in him, a ruthlessness that seemed like a work of art. He seemed like a work of art himself, as though in losing the innocence he spoke of he had recreated himself.

'I often wonder about Fisher,' he remarked.

The Wiltshire twins giggled. 'What's so great about this bloody Fisher?' the older Arrowsmith boy murmured, nudging his brother with an elbow.

'What're you doing these days?' Wiltshire asked, interrupting Mace-Hamilton, who had also begun to say something.

'I make buttons,' Torridge replied. 'You may recall my father made buttons.'

'Ah, here're the drinks,' Arrowsmith rowdily observed.

'I don't much keep up with the school,' Torridge said as the waiter placed a glass of Chartreuse in front of him. 'I don't so much as think about it except for wondering about poor old Fisher. Our headmaster was a cretin,' he informed Mrs Wiltshire.

Again the Wiltshire twins giggled. The Arrowsmith girl yawned and her brothers giggled also, amused that the name of Fisher had come up again.

'You will have coffee, Mr Torridge?' Mrs Mace-Hamilton offered, for the waiter had brought a fresh pot to the table.

She held it poised above a cup. Torridge smiled at her and nodded. She said:

'Pearl buttons d'you make?'

'No, not pearl.'

'Remember those awful packet peas we used to have?' Arrowsmith enquired. Wiltshire said:

'Use plastics at all? In your buttons, Porridge?'

'No, we don't use plastics. Leathers, various leathers. And horn. We specialise.'

'How very interesting!' Mrs Mace-Hamilton exclaimed.

'No, no. It's rather ordinary really.' He paused, and then added, 'Someone once told me that Fisher went into a timber business. But of course that was far from true.'

'A chap was expelled a year ago,' the younger Arrowsmith boy said, contributing this in order to cover up a fresh outburst of sniggering. 'For stealing a transistor.'

Torridge nodded, appearing to be interested. He asked the Arrowsmith boys where they were at school. The older one said Charterhouse and his brother gave the name of his preparatory school. Torridge nodded again and asked their sister and she said she was waiting to go to university. He had quite a chat with the Wiltshire twins about their school. They considered it pleasant the way he bothered, seeming genuinely to want to know. The giggling died away.

'I imagined Fisher wanted me for his *bijou*,' he said when all that was over, still addressing the children. 'Our place was riddled with fancy larks like that. Remember?' he added, turning to Mace-Hamilton.

'*Bijou*?' one of the twins asked before Mace-Hamilton could reply.

'A male tart,' Torridge explained.

The Arrowsmith boys gaped at him, the older one with his mouth actually open. The Wiltshire twins began to giggle again. The Arrowsmith girl frowned, unable to hide her interest.

'The Honourable Anthony Swain,' Torridge said, 'was no better than a whore.'

Mrs Arrowsmith, who for some minutes had been engaged with her own thoughts, was suddenly aware that the man who was in the button business was talking about sex. She gazed diagonally across the table at him, astonished that he should be talking in this way.

'Look here, Torridge,' Wiltshire said, frowning at him and shaking his head. With an almost imperceptible motion he gestured towards the wives and children.

'Andrews and Butler. Dillon and Pratt. Tothill and Gold-fish Stewart. Your dad,' Torridge said to the Arrowsmith girl, 'was always very keen. Sainsbury Major in particular.'

'Now look here,' Arrowsmith shouted, beginning to get to his feet and then changing his mind.

'My gosh, how they broke chaps' hearts, those three!'

'Please don't talk like this.' It was Mrs Wiltshire who protested, to everyone's surprise, most of all her own. 'The children are quite young, Mr Torridge.'

Her voice had become a whisper. She could feel herself reddening with embarrassment, and a little twirl of sickness occurred in her stomach. Deferentially, as though appreciating the effort she had made, Torridge apologised.

'I think you'd better go,' Arrowsmith said.

'You were right about God Harvey, Arrows. Gay as a grig he was, beneath that cassock. So was Old Frosty, as a matter of fact.'

'Really!' Mrs Mace-Hamilton cried, her bewilderment turning into outrage. She glared at her husband, demanding with her eyes that instantly something should be done. But her husband and his two friends were briefly stunned by what Torridge had claimed for God Harvey. Their schooldays leapt back at them, possessing them for a vivid moment: the dormitory, the dining-hall, the glances and the invitations, the meetings behind Chapel. It was somehow in keeping with the school's hypocrisy that God Harvey had had inclinations himself, that a rumour begun as an outrageous joke should have contained the truth.

'As a matter of fact,' Torridge went on, 'I wouldn't be what I am if it hadn't been for God Harvey. I'm what they call queer,' he explained to the children. 'I perform sexual acts with men.'

'For God's sake, Torridge,' Arrowsmith shouted, on his feet, his face the colour of ripe strawberry, his watery eyes quivering with rage.

'It was nice of you to invite me tonight, Arrows. Our *alma mater* can't be too proud of chaps like me.'

People spoke at once, Mrs Mace-Hamilton and Mrs Wiltshire, all three men. Mrs Arrowsmith sat still. What she was thinking was that she had become quietly drunk while her husband had more boisterously reached the same condition. She was thinking, as well, that by the sound of things he'd possessed as a boy a sexual urge that was a lot livelier than the one he'd once exposed her to and now hardly ever did. With boys who had grown to be men he had had a whale of a time. Old Frosty had been a kind of Mr Chips, she'd been told. She'd never ever heard of Sainsbury Major or God Harvey.

'It's quite disgusting,' Mrs Mace-Hamilton's voice cried out above the other voices. She said the police should be called. It was scandalous to have to listen to unpleasant conversation like this. She began to say the children should leave the dining-room, but changed her mind because it appeared that Torridge himself was about to go. 'You're a most horrible man,' she cried.

Confusion gathered, like a fog around the table. Mrs Wiltshire, who knew that her husband had committed adultery with Mrs Arrowsmith, felt another bout of nerves in her stomach. 'Because she was starved, that's why,' her husband had almost violently confessed when she'd discovered. 'I was putting her out of her misery.' She had wept then and he had comforted her as best he could. She had not told him that he had never succeeded in arousing in her the desire to make love: she had always assumed that to be a failing in herself, but now for some reason she was not so sure. Nothing had been directly said that might have caused this doubt, but an instinct informed Mrs Wiltshire that the doubt should be there. The man beside her smiled his brittle, malevolent smile at her, as if in sympathy.

With his head bent over the table and his hands half hiding his face, the younger Arrowsmith boy examined his father by glancing through his fingers. There were men whom his parents warned him against, men who would sit beside you in buses or try to give you a lift in a car. This man who had come tonight, who had been such a joke up till now, was apparently one of these, not a joke at all. And the confusion was greater: at one time, it seemed, his father had been like that too.

The Arrowsmith girl considered her father also. Once she had walked into a room in Lagos to find her mother in the arms of an African clerk. Ever since she had felt sorry for her father. There'd been an unpleasant scene at the time, she'd screamed at her mother and later in a fury had told her father what she'd seen. He'd nodded, wearily seeming not to be surprised, while her mother had miserably wept. She'd put her arms around her father, comforting him; she'd felt no mercy for her mother, no sympathy or understanding. The scene formed vividly in her mind as she sat at the dinner table: it appeared to be relevant in the confusion and yet not clearly so. Her parents' marriage was messy, messier than it had looked. Across the table her mother grimly smoked, focussing her eyes with difficulty. She smiled at her daughter, a soft, inebriated smile.

The older Arrowsmith boy was also aware of the confusion. Being at a school where the practice which had
been spoken of was common enough, he could easily believe the facts that had been thrown about. Against his
will, he was forced to imagine what he had never imagined
before: his father and his friends as schoolboys, engaged in
passion with other boys. He might have been cynical about
this image but he could not. Instead it made him want to
gasp. It knocked away the smile that had been on his face
all evening.

The Wiltshire twins unhappily stared at the white table-
cloth, here and there stained with wine or gravy. They, too,
found they'd lost the urge to smile and instead shakily
blinked back tears.

'Yes, perhaps I'd better go,' Torridge said.

With impatience Mrs Mace-Hamilton looked at her husband, as if expecting him to hurry Torridge off or at least to
say something. But Mace-Hamilton remained silent. Mrs
Mace-Hamilton licked her lips, preparing to speak herself.
She changed her mind.

'Fisher didn't go into a timber business,' Torridge said,
'because poor old Fisher was dead as a doornail. Which is
why our cretin of a headmaster, Mrs Mace-Hamilton, had that
Assembly.'

'Assembly?' she said. Her voice was weak, although she'd
meant it to sound matter-of-fact and angry.

'There was an Assembly that no one understood. Poor old
Fisher had strung himself up in a barn on his father's farm.
I discovered that,' Torridge said, turning to Arrowsmith,
'years later: from God Harvey actually. The poor chap left a
note but the parents didn't care to pass it on. I mean it was
for you, Arrows.'

Arrowsmith was still standing, hanging over the table.
'Note?' he said. 'For me?'

'Another note. Why d'you think he did himself in, Arrows?'

Torridge smiled, at Arrowsmith and then around the table.

'None of that's true,' Wiltshire said.

'As a matter of fact it is.'

He went, and nobody spoke at the dinner table. A body of a schoolboy hung from a beam in a barn, a note on the straw below his dangling feet. It hung in the confusion that had been caused, increasing the confusion. Two waiters hovered by a sideboard, one passing the time by arranging sauce bottles, the other folding napkins into cone shapes. Slowly Arrowsmith sat down again. The silence continued as the conversation of Torridge continued to haunt the dinner table. He haunted it himself, with his brittle smile and his tap dancer's elegance, still faithful to the past in which he had so signally failed, triumphant in his middle age.

Then Mrs Arrowsmith quite suddenly wept and the Wiltshire twins wept and Mrs Wiltshire comforted them. The Arrowsmith girl got up and walked away, and Mrs Mace-Hamilton turned to the three men and said they should be ashamed of themselves, allowing all this to happen.

Flights of Fancy

In her middle age Sarah Machaen had developed the habit of nostalgically slipping back into her childhood. Often, on a bus or at a dinner party, she would find herself caught in a mesh of voices and events that had been real forty years ago. There were summer days in the garden of her father's rectory, her brothers building another tree-house, her father asleep in a brown-and-orange-striped deck-chair. In the cool untidy kitchen she helped her mother to make strawberry cake; she walked with the old spaniel, Dodge, to Mrs Rolleston's Post Office and Stores in the village, her shoes dusty as soon as she took a single step. On wet winter afternoons, cosy by the fire in the drawing-room, the family played consequences or card games, or listened to the wireless. The war brought black-out curtains and rationing, and two evacuees.

At forty-seven Sarah Machaen was reconciled to the fact that her plainness wasn't going to go away. As a child she had believed that growing up would put paid to the face she couldn't care for, that it would develop prettily in girlhood, as the ugly duckling had developed. 'Oh, it's quite common,' she heard a woman say to her mother. 'Many a beauty was as plain as a pikestaff to begin with.' But no beauty dawned in Sarah's face.

Her older brother became a clergyman like their father, her younger one an engineer. She herself, in 1955, found employment she enjoyed in the firm of Pollock-Brown Lighting. She became secretary to Mr Everend, who at that time was assistant to the director in charge of publicity, whom he subsequently succeeded. The office was a busy one, and although Sarah had earlier had ambitions to work in the more cultural ambience of a museum or a publishing house she soon found herself taking a genuine interest in Pollock-Brown's range of well-designed products: light fittings that were increasingly specified by architects of taste all over Britain and Europe. The leaflets that passed through the Pollock-Brown publicity department constantly drew attention to the quality and the elegance that placed Pollock-Brown ahead of the field; the photographs in trade advertisements made many of the Pollock-Brown fitments seem like works of art. Sarah could discover no reason to argue with these claims, and was content to let Pollock-Brown become her daytime world, as a museum or a publishing house might have been. Her status in the organisation rose with the status of Mr Everend, who often stated that he wished to be served by no other secretary. The offices of the firm were in London, a large block of glass and concrete in Kingsway. Twenty miles away, in factories just beyond the Green Belt, the manufacture of the well-designed fitments took place.

Since 1960 Sarah had had a flat in Tufnell Park, which was quite convenient, the Northern line all the way to Tottenham Court Road, the Central on to Holborn. The brother who was a clergyman lived in Harrogate and did not often come to London; the one who was an engineer had spent his life building dams in Africa and returned to England only with reluctance. Sarah's parents, happily married for almost fifty years, had died within a month of one another in 1972, sharing a room in an old-persons' home that catered exclusively for the clergy and their wives.

But even so Sarah was not alone. She had many friends, made in Pollock-Brown and through the Bach choir in which she sang, and some that dated back to her schooldays. She was a popular choice as a godmother. She was invited to parties and went regularly to the theatre or to concerts, often with her friend Anna, whose marriage had failed six years ago. She lived on her own in the flat in Tufnell Park now: when first she'd lived there she'd shared it with a girl called Elizabeth, with whom she'd been at school. Elizabeth, a librarian, was bespectacled and rather fat, a chatterbox and a compulsive nibbler. She hadn't been all that easy to live with but Sarah knew her well and appreciated her kindness and her warmth. It had astonished her when Elizabeth began to go out with a man she'd met in her library, a man whom she later became engaged to. It seemed to Sarah that Elizabeth wasn't the kind of girl who became engaged, any more than she herself was, yet in the end Elizabeth married and went to live in Cricklewood, where she reared a family. Sarah took in another girl but this time the arrangement didn't work because the new girl, a stranger to Sarah, kept having men in her bedroom. Sarah asked her to go, and did not attempt to replace her.

Almost every weekend she made the journey to Cricklewood to see Elizabeth and her family. The children loved her and often said so. Elizabeth's husband enjoyed chatting to her, drinking gin and tonic, to which Sarah had become mildly addicted. It was a home-from-home, and it wasn't the only one. No husband disliked Sarah. No one found her a bore. She brought small presents when she visited. She struck the right note and fitted in.

Now and again these friends attempted to bring Sarah into contact with suitable men, but nothing ever came of such efforts. There'd been, while she was still at the secretarial college she'd attended, a man called George, who had taken her out, who had embraced her and had once, in his bedsitting-room, begun to undress her. She had enjoyed these attentions even though their perpetrator was not a person she greatly cared for. She had been quite prepared to permit him to take her clothes off and then to proceed in whatever way he wished, but he had suddenly appeared to change his mind, to lose interest or to develop nerves, it wasn't clear which. She'd felt quite sick and shaky, sitting on his lap in an armchair, while his fingers fell away from the buttons he'd been undoing. Awkwardly she had nuzzled her nose into his neck, hoping this would induce him to continue, but his arms, which hung down on either side of the armchair, had remained where they were. A moment later he'd clambered to his feet and had filled a kettle for tea. As an experience, it was one that Sarah was destined never to forget. She recalled it often as she lay alone in bed at night, extending her companion's desire and sometimes changing his identity before she did so. In middle age his bed-sitting-room was still as vivid as it had ever been, and she could still recall the feel of the blood draining away from her face and the sickness that developed when he seemed suddenly to reject her.

Sarah was not obsessed by this and she made efforts not to dwell on it, but it often struck her that it was unfair that she should be deprived of a side of life which was clearly pleasant. There was an assumption that girls without much in the way of looks didn't possess the kind of desire that looks appeared to indicate, but this of course was not true. When politely dancing with men or even when just talking to them she had more than once experienced what privately she designated as a longing to be loved by them. Her expression on these occasions did not ever betray her, and her plainness trailed a modesty that prevented her from ever being forward. She learnt to live with her frustrations, wondering as she grew older if some elderly widower, no longer moved by physical desire but seeking only an agreeable companion, might not one day propose marriage to her. She might accept, she vaguely thought. She wasn't at all sure what it would be like being married to an elderly widower, but some instinct informed her that she'd prefer it to being on her own in the flat in Tufnell Park all through her middle age. Alone at night her thoughts went further, creating the widower as a blind man who could not even sense her plainness, whose fingers caressing her face felt a beauty that was not there. Other scenes took place in which the widower ended by finding a vigour he thought he'd lost. It often astonished her in the daytime that she had imagined so.

On the other hand, her friend Anna, the one whose marriage had failed, lived a rackety life with men and sometimes said she envied Sarah the quietness of hers. Now and again, having dinner together after a visit to the theatre or a concert, Anna would refer to the lovers she'd had, castigating most of them as selfish. 'How right you are,' she had a way of saying, 'to steer clear of all that.' Sarah always laughed when Anna said that, pointing out that it hadn't been her choice. 'Oh, choice or not, by God you're better off,' Anna would insist. 'I really swear.' Then Anna met a Canadian, who married her and took her off to Montreal.

That was another person to miss, as she had missed the people of her childhood, and her friend Elizabeth – for it naturally wasn't the same after Elizabeth married. She had often thought of telling Anna about her longing for a relationship with a man, but shyness had always held her back. The shyness had to do with not knowing enough, with having so little experience, the very opposite of Anna. Yet once, when they'd both had quite a lot of wine to drink, she'd almost asked her what she should do. 'Just because I'm so wretchedly plain,' she'd almost said, 'doesn't mean I can do without things.' But she hadn't said that, and now Anna was gone and there was no one else who wouldn't have been just a little shocked to hear stuff like that. Not in a million years could she have said it to Elizabeth.

And so it remained. No widower, elderly or otherwise,

proposed marriage; no blind man proclaimed love. What happened was rather different from all that. Once a year, as Christmas approached, Pollock-Brown held its annual staff party at the factories beyond the Green Belt. Executive and clerical staff from the building in Kingsway met the factory workers in their huge canteen, richly decorated now with Christmas hangings. Dancing took place. There was supper, and unlimited drinks at the firm's expense. The managing director made a speech and the present chairman, Sir Robert Quinn, made a speech also, in the course of which he thanked his workers for their loyalty. A thousand Pollock-Brown employees let their hair down, typists and secretaries, directors, executives who would soon be directors, tea-women, mould-makers, van-drivers, lorry-drivers, ware-housemen, finishers, polishers. In a formal manner Mr Everend always reserved the first dance for Sarah and she felt quite proud to be led on to the floor in the wake of Sir Robert and his secretary and the managing director and his secretary, a woman called Mrs Mykers. After that the Christmas spirit really got going. Paper hats were supplied to everyone, including Sir Robert Quinn, Mr Everend, and the managing director. One of the dispatch boys had once poured a little beer over Mr Everend, because Mr Everend always so entered into the spirit of things that horseplay with beer seemed quite in order. There were tales, many of them true, of sexual congress in out-of-the way corners, particularly in store-rooms.

'Hullo,' a girl said, addressing Sarah in what for this one evening of the year was called the Ladies' Powder Room. *Female Staff* a painted sign more ordinarily stated, hidden now beneath the festive card that bore the grander title.

'Hullo,' Sarah replied, unable to place the girl. She was small, with short black hair that was smooth and hung severely straight on either side of her face. She was pretty:

an oval face with eyes almost as black as her hair, and a mouth that slightly pouted, dimpling her cheeks. Sarah frowned as the dimples came and went. The girl smiled in a friendly way. She said her name was Sandra Pond.

'You're Everend's girl,' she added.

'Secretary,' Sarah said.

'I meant that.' She laughed and the dimples danced about. 'I didn't mean nothing suspect, Miss Machaen.'

'Suspect?'

'You know.'

She wore a black dress with lace at her neck and wrists. Her feet were neat, in shiny black shoes. Her legs were slim, black-clad also. How nice to be so attractive! Sarah thought, a familiar reflection when meeting such girls for the first time. It wouldn't even matter having a slack, lower-class accent, as this girl had. You'd give up a lot for looks like that.

'I'm in polishing,' the girl said. 'Your plastic lamp-shades.'

'You don't sound as if you like it.' Sarah laughed. She glanced at herself in the mirror above one of the two wash-basins. Hurriedly she looked away.

'It's clean,' Sandra Pond said. 'A polishing machine's quite clean to operate.'

'Yes, I suppose it would be.'

'Care for a drink at all, Miss Machaen?'

'A drink?'

'Don't you drink, Miss Machaen?'

'Well, yes, but – '

'We're meant to mix at a thing like this. The peasants and the privileged.' She gave a rasping, rather unattractive laugh. 'Come on,' she said.

Beneath the prettiness there was something hard about her. There were flashes of bitterness in the way she'd said 'the peasants and the privileged,' and in the way she'd laughed and in the way she walked out of the Ladies' Powder Room.

She walked impatiently, as if she disliked being at the Christmas party. She was a prickly girl, Sarah said to herself. She wasn't at all glad that she'd fallen into conversation with her.

They sat down at a small table at the edge of the dance-floor. 'What d'you drink?' the girl said, immediately getting to her feet again in an edgy way. 'Whisky?'

'I'd like a gin and tonic.'

The dimples came and went, cracking the brittleness. The smile seemed disposed to linger but did not. 'Don't go away now,' the slack voice commanded as she jerked quickly away herself.

'Someone looking after you?' Dancing with the wife of the dispatch manager, Mr Everend shouted jollily at Sarah. He wore a scarlet, cone-shaped paper hat. The wife of the dispatch manager was eyeing, over his shoulder, a sales executive called Chumm, with whom, whenever it was possible, she went to bed.

'Yes, thanks, Mr Everend,' Sarah answered, waving a hand to indicate that he mustn't feel responsible for her.

'Horrid brute, that man,' Sandra Pond said, returning with their drinks. 'Cheers,' she said, raising a glass of what looked like whisky and touching Sarah's glass with it.

'Cheers,' Sarah said, although it was a salutation she disliked.

'It began last year here,' Sandra said, pointing with her glass at the dispatch manager's wife. 'Her and Chumm.'

'I've never met her actually.'

'You didn't miss nothing. That Chumm's a villain.'

'He has that reputation.'

'He screwed her in a store-room. I walked in on top of them.'

'Oh.'

'Oh in-bloody-deed.' She laughed. 'You like gin and t, d'you? Your drink, Miss Machaen?'

'Please call me Sarah. Yes, I like it.'

'Whisky mac this is. I love booze. You like it, Sarah?'

'Yes, I do rather.'

'Birds of a feather.' She laughed, and paused. 'I seen you last year. Dancing with Everend and that. I noticed you.'

'I've been coming for a long time.'

'How long you been at P-B, then?'

'Since 1960.'

'Jesus!'

'I know.'

'I was only a nipper in 1960. What age'd you say I was, Sarah?'

'Twenty-five?'

'Thirty. Don't look it, do I?'

'No, indeed.'

'You live alone, do you, Sarah?'

'Yes, I do. In Tufnell Park.'

'Nice?'

'It is quite nice.'

Sandra Pond nodded repeatedly. Tufnell Park was very nice indeed, she said, extremely nice.

'You sit there, Sarah,' she said. 'I'm going to get you another drink.'

'Oh, no. Let me. Please.' She began to get to her feet, but Sandra Pond shot out a hand, a movement like a whip's, instantly restraining her. Her small fingers pressed into the flesh of Sarah's arm. 'Stay right where you are,' she said.

An extraordinary thought occurred to Sarah as she watched the girl moving rapidly away with their two empty glasses: Sandra Pond wanted to share her flat.

'Now, now, now,' Mr Priddy from Accounts admonished, large and perspiring, staring down at her through thick spectacles. He reached for her, seemingly unaware of her protestations. His knees pressed into hers, forcing them into waltztime.

'They do an awful lot of good, these things,' Mr Priddy confidently remarked. 'People really get a chance.' He added something else, something about people getting a chance to chew the rag. Sarah nodded. 'We've had a miracle of a year,' Mr Priddy said. 'In spite of everything.'

She could see Sandra Pond standing with two full glasses, looking furious. She tried to smile at her through the dancing couples, to make some indication with her eyes that she'd had no option about dancing with Mr Priddy. But Sandra Pond, glaring into the dancers, hadn't even noticed her yet.

'Mrs Priddy couldn't come,' Mr Priddy told her. 'Tummy trouble.'

She said she was sorry, trying to remember what Mrs Priddy looked like and failing in that.

'She gets it,' Mr Priddy said.

Sandra Pond had seen them and was looking aggrieved now, her head on one side. She sat down at the table and lit a cigarette. She crossed her thin legs.

'Thank you very much,' Sarah said, and Mr Priddy smiled graciously and went away to do his duty by some other lone woman.

'Can't stand him,' Sandra Pond said. 'Clammy blooming hands.'

Sarah drank some gin and tonic. 'I say, you know,' a man called out, 'it's a hell of a party, eh?'

He wasn't sober. He swayed, with a glass in one hand, peering down at them. He was in charge of some department or other, Sarah couldn't remember which. He spent a great deal of time in a pub near the Kingsway building, not going home until the last minute. He lived with a sister, someone had once told her.

'Hey, who's she?' he demanded, wagging his glass at Sandra. 'Who's this one, Sarah?'

'Sandra Pond,' Sarah said sharply. 'In the polishing department.'

'Polishing, eh? Nice party, Sandra?'

'If you like the type of thing.'

'The drink's good.'

'It's free, you mean.'

'That's what I mean, girlie.'

He went away. Sandra Pond laughed. She was a little drunk herself, she confessed. It took her like that, quite suddenly, after the fifth or sixth whisky mac. 'How about you, Sarah?'

'I'm just about right.'

'D'you know what I'd like to do?'

'What?'

'Oh, no.' She looked away, coyly pouting, the dimples in her cheeks working. 'No, I couldn't say,' she said. 'I couldn't tell you, Sarah.'

The notion that the girl wanted to share her flat had remained with Sarah while she'd danced with Mr Priddy and while the man had swayed in front of them, saying the party was nice. It was still there now, at the very front of her mind, beginning to dominate everything else. It seemed to be an unspoken thought between them, deliberately placed there by the girl while she'd been saying that Tufnell Park was nice.

'Actually I'm quite pissed,' the girl was saying now, giggling.

The expression grated on Sarah. She could never see why people had to converse in an obscene way. It didn't in any way whatsoever make sense for the girl to say she was urinated when she meant drunk.

'Sorry,' Sandra Pond said.

'It's all right.'

'I offended you. It showed in your face. I'm sorry, Sarah.'

'Actually, it's time for me to go home.'

'Oh, God, I've driven you away.'

'It's not that.'

'Have another drink. I've spoiled your evening.'

'No, not at all.'

'You know how it is: everything smooth and unruffled and then everything going bonk! You know, Sarah?'

Sarah frowned, shaking her head.

'Like if you looked down a well and then you dropped a stone in. Know what I mean? There'd be a disturbance. I had a friend said that to me once, we was very close. Hazel she was called.'

'Well, I do know what she meant of course – '

'D'you really, Sarah?'

'Yes, of course.'

'She was talking about people, see. What happens to people. Like you meet someone, Sarah.'

It was the kind of cliché that Sarah didn't care for, still water and someone throwing a stone. It was silly and half-baked, but typical in a way of what was said at an office party.

'She was like that,' Sandra Pond said. 'She talked like that, did Hazel.'

'I see.'

'When she met me, she meant. A disturbance.'

'Yes.'

'Merry Christmas then, Sarah.'

'Merry Christmas.'

As she edged her way around the dance-floor, she felt glad she'd escaped and was thinking that when Mr Everend collided with her almost. He always gave her a lift home after the Christmas party. He offered to now, sensing that she was ready to go. But he insisted on a last dance and while they danced he thanked her for all the work she'd done during the year, and for being patient with him, which she really hadn't had to. 'A last drink,' he said as they stepped off the dance-floor, just beside where the drinks table was. He found her a gin and tonic and had a tomato juice himself.

In the arms of a black-haired youth, Sandra Pond danced by while the band played 'Just One of Those Things'; her thin arms were around the youth's neck, her head lolled on his shoulder. Her eyes were blank, Sarah noticed in the moment it took the couple to dance by.

'Merry Christmas, Sarah,' Mr Everend said.

'Merry Christmas, Mr Everend.'

*

That night she lay in bed, feeling woozy after all the gin and tonic. Not really wishing to, and yet slowly and quite care-fully, she went over everything that had happened since Sandra Pond had addressed her in the Ladies' Powder Room. She remembered the grip of the girl's fingers and the pout of her lips and her bitterness when she spoke of Pollock-Brown and even when she didn't. Had she really walked in on the dispatch manager's wife and Chumm in a store-room? It was odd the way she'd spoken to her in the Ladies' Powder Room, odd the way she'd spoken of Tufnell Park. For some minutes she imagined Sandra Pond sharing her flat with her as Elizabeth had, sharing the things in the kitchen cupboards, the Special K and the marmalade and the sugar. The girl was seventeen years younger, she didn't have the same background or presumably the same interests. Sarah smiled a little in the darkness, thinking about what people would say if she began to share her flat with a polisher of plastic lamp-shades. People would think she was mad, her brother and his wife in their Harrogate rectory, her other brother and his wife in Africa, the friends whose parties she went to, the Bach choir,

Elizabeth, Anna in Montreal. And of course they would all be right. She was well-to-do and middle-aged and plain. Side by side with Mr Everend she had found her way to the top of the firm. She would retire one day and that would be that. It didn't make sense to share a flat with someone like Sandra Pond, but she sensed that had she stayed in Sandra Pond's company the flat would have been openly mentioned. And yet surely it must be as clear to Sandra Pond as it would be to everyone else that they'd make a most ill-assorted couple? What was in the girl's mind, that she could see the picture so differently? Thinking about it, Sarah could find only a single piece of common ground between them. It wasn't even properly real, based neither on a process of deduction or indeed of observation. It was an instinct that Sandra Pond, unlike Elizabeth or Anna, wouldn't marry. And for some reason Sarah sensed that Sandra Pond wouldn't be difficult, as the girl she'd tried to share the flat with after Elizabeth's departure had been. Her mind rebelliously wandered, throwing up flights of fancy that she considered silly almost as soon as they came to her, flights of fancy in which she educated Sandra Pond and discovered in her an intelligence that was on a par with her own, in which slowly a real friendship developed, and why should it not? Clearly there was a lot that Sandra Pond didn't know. Sarah doubted that the girl had ever been inside a theatre in her life, except maybe to see something like the Black and White Minstrel Show or a Christmas pantomime. She wondered if she ever opened a book or listened to music or went to an art gallery.

For a week, at odd moments of the day, or at night, Sarah wondered about Sandra Pond. She half expected that she might hear from her, that the slack accents would drift over her telephone, suggesting a drink. But she didn't. Instead, with the flights of fancy that she considered silly, she saw herself persevering in her patience and finally rewarded as

Sandra Pond, calling on a sensitivity that had remained unaired till now, responded. Something assured Sarah that such a sensitivity was there: increasingly unable to prevent herself, she went over the course of their conversation in search of signs of it. And then, as if rejecting the extravagances of a dream in the first moments of consciousness, she would reject the fantasies that had not required a surrender to sleep. But all of them returned.

*

Sarah spent Christmas that year with Elizabeth and her family in Cricklewood. She relaxed with gin and tonic, listened to Elizabeth's husband complaining about his sister, from whom he'd just bought a faulty car. She received presents and gave them, she helped to cook the Christmas dinner. Preparing stuffing for the turkey, she heard herself saying:

'It's the only thing that worries me, being alone when I'm old.'

Elizabeth, plumper than ever this Christmas, expressed surprise by wrinkling her nose, which was a habit with her.

'Oh, but you manage so well.'

'Actually the future looks a little bleak.'

'Oh, Sarah, what nonsense!'

It was, and Sarah knew it was: she had learnt how to live alone. There was nothing nicer than coming back to the flat and putting a record on, pouring herself a drink and just sitting there listening to Mozart. There was nothing nicer than not having to consider someone else. She'd only shared the flat with Elizabeth in the first place because it had been necessary financially. That period was past.

'It's just that whatever shall I do when I finish at Pollock-Brown?'

'But that's years away.'

165

'Not really. Thirteen years. When I'm sixty.'

'They'll keep you on, surely? If you want to stay?'

'Mr Everend will be gone. I don't think I'd want to work for anyone else. No, I'll retire at sixty. According to the book.'

'But, my dear, you'll be perfectly all right.'

'I keep thinking of the flat, alone in it.'

'You've been alone in it for years.'

'I know.'

She placed more stuffing in the turkey and pressed it down with a wooden spoon. Sandra Pond would be forty-three when she was sixty. She'd probably look much the same, a little grey in her hair perhaps; she'd never run to fat.

'How are things going?' Elizabeth's husband demanded, coming into the kitchen in a breezy mood. 'Drink for Sarah?'

She smiled at him as he took tonic bottles from the fridge. 'I think she's got the change,' she heard Elizabeth saying to him later. 'Poor thing's gone all jittery.'

Sarah didn't mention the subject of her flat again that Christmas.

*

Well Im a les and I thought you was as well, the letter said. *Im sorry Sarah I didnt' mean to ofend you I didnt' no a thing about you. Ive loved other girls but not like you not as much. I really do love you Sarah. Im going to leave bloody PB because I dont want reminding every time I walk into that bloody canteen. What I wanted was to dance with you remember when I said I wanted to do something? Thats what I ment when I said that. Sandra Pond.*

*

Sarah tried not to think about the letter, which both upset and shocked her. She tried to forget the whole thing, the meeting with Sandra Pond and how she'd felt herself drawn towards having a friendship with the girl. It made her shiver when she thought about all that the letter suggested, it even made her feel a little sick.

Such relationships between women had been talked about at school and often occurred in newspaper reports and in books, on the television even. Sarah had occasionally wondered if this woman or that might possibly possess lesbian tendencies but she had done so without much real interest and had certainly never wondered about such tendencies in relation to herself. But now, just as she had been unable to prevent her mind from engaging in flights of fancy after her meeting with Sandra Pond, she was unable to prevent it from straying about in directions that were inspired by the girl's letter. The man called George, who over the years had become the root of many fantasies, lost his identity to that of Sandra Pond. Yet it was all different because revulsion, not present before, seemed everywhere now. Was it curiosity of a kind, Sarah wondered, that drove her on, enslaving her to fancies she did not care for? No longer did she think of them as silly; malicious rather, certainly malign, like the stuff of nightmares. Grimly she watched while Sandra Pond crossed the floor of a room, coming closer to her, smiling at her. As the man called George had, the hands of the girl undid the buttons of her dress, and then it seemed that fear was added to revulsion. 'I really do love you, Sarah,' the slack voice said, as it had said in the letter, as no other voice had ever said. The passion had a cloying kind of headiness about it, like drunkenness. It was adoration, the girl said, whispering now: it was adoration for every inch of skin and every single hair that grew from Sarah's body and every light in her eyes, and the beauty of her plainness. The pouting lips came closer to her own, the dimples danced. And Sarah, then, would find herself weeping.

She never knew why she wept and assumed it was simply an extension of her revulsion. She felt no desire to have this kind of relationship with a person of her own sex. She didn't want a girl's lips leaving lipstick on her own, she didn't want to experience their softness or the softness of the body that went with them. She didn't want to experience a smell of scent or painted fingernails.

In rational moments Sarah said to herself that as time passed this nightmare would fog over, as other occurrences in her life had fogged over with the passing of time. She had destroyed the letter almost as soon as she'd read it. She had made enquiries: Sandra Pond, as she'd promised, had left Pollock-Brown.

Sarah visited Elizabeth and her family more frequently, she spent a weekend with her brother and his wife in Harrogate, she wrote at length to her other brother, saying they must not lose touch. She forced her mind back into childhood, to which it had regularly and naturally drifted before its invasion by Sandra Pond. It was a deliberate journey now, requiring discipline and concentration, but it was possible to make. Her father ambled into the sitting-room of the rectory, the spaniel called Dodge ambling after him. The wood fire brightly burned as indoor games were played, no one sulky or out of temper. 'And the consequences were,' her brother who was an engineer said, 'fire over England.' In the sunny garden she read about the girls of the Châlet School. Her brothers, in short trousers and flannel shirts, ran about catching wasps in jam-jars. 'The peace of God,' her father's voice murmured, drifting over his small congregation. 'Of course you'll grow up pretty,' her mother softly promised, wiping away her tears.

The passing of time did help. The face of Sandra Pond faded a little, the wording of the ill-written letter became jumbled and uncertain. She would never hear of the girl again, she said to herself, and with an effort that lessened as more months passed by she continued to conjure up the distant world of the rectory.

★

Then, one Saturday morning in November, nearly a year after the Christmas party, Sandra Pond was there in the flesh again. She was in the Express Dairy, where Sarah always did her Saturday-morning shopping, and as soon as she saw her Sarah knew the girl had followed her into the shop. She felt faint and sickish when Sandra Pond smiled her pouting smile and the two dimples danced. She felt the blood draining away from her face and a tightening in her throat.

'Sorry,' Sandra Pond said instead of saying hullo, just standing there.

Sarah had a tin of Crosse and Blackwell's soup in one hand and a wire shopping basket in the other. She didn't know what to say. She thought she probably couldn't say anything even if she tried.

'I just wanted to say I was sorry,' Sandra Pond said. 'I've had it on my mind, Miss Machaen.'

Sarah shook her head. She put the Crosse and Blackwell's soup back on the stack of tins.

'I shouldn't have written that letter's what I mean.'

The girl didn't look well. She seemed to have a cold. She didn't look as pretty as she had at the Christmas party. She wore a brown tweed coat which wasn't very smart. Her shoes were cheap-looking.

'I don't know why I did it, Miss Machaen.'

Sarah tried to smile because she didn't want to be unkind. She ran her tongue about the inside of her mouth, which was dry, as though she'd eaten salt. She said:

'It doesn't matter.'

'It does to me. I couldn't sleep nights.'

'It was just a misunderstanding.'

Sandra Pond didn't say anything. She let a silence gather, and Sarah realised that she was doing so deliberately. Sandra Pond had come back to see how things were, to discover if, with time, the idea appealed to Sarah now, if she'd come to terms with the strangeness of it. As she stood there with the wire basket, she was aware that Sandra Pond had waited for an answer to her letter, that even before that, at the Christmas party, she had hoped for some sign. The girl was staring down at the cream-coloured tiles of the floor, her hands awkwardly by her sides.

The flights of fancy tumbled into Sarah's mind, jogging each other for precedence. They came in flashes: she and Sandra Pond sitting down to a meal, and walking into the foyer of a theatre, and looking at the'Madonna of the Meadow' in the National Gallery, and then a scene like the scene with the man called George occurred.

Sandra Pond looked up and at once the flights of fancy snapped out, like lights extinguished. What would people say? Sarah thought again, as she had on the night of the party. What would her brothers say to see passion thumping at their sister from the eyes of Sandra Pond? What would Elizabeth say, or Anna, or Mr Everend, or her dead father and mother? Would they cry out, amazed and yet delighted, that her plainness should inspire all this, that her plainness at last was beauty? Or would they shudder with disgust?

'I can't help being,' Sandra Pond said, 'the way I am.'

Sarah shook her head, trying to make the gesture seem sympathetic. She wanted to explain that she knew the girl had come specially back, to see what passing time had done, but she could not bring herself to. To have mentioned passing time in that way would have begun another kind of conversation. It was all ridiculous, standing here in the Express Dairy.

'I just wanted to say that and to say I was sorry. Thank you for listening, Miss Machaen.'

She was moving away, the heels of her shoes making a clicking noise on the cream-tiled floor. The smooth back of her head was outlined against packets of breakfast cereals and then against stacks of Mother's Pride bread. Something about her shoulders suggested to Sarah that she was holding back tears.

'Excuse me, dear,' a woman said, poking around Sarah to reach for oxtail soup.

'Oh, sorry.' Mechanically she smiled. She felt shaky and wondered if her face had gone pale. She couldn't imagine eating any of the food she'd selected. She couldn't imagine opening a tin or unwrapping butter without being overcome by the memory of Sandra Pond's sudden advent in the shop. Her instinct was to replace the goods on the shelves and she almost did so. But it seemed too much of a gesture, and too silly. Instead she carried the wire basket to the cashier and paid for what she'd chosen, transferring everything into her shopping-bag.

She walked away from the Express Dairy, by the newsagent's and the butcher's and the Martinez Dry Cleaners, who were offering a bargain, three garments cleaned for the normal price of one. She felt, as she had when the man called George had suddenly lost interest in her body, a pain inside her somewhere.

There was a bus-stop, but Sandra Pond was not standing by it. Nor was she on the pavements that stretched on either side of a road that was busy with Saturday-morning traffic. Nor did she emerge from the telephone box, nor from the newsagent's, nor from Walton's the fruiterer's.

Sarah waited, still looking about. Sandra Pond had been genuinely sorry; she'd meant it when she'd said she'd hated causing the upset. 'Please come and have coffee,' were the words Sarah had ready to say now. 'It's really quite all right.' But she did not say them, because Sandra Pond had not lingered. And in a million years, Sarah thought, she would not ever find her.

Death in Jerusalem

'Till then,' Father Paul said, leaning out of the train window. 'Till Jerusalem, Francis.'

'Please God, Paul.' As he spoke the Dublin train began to move and his brother waved from the window and he waved back, a modest figure on the platform. Everyone said Francis might have been a priest as well, meaning that Francis's quietness and meditative disposition had an air of the cloister about them. But Francis contented himself with the running of Daly's hardware business, which his mother had run until she was too old for it. 'Are we game for the Holy Land next year?' Father Paul had asked that July. 'Will we go together, Francis?' He had brushed aside all Francis's protestations, all attempts to explain that the shop could not be left, that their mother would be confused by the absence of Francis from the house. Rumbustiously he'd pointed out that there was their sister Kitty, who was in charge of the household of which Francis and their mother were part and whose husband, Myles, could surely be trusted to look after the shop for a single fortnight. For thirty years, ever since he was seven, Francis had wanted to go to the Holy Land. He had savings which he'd never spent a penny of: you couldn't take them with you, Father Paul had more than once stated that July.

On the platform Francis watched until the train could no longer be seen, his thoughts still with his brother. The priest's ruddy countenance smiled again behind cigarette smoke; his bulk remained impressive in his clerical clothes, the collar pinching the flesh of his neck, his black shoes scrupulously polished. There were freckles on the backs of

his large, strong hands; he had a fine head of hair, grey and
crinkly. In an hour and a half's time the train would creep
into Dublin, and he'd take a taxi. He'd spend a night in the
Gresham Hotel, probably falling in with another priest,
having a drink or two, maybe playing a game of bridge after
his meal. That was his brother's way and always had been –
an extravagant, easy kind of way, full of smiles and good
humour. It was what had taken him to America and made
him successful there. In order to raise money for the church
that he and Father Steigmuller intended to build before 1980
he took parties of the well-to-do from San Francisco to Rome
and Florence, to Chartres and Seville and the Holy Land.
He was good at raising money, not just for the church but
for the boys' home of which he was president, and for the
Hospital of Our Saviour, and for St Mary's Old People's
Home on the west side of the city. But every July he flew
back to Ireland, to the town in Co. Tipperary where his
mother and brother and sister still lived. He stayed in the
house above the shop which he might have inherited himself
on the death of his father, which he'd rejected in favour of
the religious life. Mrs Daly was eighty now. In the shop she
sat silently behind the counter, in a corner by the chicken-
wire, wearing only clothes that were black. In the evenings
she sat with Francis in the lace-curtained sitting-room, while
the rest of the family occupied the kitchen. It was for her
sake most of all that Father Paul made the journey every
summer, considering it his duty.

Walking back to the town from the station, Francis was
aware that he was missing his brother. Father Paul was
fourteen years older and in childhood had often taken the
place of their father, who had died when Francis was five.
His brother had possessed an envied strength and knowledge;
he'd been a hero, quite often worshipped, an example of success. In later life he had become an example of generosity as

well: ten years ago he'd taken their mother to Rome, and
their sister Kitty and her husband two years later; he'd paid
the expenses when their sister Edna had gone to Canada; he'd
assisted two nephews to make a start in America. In childhood Francis hadn't possessed his brother's healthy freckled
face, just as in middle age he didn't have his ruddy complexion
and his stoutness and his easiness with people. Francis was
slight, his sandy hair receding, his face rather pale. His
breathing was sometimes laboured because of wheeziness in
the chest. In the ironmonger's shop he wore a brown cotton
coat.

'Hullo, Mr Daly,' a woman said to him in the main street
of the town. 'Father Paul's gone off, has he?'

'Yes, he's gone again.'

'I'll pray for his journey so,' the woman promised, and
Francis thanked her.

*

A year went by. In San Francisco another wing of the boys'
home was completed, another target was reached in Father
Paul and Father Steigmuller's fund for the church they
planned to have built by 1980. In the town in Co. Tipperary
there were baptisms and burial services and First Com-
munions. Old Loughlin, a farmer from Bansha, died in
Flynn's grocery and bar, having gone there to celebrate a
good price he'd got for a heifer. Clancy, from behind the
counter in Doran's drapery, married Maureen Talbot; Mr
Nolan's plasterer married Miss Driscoll; Johneen Lynch
married Seamus in the chip shop, under pressure from her
family to do so. A local horse, from the stables on the Limerick
road, was said to be an entry for the Fairyhouse Grand
National, but it turned out not to be true. Every evening of
that year Francis sat with his mother in the lace-curtained
sitting-room above the shop. Every weekday she sat in her

corner by the chicken-wire, watching while he counted out screws and weighed staples, or advised about yard brushes or tap-washers. Occasionally, on a Saturday, he visited the three Christian Brothers who lodged with Mrs Shea and afterwards he'd tell his mother about how the authority was slipping these days from the nuns and the Christian Brothers, and how Mrs Shea's elderly maid, Agnes, couldn't see to cook the food any more. His mother would nod and hardly ever speak. When he told a joke—what young Hogan had said when he'd found a nail in his egg or how Agnes had put mint sauce into a jug with milk in it—she never laughed and looked at him in surprise when he laughed himself. But Dr Grady said it was best to keep her cheered up.

All during that year Francis talked to her about his forth-coming visit to the Holy Land, endeavouring to make her understand that for a fortnight next spring he would be away from the house and the shop. He'd been away before for odd days, but that was when she'd been younger. He used to visit an aunt in Tralee, but three years ago the aunt had died and he hadn't left the town since.

Francis and his mother had always been close. Before his birth two daughters had died in infancy, and his very survival had often struck Mrs Daly as a gift. He had always been her favourite, the one among her children whom she often con-sidered least able to stand on his own two feet. It was just like Paul to have gone blustering off to San Francisco instead of remaining in Co. Tipperary. It was just like Kitty to have married a useless man. 'There's not a girl in the town who'd touch him,' she'd said to her daughter at the time, but Kitty had been headstrong and adamant, and there was Myles now, doing nothing whatsoever except cleaning other people's windows for a pittance and placing bets in Donovan's the turf accountant's. It was the shop and the arrangement Kitty had with Francis and her mother that kept her and the children going, three of whom had already left the town, which in Mrs Daly's opinion they mightn't have done if they'd had a better type of father. Mrs Daly often wondered what her own two babies who'd died might have grown up into, and imagined they might have been like Francis, about whom she'd never had a moment's worry. Not in a million years would he give you the feeling that he was too big for his boots, like Paul sometimes did with his lavishness and his big talk of America. He wasn't silly like Kitty, or so sinful you couldn't forgive him, like you couldn't forgive Edna, even though she was dead and buried in Toronto.

Francis understood how his mother felt about the family. She'd had a hard life, left a widow early on, trying to do the best she could for everyone. In turn he did his best to compensate for the struggles and disappointments she'd suffered, cheering her in the evenings while Kitty and Myles and the youngest of their children watched the television in the kitchen. His mother had ignored the existence of Myles for ten years, ever since the day he'd taken money out of the till to pick up the odds on Gusty Spirit at Phoenix Park. And although Francis got on well enough with Myles he quite understood that there should be a long aftermath to that day. There'd been a terrible row in the kitchen, Kitty screaming at Myles and Myles telling lies and Francis trying to keep them calm, saying they'd give the old woman a heart attack.

She didn't like upsets of any kind, so all during the year before he was to visit the Holy Land Francis read the New Testament to her in order to prepare her. He talked to her about Bethlehem and Nazareth and the miracle of the loaves and fishes and all the other miracles. She kept nodding, but he often wondered if she didn't assume he was just casually referring to episodes in the Bible. As a child he had listened to such talk himself, with awe and fascination, imagining the walking on the water and the temptation in the wilderness. He had imagined the cross carried to Calvary, and the rock rolled back from the tomb, and the rising from the dead on the third day. That he was now to walk in such places seemed extraordinary to him, and he wished his mother was younger so that she could appreciate his good fortune and share it with him when she received the postcards he intended, every day, to send her. But her eyes seemed always to tell him that he was making a mistake, that somehow he was making a fool of himself by doing such a showy thing as going to the Holy Land. *I have the entire itinerary mapped out*, his brother wrote from San Francisco. *There's nothing we'll miss.*

*

It was the first time Francis had been in an aeroplane. He flew by Aer Lingus from Dublin to London and then changed to an El Al flight to Tel Aviv. He was nervous and he found it exhausting. All the time he seemed to be eating, and it was strange being among so many people he didn't know. 'You will taste honey such as never before,' an Israeli businessman in the seat next to his assured him. 'And Galilean figs. Make certain to taste Galilean figs.' Make certain too, the businessman went on, to experience Jerusalem by night and in the early dawn. He urged Francis to see places he had never heard of, the Yad Va-Shem, the treasures of the Shrine of the Book. He urged him to honour the martyrs of Masada and to learn a few words of Hebrew as a token of respect. He told him of a shop where he could buy mementoes and warned him against Arab street traders.

'The hard man, how are you?' Father Paul said at Tel Aviv airport, having flown in from San Francisco the day before. Father Paul had had a drink or two and he suggested another when they arrived at the Plaza Hotel in Jerusalem. It was half-past nine in the evening. 'A quick little nightcap,' Father Paul insisted, 'and then hop into bed with you, Francis.' They sat in an enormous open lounge with low, round tables and square modern armchairs. Father Paul said it was the bar.

They had said what had to be said in the car from Tel Aviv to Jerusalem. Father Paul had asked about their mother, and Kitty and Myles. He'd asked about other people in the town, old Canon Mahon and Sergeant Malone. He and Father Steigmuller had had a great year of it, he reported: as well as everything else, the boys' home had turned out two tip-top footballers. 'We'll start on a tour at half-nine in the morning,' he said. 'I'll be sitting having breakfast at eight.'

Francis went to bed and Father Paul ordered another whisky, with ice. To his great disappointment there was no Irish whisky in the hotel so he'd had to content himself with Haig. He fell into conversation with an American couple, making them promise that if they were ever in Ireland they wouldn't miss out Co. Tipperary. At eleven o'clock the barman said he was wanted at the reception desk and when Father Paul went there and announced himself he was given a message in an envelope. It was a telegram that had come, the girl said in poor English. Then she shook her head, saying it was a telex. He opened the envelope and learnt that Mrs Daly had died.

*

Francis fell asleep immediately and dreamed that he was a boy again, out fishing with a friend whom he couldn't now identify.

On the telephone Father Paul ordered whisky and ice to be brought to his room. Before drinking it he took his jacket off and knelt by his bed to pray for his mother's salvation. When he'd completed the prayers he walked slowly up and down the length of the room, occasionally sipping at his whisky. He argued with himself and finally arrived at a decision.

*

For breakfast they had scrambled eggs that looked like yellow ice-cream, and orange juice that was delicious. Francis wondered about bacon, but Father Paul explained that bacon was not readily available in Israel.

'Did you sleep all right?' Father Paul enquired. 'Did you have the jet-lag?'

'Jet-lag?'

'A tiredness you get after jet flights. It'd knock you out for days.'

'Ah, I slept great, Paul.'

'Good man.'

They lingered over breakfast. Father Paul reported a little more of what had happened in his parish during the year, in particular about the two young footballers from the boys' home. Francis told about the decline in the cooking at Mrs Shea's boarding-house, as related to him by the three Christian Brothers. 'I have a car laid on,' Father Paul said, and twenty minutes later they walked out into the Jerusalem sunshine.

The hired car stopped on the way to the walls of the old city. It drew into a lay-by at Father Paul's request and the two men got out and looked across a wide valley dotted with houses and olive trees. A road curled along the distant slope opposite. 'The Mount of Olives,' Father Paul said. 'And that's the road to Jericho.' He pointed more particularly. 'You see that group of eight big olives? Just off the road, where the church is?'

Francis thought he did, but was not sure. There were so many olive trees, and more than one church. He glanced at

his brother's pointing finger and followed its direction with
his glance.

'The Garden òf Gethsemane,' Father Paul said.

Francis did not say anything. He continued to gaze at the
distant church, with the clump of olive trees beside it. Wild
flowers were profuse on the slopes of the valley, smears of
orange and blue on land that looked poor. Two Arab women
herded goats.

'Could we see it closer?' he asked, and his brother said that
definitely they would. They returned to the waiting car and
Father Paul ordered it to the Gate of St Stephen.

Tourists heavy with cameras thronged the Via Dolorosa.
Brown, bare-foot children asked for alms. Stall-keepers
pressed their different wares, cotton dresses, metal-ware,
mementoes, sacred goods. 'Get out of the way,' Father Paul
kept saying to them, genially laughing to show he wasn't
being abrupt. Francis wanted to stand still and close his eyes,
to visualise for a moment the carrying of the Cross. But the
ceremony of the Stations, familiar to him for as long as he
could remember, was unreal. Try as he would, Christ's journey refused to enter his imagination, and his own plain
church seemed closer to the heart of the matter than the
noisy lane he was now being jostled on. 'God damn it, of
course it's genuine,' an angry American voice proclaimed, in
reply to a shriller voice which insisted that cheating had taken
place. The voices argued about a piece of wood, neat beneath
plastic in a little box, a sample or not of the cross that had
been carried.

They arrived at the Church of the Holy Sepulchre, and at the
Chapel of the Nailing to the Cross, where they prayed. They
passed through the Chapel of the Angel, to the tomb of
Christ. Nobody spoke in the marble cell, but when they left
the church Francis overhead a quiet man with spectacles saying it was unlikely that a body would have been buried within

the walls of the city. They walked to Hezekiah's Pool and out of the old city at the Jaffa Gate, where their hired car was waiting for them. 'Are you peckish?' Father Paul asked, and although Francis said he wasn't they returned to the hotel.

Delay funeral till Monday was the telegram Father Paul had sent. There was an early flight on Sunday, in time for an afternoon one from London to Dublin. With luck there'd be a late train on Sunday evening and if there wasn't they'd have to fix a car. Today was Tuesday. It would give them four and a half days. *Funeral eleven Monday* the telegram at the reception desk now confirmed. 'Ah, isn't that great?' he said to himself, bundling the telegram up.

'Will we have a small one?' he suggested in the open area that was the bar. 'Or better still a big one.' He laughed. He was in good spirits in spite of the death that had taken place. He gestured at the barman, wagging his head and smiling jovially.

His face had reddened in the morning sun; there were specks of sweat on his forehead and his nose. 'Bethlehem this afternoon,' he laid down. 'Unless the jet-lag . . . ?'

'I haven't got the jet-lag.'

In the Nativity Boutique Francis bought for his mother a small metal plate with a fish on it. He had stood for a moment, scarcely able to believe it, on the spot where the manger had been, in the Church of the Nativity. As in the Via Dolorosa it had been difficult to rid the imagination of the surroundings that now were present, of the exotic Greek Orthodox trappings, the foreign-looking priests, the oriental smell. Gold, frankincense and myrrh, he'd kept thinking, for somehow the church seemed more the church of the kings than of Joseph and Mary and their child. Afterwards they returned to Jerusalem, to the Tomb of the Virgin and the Garden of Gethsemane. 'It could have been anywhere,' he heard the quiet, bespectacled sceptic remarking in Gethsemane. 'They're only guessing.'

*

Father Paul rested in the late afternoon, lying down on his bed with his jacket off. He slept from half-past five until a quarter-past seven and awoke refreshed. He picked up the telephone and asked for whisky and ice to be brought up and when it arrived he undressed and had a bath, relaxing in the warm water with the drink on a ledge in the tiled wall beside him. There would be time to take in Nazareth and Galilee. He was particularly keen that his brother should see Galilee because Galilee had atmosphere and was beautiful. There wasn't, in his own opinion, very much to Nazareth but it would be a pity to miss it all the same. It was at the Sea of Galilee that he intended to tell his brother of their mother's death.

We've had a great day, Francis wrote on a postcard that showed an aerial view of Jerusalem. *The Church of the Holy Sepulchre, where Our Lord's tomb is, and Gethsemane and Bethlehem. Paul's in great form.* He addressed it to his mother, and then wrote other cards, to Kitty and Myles and to the three Christian Brothers in Mrs Shea's, and to Canon Mahon. He gave thanks that he was privileged to be in Jerusalem. He read St Mark and some of St Matthew. He said his rosary.

'Will we chance the wine?' Father Paul said at dinner, not that wine was something he went in for, but a waiter had come up and put a large padded wine-list into his hand.

'Ah, no, no,' Francis protested, but already Father Paul was running his eye down the listed bottles.

'Have you local wine?' he enquired of the waiter. 'A nice red one?'

The waiter nodded and hurried away, and Francis hoped he wouldn't get drunk, the red wine on top of the whisky he'd had in the bar before the meal. He'd only had the one whisky, not being much used to it, making it last through his brother's three.

'I heard some gurriers in the bar,' Father Paul said, 'making a great song and dance about the local red wine.'

Wine made Francis think of the Holy Communion, but he didn't say so. He said the soup was delicious and he drew his brother's attention to the custom there was in the hotel of a porter ringing a bell and walking about with a person's name chalked on a little blackboard on the end of a rod.

'It's a way of paging you,' Father Paul explained. 'Isn't it nicer than bellowing out some fellow's name?' He smiled his easy smile, his eyes beginning to water as a result of the few drinks he'd had. He was beginning to feel the strain: he kept thinking of their mother lying there, of what she'd say if she knew what he'd done, how she'd savagely upbraid him for keeping the fact from Francis. Out of duty and humanity he had returned each year to see her because, after all, you only had the one mother. But he had never cared for her.

Francis went for a walk after dinner. There were young soldiers with what seemed to be toy guns on the streets, but he knew the guns were real. In the shop windows there were television sets for sale, and furniture and clothes, just like anywhere else. There were advertisements for some film or other, two writhing women without a stitch on them, the kind of thing you wouldn't see in Co. Tipperary. 'You want something, sir?' a girl said, smiling at him with broken front teeth. The siren of a police car or an ambulance shrilled urgently near by. He shook his head at the girl. 'No, I don't want anything,' he said, and then realised what she had meant. She was small and very dark, no more than a child. He hurried on, praying for her.

When he returned to the hotel he found his brother in the lounge with other people, two men and two women. Father Paul was ordering a round of drinks and called out to the

barman to bring another whisky. 'Ah, no, no,' Francis protested, anxious to go to his room and to think about the day,
to read the New Testament and perhaps to write a few more
postcards. Music was playing, coming from speakers that
could not be seen.

'My brother Francis,' Father Paul said to the people he
was with, and the people all gave their names, adding that
they came from New York. 'I was telling them about Tipp,'
Father Paul said to his brother, offering his packet of cigarettes around.

'You like Jerusalem, Francis?' one of the American women
asked him, and he replied that he hadn't been able to take it
in yet. Then, feeling that that didn't sound enthusiastic
enough, he added that being there was the experience of a
lifetime.

Father Paul went on talking about Co. Tipperary and then
spoke of his parish in San Francisco, the boys' home and the
two promising footballers, the plans for the new church. The
Americans listened and in a moment the conversation drifted
on to the subject of their travels in England, their visit to
Istanbul and Athens, an argument they'd had with the
Customs at Tel Aviv. 'Well, I'm for the hay-pile,' one of the
men announced eventually, standing up.

The others stood up too and so did Francis. Father Paul
remained where he was, gesturing again in the direction of
the barman. 'Sit down for a nightcap,' he urged his brother.

'Ah, no, no –' Francis began.

'Bring us two more of those,' the priest ordered with a
sudden abruptness, and the barman hurried away. 'Listen,'
said Father Paul. 'I've something to tell you.'

After dinner, while Francis had been out on his walk, before he'd dropped into conversation with the Americans,
Father Paul had said to himself that he couldn't stand the
strain. It was the old woman stretched out above the hardware

shop, as stiff as a board already, with the little lights burning in her room: he kept seeing all that, as if she wanted him to, as if she was trying to haunt him. Nice as the idea was, he didn't think he could continue with what he'd planned, with waiting until they got up to Galilee.

Francis didn't want to drink any more. He hadn't wanted the whisky his brother had ordered him earlier, nor the one the Americans had ordered for him. He didn't want the one that the barman now brought. He thought he'd just leave it there, hoping his brother wouldn't see it. He lifted the glass to his lips, but he managed not to drink any.

'A bad thing has happened,' Father Paul said.

'Bad? How d'you mean, Paul?'

'Are you ready for it?' He paused. Then he said, 'She died.'

Francis didn't know what he was talking about. He didn't know who was meant to be dead, or why his brother was behaving in an odd manner. He didn't like to think it but he had to: his brother wasn't fully sober.

'Our mother died,' Father Paul said. 'I'm after getting a telegram.'

The huge area that was the lounge of the Plaza Hotel, the endless tables and people sitting at them, the swiftly moving waiters and barmen, seemed suddenly a dream. Francis had a feeling that he was not where he appeared to be, that he wasn't sitting with his brother, who was wiping his lips with a handkerchief. For a moment he appeared in his confusion to be struggling his way up the Via Dolorosa again and then in the Nativity Boutique.

'Take it easy, boy,' his brother was saying. 'Take a mouthful of whisky.'

Francis didn't obey that injunction. He asked his brother to repeat what he had said, and Father Paul repeated that their mother had died.

Francis closed his eyes and tried as well to shut away the sounds around them. He prayed for the salvation of his mother's soul. 'Blessed Virgin, intercede,' his own voice said in his mind. 'Dear Mary, let her few small sins be forgiven.'

Having rid himself of his secret, Father Paul felt instant relief. With the best of intentions in the world it had been a foolish idea to think he could maintain the secret until they arrived in a place that was perhaps the most suitable in the world to hear about the death of a person who'd been close to you. He took a gulp of his whisky and wiped his mouth with his handkerchief again. He watched his brother, waiting for his eyes to open.

'When did it happen?' Francis asked eventually.

'Yesterday.'

'And the telegram only came – '

'It came last night, Francis. I wanted to save you the pain.'

'Save me? How could you save me? I sent her a postcard, Paul.'

'Listen to me, Francis – '

'How could you save me the pain?'

'I wanted to tell you when we got up to Galilee.'

Again Francis felt he was caught in the middle of a dream. He couldn't understand his brother: he couldn't understand what he meant by saying a telegram had come last night, why at a moment like this he was talking about Galilee. He didn't know why he was sitting in this noisy place when he should be back in Ireland.

'I fixed the funeral for Monday,' Father Paul said.

Francis nodded, not grasping the significance of this arrangement. 'We'll be back there this time tomorrow,' he said.

'No need for that, Francis. Sunday morning's time enough.'

'But she's dead – '

'We'll be there in time for the funeral.'

187

'We can't stay here if she's dead.'

It was this, Father Paul realised, he'd been afraid of when he'd argued with himself and made his plan. If he'd have knocked on Francis's door the night before, Francis would have wanted to return immediately without seeing a single stone of the land he had come so far to be moved by.

'We could go straight up to Galilee in the morning,' Father Paul said quietly. 'You'll find comfort in Galilee, Francis.'

But Francis shook his head. 'I want to be with her,' he said.

Father Paul lit another cigarette. He nodded at a hovering waiter, indicating his need of another drink. He said to himself that he must keep his cool, an expression he was fond of.

'Take it easy, Francis,' he said.

'Is there a plane out in the morning? Can we make arrangements now?' He looked about him as if for a member of the hotel staff who might be helpful.

'No good'll be done by tearing off home, Francis. What's wrong with Sunday?'

'I want to be with her.'

Anger swelled within Father Paul. If he began to argue his words would become slurred: he knew that from experience. He must keep his cool and speak slowly and clearly, making a few simple points. It was typical of her, he thought, to die inconveniently.

'You've come all this way,' he said as slowly as he could without sounding peculiar. 'Why cut it any shorter than we need? We'll be losing a week anyway. She wouldn't want us to go back.'

'I think she would.'

He was right in that. Her possessiveness in her lifetime would have reached out across a dozen continents for Francis. She'd known what she was doing by dying when she had.

'I shouldn't have come,' Francis said. 'She didn't want me to come.'

'You're thirty-seven years of age, Francis.'

'I did wrong to come.'

'You did no such thing.'

The time he'd taken her to Rome she'd been difficult for the whole week, complaining about the food, saying everywhere was dirty. Whenever he'd spent anything she'd disapproved. All his life, Father Paul felt, he'd done his best for her. He had told her before anyone else when he'd decided to enter the priesthood, certain that she'd be pleased. 'I thought you'd take over the shop,' she'd said instead.

'What difference could it make to wait, Francis?'

'There's nothing to wait for.'

As long as he lived Francis knew he would never forgive himself. As long as he lived he would say to himself that he hadn't been able to wait a few years, until she'd passed quietly on. He might even have been in the room with her when it happened.

'It was a terrible thing not to tell me,' he said. 'I sat down and wrote her a postcard, Paul. I bought her a plate.'

'So you said.'

'You're drinking too much of that whisky.'

'Now, Francis, don't be silly.'

'You're half drunk and she's lying there.'

'She can't be brought back no matter what we do.'

'She never hurt anyone,' Francis said.

Father Paul didn't deny that, although it wasn't true. She had hurt their sister Kitty, constantly reproaching her for marrying the man she had, long after Kitty was aware she'd made a mistake. She'd driven Edna to Canada after Edna, still unmarried, had had a miscarriage that only the family knew about. She had made a shadow out of Francis although Francis didn't know it. Failing to hold on to her other children, she had grasped her last-born to her, as if she had borne him to destroy him.

'It'll be you'll say a mass for her?' Francis said.

'Yes, of course it will.'

'You should have told me.'

Francis realised why, all day, he'd been disappointed. From the moment when the hired car had pulled into the lay-by and his brother had pointed across the valley at the Garden of Gethsemane he'd been disappointed and had not admitted it. He'd been disappointed in the Via Dolorosa and in the Church of the Holy Sepulchre and in Bethlehem. He remembered the bespectacled man who'd kept saying that you couldn't be sure about anything. All the people with cameras made it impossible to think, all the jostling and pushing was distracting. When he'd said there'd been too much to take in he'd meant something different.

'Her death got in the way,' he said.

'What d'you mean, Francis?'

'It didn't feel like Jerusalem, it didn't feel like Bethlehem.'

'But it is, Francis, it is.'

'There are soldiers with guns all over the place. And a girl came up to me on the street. There was that man with a bit of the Cross. There's you, drinking and smoking in this place – '

'Now, listen to me, Francis – '

'Nazareth would be a disappointment. And the Sea of Galilee. And the Church of the Loaves and Fishes.' His voice had risen. He lowered it again. 'I couldn't believe in the Stations this morning. I couldn't see it happening the way I do at home.'

'That's nothing to do with her death, Francis. You've got a bit of jet-lag, you'll settle yourself up in Galilee. There's an atmosphere in Galilee that nobody misses.'

'I'm not going near Galilee.' He struck the surface of the table, and Father Paul told him to contain himself. People turned their heads, aware that anger had erupted in the pale-faced man with the priest.

'Quieten up,' Father Paul commanded sharply, but Francis didn't.

'She knew I'd be better at home,' he shouted, his voice shrill and reedy. 'She knew I was making a fool of myself, a man out of a shop trying to be big – '

'Will you keep your voice down? Of course you're not making a fool of yourself.'

'Will you find out about planes tomorrow morning?'

Father Paul sat for a moment longer, not saying anything, hoping his brother would say he was sorry. Naturally it was a shock, naturally he'd be emotional and feel guilty, in a moment it would be better. But it wasn't and Francis didn't say he was sorry. Instead he began to weep.

'Let's go up to your room,' Father Paul said, 'and I'll fix about the plane.'

Francis nodded but did not move. His sobbing ceased, and then he said, 'I'll always hate the Holy Land now.'

'No need for that, Francis.'

But Francis felt there was and he felt he would hate, as well, the brother he had admired for as long as he could remember. In the lounge of the Plaza Hotel he felt mockery surfacing everywhere. His brother's deceit, and the endless whisky in his brother's glass, and his casualness after a death, seemed like the scorning of a Church which honoured so steadfastly the mother of its founder. Vivid in his mind, his own mother's eyes reminded him that they'd told him he was making a mistake, and upbraided him for not heeding her. Of course there was mockery everywhere, in the splinter of wood beneath plastic, and in the soldiers with guns that were not toys, and the writhing nakedness in the Holy City. He'd become part of it himself, sending postcards to the dead. Not speaking again to his brother, he went to his room to pray.

'Eight a.m., sir,' the girl at the reception desk said, and Father Paul asked that arrangements should be made to book two seats on the plane, explaining that it was an emergency, that a death had occurred. 'It will be all right, sir,' the girl promised.

He went slowly downstairs to the bar. He sat in a corner and lit a cigarette and ordered two whiskies and ice, as if expecting a companion. He drank them both himself and ordered more. Francis would return to Co. Tipperary and after the funeral he would take up again the life she had ordained for him. In his brown cotton coat he would serve customers with nails and hinges and wire. He would regularly go to Mass and to Confession and to Men's Confraternity. He would sit alone in the lace-curtained sitting-room, lonely for the woman who had made him what he was, married forever to her memory.

Father Paul lit a fresh cigarette from the butt of the last one. He continued to order whisky in two glasses. Already he could sense the hatred that Francis had earlier felt taking root in himself. He wondered if he would ever again return in July to Co. Tipperary, and imagined he would not.

At midnight he rose to make the journey to bed and found himself unsteady on his feet. People looked at him, thinking it disgraceful for a priest to be drunk in Jerusalem, with cigarette ash all over his clerical clothes.

Attracta

Attracta read about Penelope Vade in a newspaper, an item
that upset her. It caused her to wonder if all her life as a
teacher she'd been saying the wrong things to the children in
her care. It saddened her when she thought about the faces
that had passed through her schoolroom, ever since 1937. She
began to feel she should have told them about herself.

She taught in a single schoolroom that hadn't altered much
since the days when she'd been a pupil in it herself. There
were portraits of England's kings and queens around the
walls, painted by some teacher in the past. There were other
pictures, added at some later date, of Irish heroes: Niall of
the Nine Hostages, Lord Edward FitzGerald, Wolfe Tone
and Grattan. Maps of Europe and of Ireland and of England,
Wales and Scotland hung side by side. A new blackboard,
attached to the wall, had ten years ago replaced the old
pedestal one. The globe had always been there in Attracta's
time, but since it did not designate political boundaries it
wasn't much out of date. The twenty-five wooden desks more
urgently needed to be replaced.

In the schoolroom Attracta taught the sixteen Protestant
children of the town. The numbers had been sometimes
greater in the past, and often fewer; sixteen was an average, a
number she found easy to manage when divided into the four
classes that the different ages demanded. The room was large,
the desks arranged in groups, discipline had never been a
problem. The country children brought sandwiches for
lunch, the children of the town went home at midday.
Attracta went home herself, to the house in North Street

which she'd inherited from her Aunt Emmeline and where now she lived alone. She possessed an old blue Morris Minor but she did not often drive it to and from her schoolroom, preferring to make the journey on foot in order to get fresh air and exercise. She was a familiar figure, the Protestant teacher with her basket of groceries or exercise-books. She had never married, though twice she'd been proposed to: by an exchange clerk in the Provincial Bank and by an English visitor who'd once spent the summer in the area with his parents. All that was a long time ago now, for Attracta was sixty-one. Her predecessor in the schoolroom, Mr Ayrie, hadn't retired until he was over seventy. She had always assumed she'd emulate him in that.

Looking back on it, Attracta didn't regret that she had not married. She hadn't much cared for either of the men who'd proposed to her and she didn't mind being alone at sixty-one in her house in North Street. She regularly went to church, she had friends among the people who had been her pupils in the past. Now and again in the holidays she drove her Morris Minor to Cork for a day's shopping and possibly a visit to the Savoy or the Pavilion, although the films they offered were not as good as they'd been in the past. Being on her own was something she'd always known, having been both an only child and an orphan. There'd been tragedy in her life but she considered that she had not suffered. People had been good to her.

English Girl's Suicide in Belfast the headline about Penelope Vade said, and below it there was a photograph, a girl with a slightly crooked smile and freckled cheeks. There was a photograph of her husband in army uniform, taken a few weeks before his death, and of the house in Belfast in which she had later rented a flat. *From the marks of blood on carpets and rugs*, the item said, *it is deduced that Mrs Vade dragged herself across the floors of two rooms. She appears repeatedly to have fainted before she reached a bottle of aspirins in a kitchen cupboard.* She had been twenty-three at the time of her death.

It was Penelope Vade's desire to make some kind of gesture, a gesture of courage and perhaps anger, that had caused her to leave her parents' home in Haslemere and to go to Belfast. Her husband, an army officer, had been murdered in Belfast; he'd been decapitated as well. His head, wrapped in cotton-wool to absorb the ooze of blood, secured within a plastic bag and packed in a biscuit-tin, had been posted to Penelope Vade. Layer by layer the parcel had been opened by her in Haslemere. She hadn't known that he was dead before his dead eyes stared into hers.

Her gesture was her mourning of him. She went to Belfast to join the Women's Peace Movement, to make the point that somehow neither he nor she had been defeated. But her gesture, publicly reported, had incensed the men who'd gone to the trouble of killing him. One after another, seven of them had committed acts of rape on her. It was after that that she had killed herself.

A fortnight after Attracta had first read the newspaper item it still upset her. It haunted her, and she knew why it did, though only imprecisely. Alone at night, almost catching her unawares, scenes from the tragedy established themselves in her mind: the opening of the biscuit-box, the smell of death, the eyes, blood turning brown. As if at a macabre slide-show, the scene would change: before people had wondered about her whereabouts Penelope Vade had been dead for four days; mice had left droppings on her body.

One afternoon, in order to think the matter over in peace and quiet, Attracta drove her Morris Minor to the sea at Cedarstrand, eight miles from the town. She clambered from the strand up to the headland and paused there, gazing down into the bay, at the solitary island it held. No one had ever lived on the island because its smallness would have made a self-supporting existence impossible. When she'd been growing up she'd often wondered what it would be like to live alone on the rocky fastness, in a wooden hut or a cottage built of stones. Not very agreeable, she'd thought, for she'd always been sociable. She thought it again as she turned abruptly from the sea and followed a path inland through wiry purple heather.

Two fishermen, approaching her on the path, recognised her as the Protestant teacher from the town eight miles away and stood aside for her to pass. She was thinking that nothing she might ever have said in her schoolroom could possibly have prevented the death of a girl in a city two hundred miles away. Yet in a way it seemed ridiculous that for so long she had been relating the details of Cromwell's desecration and the laws of Pythagoras, when she should have been talking about Mr Devereux and Geraldine Carey. And it was Mr Purce she should have recalled instead of the Battle of the Boyne.

The fishermen spoke to her as she passed them by but she didn't reply. It surprised them that she didn't, for they hadn't heard that the Protestant teacher had recently become deaf or odd. Just old, they supposed, as they watched her progressing slowly: an upright figure, spare and seeming fragile, a certain stiffness in her movement.

*

What made Attracta feel close to the girl in the newspaper item was the tragedy in her own life: the death of her mother and her father when she was three. Her parents had gone away, she had been told, and at first she had wept miserably and would not be comforted. But as days passed into weeks, and weeks into months, this unhappiness gradually left her. She ceased to ask about her parents and became used to living in her Aunt Emmeline's house in North Street. In time she no longer remembered the morning she'd woken up in this house in a bed that was strange to her; nor could she recollect her parents' faces. She grew up assuming they were no longer alive and when once she voiced this assumption her aunt did not contradict it. It wasn't until later in her childhood, when she was eleven, that she learnt the details of the tragedy from Mr Purce, a small man in a hard black hat, who was often to be seen on the streets of the town. He was one of the people she noticed in her childhood, like the elderly beggar-woman called Limerick Nancy and the wild-looking builder's labourer who could walk a hundred miles without stopping, who never wore a jersey or a coat over his open shirt even on the coldest winter days. There were other people too: priests going for a walk in pairs, out along the road that led to the golf-course and to Cedarstrand by the longer route. Strolling through the afternoon sunshine there were nuns in pairs also, and there was Redmond the solicitor hurrying about with his business papers, and Father Quinn on his bicycle. At night there were the red-fleshed country bachelors tipsily smiling through cigarette smoke, lips glistening in the street-light outside Keogh's public house. At all times of day, at all the town's corners, the children of the poor waited for nothing in particular.

The town was everything in Attracta's childhood, and only some of it had changed in the fifty years that had passed. Without nostalgia she remembered now the horses and carts with milk churns for the creamery, slowly progressing on narrow streets between colour-washed houses. On fair-days the pavements had been slithery with dung, and on fair-days they still were. Farmers stood by their animals, their shirts clean for the occasion, a stud at their throats, without collar or tie. Dogs slouched in a manner that was characteristic of the dogs of the town; there was a smell of stout and sawdust. In her childhood there had been O'Mara's Picture House, dour grey cement encasing the dreamland of Fred Astaire and Ginger Rogers. Built with pride in 1929, O'Mara's was a ruin now.

Within the world of the town there was for Attracta a smaller, Protestant world. Behind green railings there was Mr Ayrie's Protestant schoolroom. There was the Church of Ireland church, with its dusty flags of another age, and Archdeacon Flower's prayers for the English royal family. There were the Sunday-school classes of Mr and Mrs Bell, and the patience of her aunt, which seemed like a Protestant thing also – the Protestant duty of a woman who had never expected to find herself looking after a child. There was Mr Devereux, a Protestant who never went to church.

No one in the town, not even her aunt, was kinder to Attracta than Mr Devereux. On her birthday he came himself to the house in North Street with a present carefully wrapped, a dolls' house once, so big he'd had to ask the man next door to help him out of the dickey of his motor-car with it. At Christmas he had a Christmas tree in his house, and other children in the town, her friends from school, were invited to a party. Every Saturday she spent the afternoon with him, eating his housekeeper's delicious orange cake for tea and sticking stamps into the album he'd given her, listening to his gramophone in the room he called his office. He loved getting a huge fire going in his office, banking up the coals so that they'd glow and redden her cheeks. In summer he sat in his back garden with her, sometimes reading *Coral Island* aloud. He made her run away to the raspberry canes and come back with a punnet of fruit which they'd have at suppertime. He was different from her aunt and from Mr Ayrie and Arch-deacon Flower. He smelt of the tobacco he smoked in his pipe. He wore tweed suits and a striped shirt with a white celluloid collar, and patterned brown shoes which Attracta greatly admired. His tie matched the tweed of his suit, a gold watch dangled from the lapel of his jacket into his top pocket. He was by trade a grain merchant.

His house was quiet and always a little mysterious. The drawing-room, full of looming furniture, was dark in the daytime. Behind layers of curtains that hung to the ground blue blinds obscured the greater part of the light: sunshine would damage the furniture, Mr Devereux's housekeeper used to say. On a summer's afternoon this woman would light a paraffin lamp so that she could polish the mahogany surfaces of the tables and the grand piano. Her name was Geraldine Carey: she added to the house's mystery.

Mr Devereux's smile was slow. There was a laziness about it, both in its leisurely arrival and the way it lingered. His eyes had a weary look, quite out of keeping with all the efforts he made to promote his friendship with Attracta and her aunt. Yet the efforts seemed natural to Attracta, as were the efforts of Geraldine Carey, who was the quietest person Attracta had ever met. She spoke in a voice that was often hard to hear. Her hair was as black as coal, drawn back from her face and arranged in a coiled bun at the back of her head. Her eyes were startlingly alive, seeming to be black also, often cast down. She had the kind of beauty that Attracta would like one day to possess herself, but knew she would not. Geraldine Carey was like a nun because of the dark clothes she wore, and she had a nun's piety. In the town it was said she couldn't go to mass often enough. 'Why weren't you a nun, Geraldine?' Attracta asked her once, watching her making bread in her big, cool kitchen. The habit would have suited her, she added, already imagining the housekeeper's face framed by the coif, and the black voluminous skirts. But Geraldine Carey replied that she'd never heard God calling her. 'Only the good are called,' she said.

There'd been a time, faintly remembered by Attracta, when her Aunt Emmeline hadn't been well disposed towards Mr

Devereux and Geraldine Carey. There'd been suspicion of some kind, a frowning over the presents he brought, an agitation whenever Attracta was invited to tea. Because of her own excitement over the presents and the invitations Attracta hadn't paid much attention to the nature of her aunt's concern, and looking back on it years later could only speculate. Her Aunt Emmeline was a precise person, a tall woman who had never married, reputed to be delicate. Her house in North Street, very different from Mr Devereux's, reflected her: it was neat as a new pin, full of light, the windows of its small rooms invariably open at the top to let in fresh air. The fan-light above the hall-door was always gleaming, filling the hall with morning sunlight. Attracta's Aunt Emmeline had a fear of dankness, of damp clothes and wet feet, and rain falling on the head. She worried about lots of things.

Clearly she had worried about Mr Devereux. There was an occasion when Archdeacon Flower had been specially invited to tea, when Attracta had listened at the sitting-room door because she'd sensed from her aunt's flustered manner that something important was to be discussed. 'Oh, have no worry in that direction at all,' she heard the Archdeacon say. 'Gentle as a lamb that man's become.' Her aunt asked a question Attracta could not hear because of the sound of a tea-cup being replaced on a saucer. 'He's doing the best he can,' the Archdeacon continued, 'according to his lights.' Her aunt mentioned Geraldine Carey, and again the Archdeacon reassured her. 'Bygones are bygones,' he said. 'Isn't it a remarkable thing when a man gets caught in his own snare?' He commented on the quality of her aunt's fruitcake, and then said that everyone should be charitably disposed towards Mr Devereux and Geraldine Carey. He believed, he said, that that was God's wish.

After that, slowly over the years, Attracta's aunt began to

think more highly of Mr Devereux, until in the end there was no one in the entire town, with the possible exception of Archdeacon Flower, whom she held in greater esteem. Once when Phelan the coal merchant insisted that she hadn't paid for half a ton of coal and she recollected perfectly giving the money to the man who'd delivered it, Mr Devereux had come to her aid. 'A right old devil, Phelan is,' Attracta heard him saying in the hall, and that was the end her aunt had ever heard of the matter. On Saturday evenings, having kept Attracta company on her walk home, Mr Devereux might remain for a little while in the house in North Street. He sometimes brought lettuces or cuttings with him, or tomatoes or strawberries. He would take a glass of sherry in the trim little sitting-room with its delicate inlaid chairs that matched the delicacy of Attracta's aunt. Often he'd still be there, taking a second glass, when Attracta came down to say goodnight. Her aunt's cat, Diggory, liked to climb up on to his knees, and as if in respect of some kind Mr Devereux never lit his pipe. He and her aunt would converse in low voices and generally they'd cease when Attracta entered the room. She would kiss him good-night after she'd kissed her aunt. She imagined it was what having a father was like.

*

At the town's approximate centre there stood a grey woman on a pedestal, a statue of the Maid of Erin. It was here, only yards from this monument, that Mr Purce told Attracta the truth about her parents' death, when she was eleven. She'd always had the feeling that Mr Purce wanted to speak to her, even that he was waiting until she could understand what it was he had to say. He was a man people didn't much like; he'd settled in the town, having come there from somewhere else. He was a clerk in the court-house.

'There's a place I know where there's greenfinches,' he said, as if introducing himself. 'Ten nests of them, maybe twelve, maybe more. D'you understand me, Attracta? Would you like me to show you?'

She was on her way home from school. She had to get back to do her homework, she said to Mr Purce. She didn't want to go looking for greenfinches with him.

'Did Devereux tell you not to talk to Mr Purce?' he said, and she shook her head. As far as she could remember, Mr Devereux had never mentioned Mr Purce. 'I see you in church,' Mr Purce said.

She had seen him too, sitting in the front, over on the left-hand side. Her aunt had often remarked that the day Mr Purce didn't go to church it would be a miracle. It was like Geraldine Carey going to mass.

'I'll walk out with you,' he said. 'I have a half-day today for myself.'

They walked together, to her embarrassment. She glanced at shop-windows to catch a glimpse of their reflection, to see if they looked as awkward as she felt. He was only a head taller than she and part of that was made up by his hard black hat. His clerk's suit was double-breasted, navy-blue with a pale stripe in it, shiny here and there, in need of a good ironing. He wore black leather gloves and carried a walking-stick. He always had the gloves and the walking-stick in church, but his Sunday suit was superior to the one he wore now. Her own fair hair, pinned up under her green-brimmed hat, was what stood out between the two of them. The colour of good corn, Mr Devereux used to say, and she always considered that a compliment, coming from a grain merchant. Her face was thin and her eyes blue, but reflected in the shop-windows there was now only a blur of flesh, a thin shaft between her hat and the green coat that matched it.

'You've had misfortune, Attracta.' Solemnly he nodded,

repeating the motion of his head until she wished he'd stop.
'It was a terrible thing to be killed by mistake.'

Attracta didn't know what he was talking about. They
passed by the last of the shops in North Street, Shannon's
grocery and bar, O'Brien's bakery, the hardware that years
ago had run out of stock. The narrow street widened a bit.
Mr Purce said:

'Has she made a Catholic girl out of you, Attracta?'

'Who, Mr Purce?'

'Devereux's woman. Has she tried anything on? Has she
shown you rosary beads?'

She shook her head.

'Don't ever look at them if she does. Look away immediately if she gets them out of her apron or anything like that.
Will you promise me that, girl?'

'I don't think she would. I don't think Mr Devereux – '

'You can never tell with that crowd. There isn't a trick in
the book they won't hop on to. Will you promise me now?
Have nothing to do with carry-on like that.'

'Yes, Mr Purce.'

As they walked he prodded at the litter on the pavement
with his walking-stick. Cigarette packets and squashed
match-boxes flew into the gutter, bits of the *Cork Examiner*,
sodden paper-bags. He was known for this activity in the
town, and even when he was on his own his voice was often
heard protesting at the untidiness.

'I'm surprised they never told you, Attracta,' he said. 'What
are you now, girl?'

'I'm eleven.'

'A big girl should know things like that.'

'What things, Mr Purce?'

He nodded in his repetitious manner, and then he explained
himself. The tragedy had occurred in darkness, at night: her
parents had accidentally become involved with an ambush

meant for the Black and Tan soldiers who were in force in the area at the time. She herself had long since been asleep at home, and as he spoke she remembered waking up to find herself in a bed in her aunt's house, without knowing how she got there. 'That's how they got killed, Attracta,' Mr Purce said, and then he said an extraordinary thing. 'You've got Devereux and his woman to thank for it.'

She knew that the Black and Tan soldiers had been camped near the town; she knew there'd been fighting. She realised that the truth about the death had been counted too terrible for a child to bear. But that her parents should have been shot, and shot in error, that the whole thing had somehow been the responsibility of Mr Devereux and Geraldine Carey, seemed inconceivable to Attracta.

'They destroyed a decent Protestant pair,' Mr Purce continued, still flicking litter from the pavement. 'Half-ten at night on a public road, destroyed like pests.'

The sun, obscured by clouds while Attracta and Mr Purce had made the journey from the centre of the town, was suddenly warm on Attracta's face. A woman in a horse and cart, attired in the black hooded cloak of the locality, passed slowly by. There were sacks of meal in the cart which had probably come from Mr Devereux's mill.

'Do you understand what I'm saying to you, Attracta? Devereux was organising resistance up in the hills. He had explosives and booby traps, he was drilling men to go and kill people. Did nobody tell you about himself and Geraldine Carey?'

She shook her head. He nodded again, as if to indicate that little better could be expected.

'Listen to me, Attracta. Geraldine Carey was brought into this town by the man she got married to, who used to work at Devereux's mill. Six months later she'd joined up with Devereux in the type of dirty behaviour I wouldn't soil myself telling you about. Not only that, Attracta, she was gun-running with him. She was fixing explosives like a man would, dressed up like a man in uniform. Devereux was as wild as a savage. There was nothing Devereux wouldn't do, there was nothing the woman wouldn't do either. They'd put booby traps down and it didn't matter who got killed. They'd ambush the British soldiers when the soldiers didn't have a chance.'

It was impossible to believe him. It was impossible to visualise the housekeeper and Mr Devereux in the role he'd given them. No one with any sense could believe that Geraldine Carey would kill people. Was everything Mr Purce said a lie? He was a peculiar man: had he some reason for stating her mother and her father had met their deaths in this way?

'Your father was a decent man, Attracta. He was never drunk in his life. There was prayers for him in the chapel, but that was only a hypocrisy of the priests. Wouldn't the priest Quinn like to see every Protestant in this town dead and buried? Wouldn't he like to see you and me six foot down with clay in our eye-sockets?'

Attracta didn't believe that, and more certainly now it seemed to her that everything Mr Purce said was untrue. Catholics were different; they crossed themselves when they passed their chapel; they went in for crosses and confession; they had masses and candles. But it was hard to accept that Father Quinn, a jovial red-haired man, would prefer it if she were dead. She'd heard her aunt's maid, Philomena, saying that Father Doran was cantankerous and that Father Martin wasn't worth his salt, but neither of them seemed to Attracta to be the kind of man who'd wish people dead. 'Proddy-woddy green-guts,' Catholic children would shout out some-times. 'Catty-catty going to mass,' the Protestants would reply, 'riding on the Devil's ass.' But there was never much vindictiveness about any of it. The sides were unevenly matched: there were too few Protestants in the town to make a proper opposition; trouble was avoided.

'He was a traitor to his religion, Attracta. And I'll promise you this: if I was to tell you about that woman of his you wouldn't enter the house they have.' Abruptly he turned and walked away, back into the town, his walking-stick still frantically working, poking away any litter it could find.

The sun was hot now. Attracta felt sticky within her several layers of clothes. She had a chapter of her history book to read, about the Saxons coming to England. She had four long-division sums to do, and seven lines of poetry to learn. *What potions have I drunk of Syren tears*, the first one stated, a statement Attracta could make neither head nor tail of.

She didn't go straight home. Instead she turned off to the left and walked through a back street, out into the country. She passed fields of mangels and turnips, again trying to imagine the scenes Mr Purce had sketched for her, the ambush of men waiting for the soldiers, the firing of shots. It occurred to her that she had never asked anyone if her parents were buried in the Church of Ireland graveyard.

She passed by tinkers encamped on the verge of the road. A woman ran after her and asked for money, saying her husband had just died. She swore when Attracta said she hadn't any, and then her manner changed again. She developed a whine in her voice, she said she'd pray for Attracta if she'd bring her money, tomorrow or the next day.

Had Mr Purce only wished to turn her against Mr Devereux because Mr Devereux did not go to church? Was there no more to it than that? Did Mr Purce say the first thing that came into his head? As Attracta walked, the words of Archdeacon Flower came back to her: in stating that Mr Devereux was now as gentle as a lamb, was there the implication that once he hadn't been? And had her aunt, worried about Geraldine Carey, been reassured on that score also?

'It's all over now, dear,' her aunt said. She looked closely at Attracta and then put her arms round her, as if expecting tears. But tears didn't come, for Attracta was only amazed.

★

Fifty years later, walking through the heather by the sea, Attracta remembered vividly that moment of her childhood. She couldn't understand how Mr Devereux and Geraldine Carey had changed so. 'Maybe they bear the burden of guilt,' Archdeacon Flower had explained, summoned to the house the following day by her aunt. 'Maybe they look at you and feel responsible. It was an accident, but people can feel responsible for an accident.' What had happened was in the past, he reminded her, as her aunt had. She understood what they were implying, that it must all be forgotten, yet she couldn't help imagining Mr Devereux and his housekeeper laying booby traps on roads and drilling men in the hills. Geraldine Carey's husband had left the town, Mr Purce told her on a later occasion: he'd gone to Co. Louth and hadn't been heard of since. 'Whore,' Mr Purce said. 'No better than a whore she is.' Attracta, looking the word up in a dictionary, was astonished.

Having started, Mr Purce went on and on. Mr Devereux's house wasn't suitable for an eleven-year-old girl to visit, since it was the house of a murderer. Wasn't it a disgrace that a Protestant girl should set foot in a house where the deaths of British soldiers and the Protestant Irish had been planned? One Saturday afternoon, unable to restrain himself, he arrived at the house himself. He shouted at Mr Devereux from the open hall-door. 'Isn't it enough to have destroyed her father and mother without letting that woman steal her for the Pope?' His grey face was suffused beneath his hard hat, his walking-stick thrashed the air. Mr Devereux called him an Orange mason. 'I hate the bloody sight of you,' Mr

Purce said in a quieter voice, and then in his abrupt way he walked off.

That, too, Attracta remembered as she continued her walk around the headland. Mr Devereux afterwards never referred to it, and Mr Purce never spoke to her again, as if deciding that there was nothing left to say. In the town as she grew up people would reluctantly answer her when she questioned them about her parents' tragedy in an effort to discover more than her aunt or Archdeacon Flower had revealed. But nothing new emerged, the people she asked only agreeing that Mr Devereux in those days had been as wild as Mr Purce suggested. He'd drilled the local men, he'd been assisted in every way by Geraldine Carey, whose husband had gone away to Co. Louth. But everything had been different since the night of the tragedy.

Her aunt tried to explain to her the nature of Mr Purce's hatred of Mr Devereux. Mr Purce saw things in a certain light, she said, he could not help himself. He couldn't help believing that Father Quinn would prefer the town's Protestants to be dead and buried. He couldn't help believing that immorality continued in the relationship between Mr Devereux and his housekeeper when clearly it did not. He found a spark and made a fire of it, he was a bigot and was unable to do anything about it. The Protestants of the town felt ashamed of him.

Mr Purce died, and was said to have continued in his hatred with his last remaining breaths. He mentioned the Protestant girl, his bleak, harsh voice weakening. She had been contaminated and infected, she was herself no better than the people who used her for their evil purposes. She was not fit to teach the Protestant children of the town, as she was now commencing to do. 'As I lie dying,' Mr Purce said to the clergyman who had succeeded Archdeacon Flower, 'I am telling you that, sir.' But afterwards, when the story of Mr

Purce's death went round, the people of the town looked at Attracta with a certain admiration, seeming to suggest that for her the twisting of events had not been easy, neither the death of her parents nor the forgiveness asked of her by Mr Devereux, nor the bigotry of Mr Purce. She'd been caught in the middle of things, they seemed to suggest, and had survived unharmed.

Surviving, she was happy in the town. Too happy to marry the exchange clerk from the Provincial Bank or the young man who came on a holiday to Cedarstrand with his parents. *Pride goeth before destruction*, her pupils' headlines stated, and *Look before you leap*. Their fingers pressed hard on inky pens, knuckles jutting beneath the strain, tongue-tips aiding concentration. Ariadne, Finn MacCool, King Arthur's sword, Cathleen ni Houlihan: legends filled the schoolroom, with facts about the Romans and the Normans, square roots and the Gulf Stream. Children grew up and went away, returning sometimes to visit Attracta in her house in North Street. Others remained and in the town she watched them changing, grey coming into their hair, no longer moving as lithely as they had. She developed an affection for the town without knowing why, beyond the fact that it was part of her.

'Yet in all a lifetime I learnt nothing,' she said aloud to herself on the headland. 'And I taught nothing either.' She gazed out at the smooth blue Atlantic but did not see it clearly. She saw instead the brown-paper parcel that contained the biscuit-box she had read about, and the fingers of Penelope Vade undoing the string and the brown paper. She saw her lifting off the lid. She saw her frowning for a moment, before the eyes of the man she loved stared deadly into hers. Months later, all courage spent and defeated in her gesture, the body of Penelope Vade dragged itself across the floors of two different rooms. There was the bottle full of aspirins in a cupboard, and water drunk from a Wedgwood-patterned cup, like the cups Attracta drank from every day.

*

In her schoolroom, with its maps and printed pictures, the sixteen faces stared back at her, the older children at the back. She repeated her question.

'Now, what does anyone think of that?'

Again she read them the news item, reading it slowly because she wanted it to become as rooted in their minds as it was in hers. She lingered over the number of bullets that had been fired into the body of Penelope Vade's husband, and over the removal of his head.

'Can you see that girl? Can you imagine men putting a human head in a tin box and sending it through the post? Can you imagine her receiving it? The severed head of the man she loved?'

'Sure, isn't there stuff like that in the papers the whole time?' one of the children suggested.

She agreed that that was so. 'I've had a good life in this town,' she added, and the children looked at her as if she'd suddenly turned mad.

'I'm getting out of it,' one of them said after a pause. 'Back of beyond, miss.'

She began at the beginning. She tried to get into the children's minds an image of a baby sleeping while violence and death took place on the Cork road. She described her Aunt Emmeline's house in North Street, the neat feminine house it had been, her aunt's cat, Diggory, the small sitting-room, her aunt's maid, Philomena. She spoke of her own very fair hair and her thin face, and the heavy old-fashioned clothes she'd worn in those days. She spoke of the piety of Geraldine Carey, and the grain merchant's tired face. The friendship they offered her was like Penelope Vade proclaiming peace in the city where her husband had been killed; it was a gesture, too.

'His house would smell of roses on a summer's day. She'd carry his meals to him, coming out of the shadows of her kitchen. As if in mourning, the blue blinds darkened the drawing-room. It was they who bore the tragedy, not I.'

She described Mr Purce's face and his grating voice. She tried to make of him a figure they could see among the houses and shops that were familiar to them: the hard black hat, the walking-stick poking away litter. He had done his best to rescue her, acting according to his beliefs. He wanted her not to forget, not realising that there was nothing for her to remember.

'But I tried to imagine,' she said, 'as I am asking you to imagine now: my mother and father shot dead on the Cork road, and Mr Devereux and Geraldine Carey as two monstrous people, and arms being blown off soldiers, and vengeance breeding vengeance.'

A child raised a hand and asked to leave the room. Attracta gave permission and awaited the child's return before proceeding. She filled the time in by describing things that had changed in the town, the falling to pieces of O'Mara's Picture House, the closing of the tannery in 1938. When the child came back she told of Mr Purce's death, how he'd said she was not fit to teach Protestant children.

'I tried to imagine a night I'd heard about,' she said, 'when Mr Devereux's men found a man in Madden's public house whom they said had betrayed them, and how they took him out to Cedarstrand and hanged him in a barn. Were they pleased after they'd done that? Did they light cigarettes, saying the man was better dead? One of those other men must have gone to a post office with the wrapped biscuit-box. He must have watched it being weighed and paid the postage. Did he say to himself he was exceptional to have hoodwinked a post-office clerk?'

Obediently listening in their rows of worn desks, the children wondered what on earth all this was about. No geography or history lesson had ever been so bewildering; those who found arithmetic difficult would have settled for attempting to understand it now. They watched the lined face of their teacher, still thin as she'd said it had been in childhood, the fair hair grey now. The mouth twitched and rapidly moved, seeming sometimes to quiver as if it struggled against tears. What on earth had this person called Penelope Vade to do with anything?

'She died believing that hell had come already. She'd lost all faith in human life, and who can blame her? She might have stayed in Haslemere, like anyone else would have. Was she right to go to the city where her husband had been murdered, to show its other victims that her spirit had not been wholly crushed?'

No one answered, and Attracta was aware of the children's startled gaze. But the startled gaze was a natural reaction. She said to herself that it didn't matter.

'My story is one with hers,' she said. 'Horror stories, with different endings only. I think of her now and I can see quite clearly the flat she lived in in Belfast. I can see the details, correctly or not I've no idea. Wallpaper with a pattern of brownish-purple flowers on it, gaunt furniture casting shadows, a tea-caddy on the hired television set. I drag my body across the floors of two rooms, over a carpet that smells of dust and cigarette ash, over rugs and cool linoleum. I reach up in the kitchen, a hand on the edge of the sink: one by one I eat the aspirins until the bottle's empty.'

There was a silence. Feet were shuffled in the schoolroom. No one spoke.

'If only she had known,' Attracta said, 'that there was still

a faith she might have had, that God does not forever with-
hold His mercy. Will those same men who exacted that
vengeance on her one day keep bees and budgerigars? Will
they serve in shops, and be kind to the blind and the deaf?
Will they garden in the evenings and be good fathers? It is not
impossible. Oh, can't you see,' she cried, 'what happened in
this town? Here, at the back of beyond. Can't you appreciate
it? And can't you see her lying there, mice nibbling her dried
blood?'

The children still were quiet, their faces still not registering
the comment she wished to make. It was because she'd been
clumsy, she thought. All she'd meant to tell them was never
to despair. All she had meant to do was to prepare them for a
future that looked grim. She had been happy, she said again.
The conversation of Mr Purce had been full of the truth but it
hadn't made sense because the years had turned the truth
around.

To the children she appeared to be talking now to herself.
She was old, a few of them silently considered; that was it.
She didn't appear to understand that almost every day there
was the kind of vengeance she spoke of reported on the television. Bloodshed was wholesale, girls were tarred and left for
dead, children no older than they were armed with guns.

'I only hope,' they heard her saying, 'she knows that
strangers mourn her.'

Another silence lingered awkwardly and then she nodded at
a particular child and the child rose and rang a hand-bell. The
children filed away, well-mannered and docile as she had
taught them to be. She watched them in the playground,
standing in twos and threes, talking about her. It had meant
nothing when she'd said that people change. The gleam of
hope she'd offered had been too slight to be of use, irrelevant
in the horror they took for granted, as part of life. Yet she
could not help still believing that it mattered when monsters

did not remain monsters for ever. It wasn't much to put against the last bleak moments of Penelope Vade, but it was something for all that. She wished she could have made her point.

Twenty minutes later, when the children returned to the schoolroom, her voice no longer quivered, nor did it seem to struggle against tears. The older children learnt about agriculture in Sweden, the younger ones about the Pyrenees, the youngest that Munster had six counties. The day came to an end at three o'clock and when all the children had gone Attracta locked the schoolroom and walked to the house she had inherited in North Street.

A week later Archdeacon Flower's successor came to see her, his visit interrupting further violence on the television news. He beat about the bush while he nibbled biscuits and drank cups of tea by the fire; then he suggested that perhaps she should consider retiring one of these days. She was over sixty, he pointed out with his clerical laugh, and she replied that Mr Ayrie had gone on until seventy. Sixty, the clergyman repeated with another laugh, was the post's retirement age. Children were a handful nowadays.

She smiled, thinking of her sixteen docile charges. They had chattered to their parents, and the parents had been shocked to hear that they'd been told of a man decapitated and a girl raped seven times. School was not for that, they had angrily protested to the clergyman, and he had had no option but to agree. At the end of the summer term there'd be a presentation of Waterford glass.

'Every day in my schoolroom I should have honoured the small, remarkable thing that happened in this town. It matters that she died in despair, with no faith left in human life.'

He was brisk. For as long as most people could remember she had been a remarkable teacher; in no way had she failed. He turned the conversation to more cheerful topics, he ate more biscuits and a slice of cake. He laughed and even made a joke. He retailed a little harmless gossip.

Eventually she stood up. She walked with her visitor to the hall, shook hands with him and saw him out. In the sitting-room she piled the tea things on to a tray and placed it on a table by the door. She turned the television on again but when the screen lit up she didn't notice it. The face of Penelope Vade came into her mind, the smile a little crooked, the freckled cheeks.

Lovers of Their Time

Looking back on it, it seemed to have to do with that particular decade in London. Could it have happened, he wondered, at any other time except the 1960s? That feeling was intensified, perhaps, because the whole thing had begun on New Year's Day, 1963, long before that day became a bank holiday in England. 'That'll be two and nine,' she'd said, smiling at him across her counter, handing him toothpaste and emery boards in a bag. 'Colgate's, remember,' his wife had called out as he was leaving the flat. 'The last stuff we had tasted awful.'

His name was Norman Britt. It said so on a small plastic name-plate in front of his position in the travel agency where he worked, Travel-Wide as it was called. *Marie* a badge on her light-blue shop-coat announced. His wife, who worked at home, assembling jewellery for a firm that paid her on a production basis, was called Hilda.

Green's the Chemist's and Travel-Wide were in Vincent Street, a street that was equidistant from Paddington station and Edgware Road. The flat where Hilda worked all day was in Putney. Marie lived in Reading with her mother and her mother's friend Mrs Druk, both of them widows. She caught the 8.05 every morning to Paddington and usually the 6.30 back.

He was forty in 1963, as Hilda was; Marie was twenty-eight. He was tall and thin, with a David Niven moustache. Hilda was thin also, her dark hair beginning to grey, her sharply-featured face pale. Marie was well-covered, carefully made up, her reddish hair dyed blond. She smiled a lot, a

slack half-crooked smile that made her eyes screw up and
twinkle; she exuded laziness and generosity. She and her
friend Mavis went dancing a lot in Reading and had a sizeable
collection of men friends. 'Fellas' they called them.

Buying things from her now and again in Green's the
Chemist's Norman had come to the conclusion that she was
of a tartish disposition, and imagined that if ever he sat with
her over a drink in the nearby Drummer Boy the occasion
could easily lead to a hug on the street afterwards. He
imagined her coral-coloured lips, like two tiny sausages, only
softer, pressed upon his moustache and his abbreviated
mouth. He imagined the warmth of her hand in his. For all
that, she was a little outside reality: she was there to desire, to
glow erotically in the heady atmosphere of the Drummer Boy,
to light cigarettes for in a dream.

'Isn't it cold?' he said as she handed him the emery boards
and the toothpaste.

'Shocking,' she agreed, and hesitated, clearly wanting to
say something else. 'You're in that Travel-Wide,' she added
in the end. 'Me and my friend want to go to Spain this
year.'

'It's very popular. The Costa Brava?'

'That's right.' She handed him threepence change. 'In
May.'

'Not too hot on the Costa in May. If you need any help – '

'Just the bookings.'

'I'd be happy to make them for you. Look in any time.
Britt the name is. I'm on the counter.'

'If I may, Mr Britt. I could slip out maybe at four, or
roundabout.'

'Today, you mean?'

'We want to fix it up.'

'Naturally. I'll keep an eye out for you.'

It was hard not to call her madam or miss, the way he'd

normally do. He'd heard himself saying that he'd be happy to make the bookings for her, knowing that that was business jargon, knowing that the unfussy voice he'd used was a business one also. Her friend was a man, he supposed, some snazzy tough in a car. 'See you later then,' he said, but already she was serving another customer, advising about lipstick refills.

She didn't appear in Travel-Wide at four o'clock; she hadn't come when the doors closed at five-thirty. He was aware of a sense of disappointment, combined with one of anticipation: for if she'd come at four, he reflected as he left the travel agency, their bit of business would be in the past rather than the future. She'd look in some other time and he'd just have to trust to luck that if he happened to be busy with another customer she'd be able to wait. There'd be a further occasion, when she called to collect the tickets themselves.

'Ever so sorry,' she said on the street, her voice coming from behind him. 'Couldn't get away, Mr Britt.'

He turned and smiled at her, feeling the movement of his moustache as he parted his lips. He knew only too well, he said. 'Some other time then?'

'Maybe tomorrow. Maybe lunchtime.'

'I'm off myself from twelve to one. Look, you wouldn't fancy a drink? I could advise you just as easily over a drink.'

'Oh, you wouldn't have the time. No, I mustn't take advantage – '

'You're not at all. If you've got ten minutes?'

'Well, it's awfully good of you, Mr Britt. But I really feel I'm taking advantage, I really do.'

'A New Year's drink.'

He pushed open the doors of the saloon bar of the Drummer Boy, a place he didn't often enter except for office drinks at Christmas or when someone leaving the agency was being given a send-off. Ron Stocks and Mr Blackstaffe were usually there in the evenings: he hoped they'd be there now to see him in the company of the girl from Green's the Chemist's. 'What would you like?' he asked her.

'Gin and peppermint's my poison, only honestly I should pay. No, let me ask you – '

'I wouldn't dream of it. We can sit over there, look.'

The Drummer Boy, so early in the evening, wasn't full. By six o'clock the advertising executives from the firm of Dalton, Dure and Higgins, just round the corner, would have arrived, and the architects from Frine and Knight. Now there was only Mrs Gregan, old and alcoholic, known to everyone, and a red-fleshed man called Bert, with his poodle, Jimmy. It was disappointing that Ron Stocks and Mr Blackstaffe weren't there.

'You were here lunchtime Christmas Eve,' she said.

'Yes, I was.' He paused, placing her gin and peppermint on a cardboard mat that advertised Guinness. 'I saw you too.'

He drank some of his Double Diamond and carefully wiped the traces of foam from his moustache. He realised now that it would, of course, be quite impossible to give her a hug on the street outside. That had been just imagination, wishful thinking as his mother would have said. And yet he knew that when he arrived home twenty-five or so minutes late he would not tell Hilda that he'd been advising an assistant from Green's the Chemist's about a holiday on the Costa Brava. He wouldn't even say he'd been in the Drummer Boy. He'd say Blackstaffe had kept everyone late, going through the new package that Eurotours were offering in Germany and Luxembourg this summer. Hilda wouldn't in a million years suspect that he'd been sitting in a public house with a younger woman who was quite an eyeful. As a kind of joke, she quite regularly suggested that his sexual drive left something to be desired.

219

'We were thinking about the last two weeks in May,' Marie said. 'It's when Mavis can get off too.'

'Mavis?'

'My friend, Mr Britt.'

★

Hilda was watching *Z-Cars* in the sitting-room, drinking V.P. wine. His stuff was in the oven, she told him. 'Thanks,' he said.

Sometimes she was out when he returned in the evenings. She went round to friends, a Mr and Mrs Fowler, with whom she drank V.P. and played bridge. On other occasions she went to the Club, which was a place with a licence, for card-players and billiard-players. She quite liked her social life, but always said beforehand when she'd be out and always made arrangements about leaving food in the oven. Often in the daytime she'd go and make jewellery with Violet Parkes, who also went in for this occupation; and often Violet Parkes spent the day with Hilda. The jewellery-making consisted for the most part of threading plastic beads on to a string or arranging plastic pieces in the settings provided. Hilda was quick at it and earned more than she would have if she went out every day, saving the fares for a start. She was better at it than Violet Parkes.

'All right then?' she said as he carried his tray of food into the sitting-room and sat down in front of the television set. 'Want some V.P., eh?'

Her eyes continued to watch the figures on the screen as she spoke. He knew she'd prefer to be in the Fowlers' house or at the Club, although now that they'd acquired a TV set the evenings passed easier when they were alone together.

'No, thanks,' he said in reply to her offer of wine and he began to eat something that appeared to be a rissole. There were two of them, round and brown in a tin-foil container that also contained gravy. He hoped she wasn't going to be demanding in their bedroom. He eyed her, for sometimes he could tell.

'Hi,' she said, noticing the glance. 'Feeling fruity, dear?' She laughed and winked, her suggestive voice seeming odd as it issued from her thin, rather dried-up face. She was always saying things like that, for no reason that Norman could see, always talking about feeling fruity or saying she could see he was keen when he wasn't in the least. Norman considered that she was unduly demanding and often wondered what it would be like to be married to someone who was not. Now and again, fatigued after the intensity of her love-making, he lay staring at the darkness, wondering if her bedroom appetites were related in some way to the fact that she was unable to bear children, if her abandon reflected a maternal frustration. Earlier in their married life she'd gone out every day to an office where she'd been a filing clerk; in the evenings they'd often gone to the cinema.

He lay that night, after she'd gone to sleep, listening to her heavy breathing, thinking of the girl in Green's the Chemist's. He went through the whole day in his mind, seeing himself leaving the flat in Putney, hearing Hilda calling out about the emery boards and the toothpaste, seeing himself reading the *Daily Telegraph* in the Tube. Slowly he went through the morning, deliciously anticipating the moment when she handed him his change. With her smile mistily hovering, he recalled the enquiries and demands of a number of the morning's customers. 'Fix us up Newcastle and back?' a couple enquired. 'Mid-week's cheaper, is it?' A man with a squashed-up face wanted a week in Holland for himself and his sister and his sister's husband. A woman asked about Greece, another about cruises on the Nile, a third about the Scilly Isles. Then he placed the Closed sign in front of his position at the counter and went out to have lunch in Bette's

Sandwiches off the Edgware Road. 'Packet of emery boards,' he said again in Green's the Chemist's, 'and a small Colgate's.' After that there was the conversation they'd had, and then the afternoon with her smile still mistily hovering, as in fact it had, and then her presence beside him in the Drummer Boy. Endlessly she lifted the glass of gin and peppermint to her lips, endlessly she smiled. When he slept he dreamed of her. They were walking in Hyde Park and her shoe fell off. 'I could tell you were a deep one,' she said, and the next thing was Hilda was having one of her early-morning appetites.

*

'I don't know what it is about that chap,' Marie confided to Mavis. 'Something though.'

'Married, is he?'

'Oh, he would be, chap like that.'

'Now, you be careful, girl.'

'He has Sinatra's eyes. That blue, you know.'

'Now, Marie – '

'I like an older fella. He's got a nice moustache.'

'So's that fella in the International.'

'Wet behind the ears. And my God, his dandruff!'

They left the train together and parted on the platform, Marie making for the Underground, Mavis hurrying for a bus. It was quite convenient, really, living in Reading and travelling to Paddington every day. It was only half an hour and chatting on the journey passed the time. They didn't travel back together in the evenings because Mavis nearly always did an hour's overtime. She was a computer programmer.

'I talked to Mavis. It's O.K. about the insurance,' Marie said in Travel-Wide at half-past eleven that morning, having slipped out when the shop seemed slack. There'd been some details about insurance which he'd raised the evening before. He always advised insurance, but he'd quite understood when she'd made the point that she'd better discuss the matter with her friend before committing herself to the extra expenditure.

'So I'll go ahead and book you,' he said. 'There'll just be the deposit.'

'Mavis wrote the cheque.' She pushed the pink slip across the counter to him. 'Payable to Travel-Wide.'

'That's quite correct.' He glanced at it and wrote her a receipt. He said:

'I looked out another brochure or two. I'd quite like to go through them with you. So you can explain what's what to your friend.'

'Oh, that's very nice, Mr Britt. But I got to get back. I mean, I shouldn't be out in the middle of the morning.'

'Any chance of lunchtime?'

His suavity astounded him. He thought of Hilda, deftly working at her jewellery, stringing orange and yellow beads, listening to the Jimmy Young programme.

'Lunchtime, Mr Britt?'

'We'd maybe talk about the brochures.'

He fancied her, she said to herself. He was making a pass, talking about brochures and lunchtime. Well, she wasn't disagreeable. She'd meant what she'd said to Mavis: she liked an older fella and she liked his moustache, so smooth it looked as if he put something on it. She liked the name Norman.

'All right then,' she said.

He couldn't suggest Bette's Sandwiches because you stood up at a shelf on the wall and ate the sandwiches off a cardboard plate.

'We could go to the Drummer Boy,' he suggested instead. 'I'm off at twelve-fifteen.'

'Say half-past, Mr Britt.'

'I'll be there with the brochures.'

Again he thought of Hilda. He thought of her wiry, pasty limbs and the way she had of snorting. Sometimes when they were watching the television she'd suddenly want to sit on his knee. She'd get worse as she grew older; she'd get scrawnier; her hair, already coarse, would get dry and grey. He enjoyed the evenings when she went out to the Club or to her friends the Fowlers. And yet he wasn't being fair because in very many ways she did her best. It was just that you didn't always feel like having someone on your knee after a day's work.

'Same?' he said in the Drummer Boy.

'Yes please, Mr Britt.' She'd meant to say that the drinks were definitely on her, after all he'd spent last night. But in her flurry she forgot. She picked up the brochures he'd left on the seat beside her. She pretended to read one, but all the time she was watching him as he stood by the bar. He smiled as he turned and came back with their drinks. He said something about it being a nice way to do business. He was drinking gin and peppermint himself.

'I meant to pay for the drinks. I meant to say I would. I'm sorry, Mr Britt.'

'Norman, my name is.' He surprised himself again by the ease with which he was managing the situation. They'd have their drinks and then he'd suggest some of the shepherd's pie, or a ham-and-salad roll if she'd prefer it. He'd buy her another gin and peppermint to get her going. Eighteen years ago he used to buy Hilda further glasses of V.P. wine with the same thought in mind.

They finished with the brochures. She told him she lived in Reading; she talked about the town. She mentioned her mother and her mother's friend Mrs Druk, who lived with them, and Mavis. She told him a lot about Mavis. No man was mentioned, no boyfriend or fiancé.

'Honestly,' she said, 'I'm not hungry.' She couldn't have touched a thing. She just wanted to go on drinking gin with him. She wanted to get slightly drunk, a thing she'd never done before in the middle of the day. She wanted to put her arm through his.

'It's been nice meeting you,' he said.

'A bit of luck.'

'I think so too, Marie.' He ran his forefinger between the bones on the back of her hand, so gently that it made her want to shiver. She didn't take her hand away, and when she continued not to he took her hand in his.

*

After that they had lunch together every day, always in the Drummer Boy. People saw them, Ron Stocks and Mr Blackstaffe from Travel-Wide, Mr Fineman, the pharmacist from Green's the Chemist's. Other people from the travel agency and from the chemist's saw them walking about the streets, usually hand in hand. They would look together into the shop windows of Edgware Road, drawn particularly to an antique shop full of brass. In the evenings he would walk with her to Paddington station and have a drink in one of the bars. They'd embrace on the platform, as other people did.

Mavis continued to disapprove; Marie's mother and Mrs Druk remained ignorant of the affair. The holiday on the Costa Brava that June was not a success because all the time Marie kept wishing Norman Britt was with her. Occasionally, while Mavis read magazines on the beach, Marie wept and Mavis pretended not to notice. She was furious because Marie's low spirits meant that it was impossible for them to get to know fellas. For months they'd been looking forward to the holiday and now, just because of a clerk in a travel agency, it was a flop. 'I'm sorry, dear,' Marie kept saying, trying to smile; but when they returned to London the friendship declined. 'You're making a fool of yourself,' Mavis pronounced harshly, 'and it's dead boring having to hear about it.' After that they ceased to travel together in the mornings.

The affair remained unconsummated. In the hour and a quarter allotted to each of them for lunch there was nowhere they might have gone to let their passion for one another run its course. Everywhere was public: Travel-Wide and the chemist's shop, the Drummer Boy, the streets they walked. Neither could easily spend a night away from home. Her mother and Mrs Druk would guess that something untoward was in the air; Hilda, deprived of her bedroom mating, would no longer be nonchalant in front of the TV. It would all come out if they were rash, and they sensed some danger in that.

'Oh, darling,' she whispered one October evening at Paddington, huddling herself against him. It was foggy and cold. The fog was in her pale hair, tiny droplets that only he, being close to her, could see. People hurried through the lit-up station, weary faces anxious to be home.

'I know,' he said, feeling as inadequate as he always did at the station.

'I lie awake and think of you,' she whispered.

'You've made me live,' he whispered back.

'And you me. Oh, God, and you me.' She was gone before she finished speaking, swinging into the train as it moved away, her bulky red handbag the last thing he saw. It would be eighteen hours before they'd meet again.

He turned his back on her train and slowly made his way through the crowds, his reluctance to start the journey back to the flat in Putney seeming physical, like a pain, inside him. 'Oh, for God's sake!' a woman cried angrily at him, for he had been in her way and had moved in the same direction as she had in seeking to avoid her, causing a second collision. She dropped magazines on to the platform and he helped her to pick them up, vainly apologising.

It was then, walking away from this woman, that he saw the sign. *Hotel Entrance* it said in red neon letters, beyond the station's main bookstall. It was the back of the Great Western Royal, a short cut to its comforts for train travellers at the end of their journey. If only, he thought, they could share a room there. If only for one single night they were granted the privilege of being man and wife. People passed through the swing-doors beneath the glowing red sign, people hurrying, with newspapers or suitcases. Without quite knowing why, he passed through the swing-doors himself.

He walked up two brief flights of steps, through another set of doors, and paused in the enormous hall of the Great Western Royal Hotel. Ahead of him, to the left, was the long, curved reception counter and, to the right, the porter's desk. Small tables and armchairs were everywhere; it was carpeted underfoot. There were signs to lifts and to the bar and the restaurant. The stairway, gently rising to his left, was gracious, carpeted also.

They would sit for a moment in this hall, he imagined, as other people were sitting now, a few with drinks, others with pots of tea and plates half empty of assorted biscuits. He stood for a moment, watching these people, and then, as though he possessed a room in the hotel, he mounted the stairs, saying to himself that it must somehow be possible, that surely they could share a single night in the splendour of this place. There was a landing, made into a lounge, with armchairs and tables, as in the hall below. People conversed quietly; a foreign waiter, elderly and limping, collected silver-plated tea-pots; a Pekinese dog slept on a woman's lap.

The floor above was different. It was a long, wide corridor with bedroom doors on either side of it. Other corridors, exactly similar, led off it. Chambermaids passed him with lowered eyes; someone gently laughed in a room marked *Staff Only;* a waiter wheeled a trolley containing covered dishes, and a bottle of wine wrapped in a napkin. *Bathroom* a sign said, and he looked in, just to see what a bathroom in the Great Western Royal Hotel would be like. 'My God!' he whispered, possessed immediately with the idea that was, for him, to make the decade of the 1960s different. Looking back on it, he was for ever after unable to recall the first moment he beheld the bathroom on the second floor without experiencing the shiver of pleasure he'd experienced at the time. Slowly he entered. He locked the door and slowly sat down on the edge of the bath. The place was huge, as the bath itself was, like somewhere in a palace. The walls were marble, white veined delicately with grey. Two monstrous brass taps, the biggest bath taps he'd ever in his life seen, seemed to know already that he and Marie would come to the bathroom. They seemed almost to wink an invitation to him, to tell him that the bathroom was a comfortable place and not often in use since private bathrooms were now attached to most of the bedrooms. Sitting in his mackintosh coat on the edge of the bath, he wondered what Hilda would say if she could see him now.

*

He suggested it to Marie in the Drummer Boy. He led up to it slowly, describing the interior of the Great Western Royal Hotel and how he had wandered about it because he hadn't wanted to go home. 'Actually,' he said, 'I ended up in a bathroom.'

'You mean the toilet, dear? Taken short –'

'No, not the toilet. A bathroom on the second floor. Done out in marble, as a matter of fact.'

She replied that honestly he was a one, to go into a bathroom like that when he wasn't even staying in the place! He said:

'What I mean, Marie, it's somewhere we could go.'

'Go, dear?'

'It's empty half the time. Nearly all the time it must be. I mean, we could be there now. This minute if we wanted to.'

'But we're having our lunch, Norman.'

'That's what I mean. We could even be having it there.'

From the saloon bar's juke-box a lugubrious voice pleaded for a hand to be held. 'Take my hand,' sang Elvis Presley, 'take my whole life too.' The advertising executives from Dalton, Dure and Higgins were loudly talking about their hopes of gaining the Canadian Pacific account. Less noisily the architects from Frine and Knight complained about local planning regulations.

'In a bathroom, Norman? But we couldn't just go into a bathroom.'

'Why not?'

'Well, we couldn't. I mean, we *couldn't*.'

'What I'm saying is we could.'

'I want to marry you, Norman. I want us to be together. I don't want just going to a bathroom in some hotel.'

'I know; I want to marry you too. But we've got to work it out. You know we've got to work it out, Marie – getting married.'

'Yes, I know.'

It was a familiar topic of conversation between them. They took it for granted that one day, somehow, they would be married. They had talked about Hilda. He'd described Hilda to her, he'd drawn a picture in Marie's mind of Hilda bent over her jewellery-making in a Putney flat, or going out to drink V.P. with the Fowlers or at the Club. He hadn't presented a flattering picture of his wife, and when Marie had quite timidly said that she didn't much care for the sound of her he had agreed that naturally she wouldn't. The only aspect of Hilda he didn't touch upon was her bedroom appetite, night starvation as he privately dubbed it. He didn't mention it because he guessed it might be upsetting.

What they had to work out where Hilda was concerned were the economics of the matter. He would never, at Travel-Wide or anywhere else, earn a great deal of money. Familiar with Hilda's nature, he knew that as soon as a divorce was mooted she'd set out to claim as much alimony as she possibly could, which by law he would have to pay. She would state that she only made jewellery for pin-money and increasingly found it difficult to do so due to a developing tendency towards chilblains or arthritis, anything she could think of. She would hate him for rejecting her, for depriving her of a tame companion. Her own resentment at not being able to have children would somehow latch on to his unfaithfulness: she would see a pattern which wasn't really there, bitterness would come into her eyes.

Marie had said that she wanted to give him the children he had never had. She wanted to have children at once and she knew she could. He knew it too: having children was part of her, you'd only to look at her. Yet that would mean she'd have to give up her job, which she wanted to do when she married anyway, which in turn would mean that all three of them would have to subsist on his meagre salary. And not just all three, the children also.

It was a riddle that mocked him: he could find no answer, and yet he believed that the more he and Marie were together, the more they talked to one another and continued to be in love, the more chance there was of suddenly hitting upon a solution. Not that Marie always listened when he went on about it. She agreed they had to solve their problem, but now and again just pretended it wasn't there. She liked to forget about the existence of Hilda. For an hour or so when she was with him she liked to assume that quite soon, in July or even June, they'd be married. He always brought her back to earth.

'Look, let's just have a drink in the hotel,' he urged. 'Tonight, before the train. Instead of having one in the buffet.'

'But it's a hotel, Norman. I mean, it's for people to stay in –'

'Anyone can go into a hotel for a drink.'

That evening, after their drink in the hotel bar, he led her to the first-floor landing that was also a lounge. It was warm in the hotel. She said she'd like to sink down into one of the armchairs and fall asleep. He laughed at that; he didn't suggest an excursion to the bathroom, sensing that he shouldn't rush things. He saw her on to her train, abandoning her to her mother and Mrs Druk and Mavis. He knew that all during the journey she would be mulling over the splendours of the Great Western Royal.

December came. It was no longer foggy, but the weather was colder, with an icy wind. Every evening, before her train, they had their drink in the hotel. 'I'd love to show you that bathroom,' he said once. 'Just for fun.' He hadn't been pressing it in the least; it was the first time he'd mentioned the bathroom since he'd mentioned it originally. She giggled and said he was terrible. She said she'd miss her train if she went looking at bathrooms, but he said there'd easily be time. 'Gosh!' she whispered, standing in the doorway, looking in. He put his arm around her shoulders and drew her inside, fearful in case a chambermaid should see them loitering there. He locked the door and kissed her. In almost twelve months it was their first embrace in private.

They went to the bathroom during the lunch hour on New Year's Day, and he felt it was right that they should celebrate in this way the anniversary of their first real meeting. His early impression of her, that she was of a tartish disposition, had long since been dispelled. Voluptuous she might seem to the eye, but beneath that misleading surface she was prim and proper. It was odd that Hilda, who looked dried-up and wholly uninterested in the sensual life, should also belie her appearance. 'I've never done it before,' Marie confessed in the bathroom, and he loved her the more for that. He loved her simplicity in this matter, her desire to remain a virgin until her wedding. But since she repeatedly swore that she could marry no one else, their anticipating of their wedding night did not matter. 'Oh, God, I love you,' she whispered, naked for the first time in the bathroom. 'Oh, Norman, you're so good to me.'

After that it became a regular thing. He would saunter from the hotel bar, across the huge entrance lounge, and take a lift to the second floor. Five minutes later she would follow, with a towel brought specially from Reading in her handbag. In the bathroom they always whispered, and would sit together in a warm bath after their love-making, still murmuring about the future, holding hands beneath the surface of the water. No one ever rapped on the door to ask what was going on in there. No one ever questioned them as they returned, separately, to the bar, with the towel they'd shared damping her compact and her handkerchief.

Years instead of months began to go by. On the juke-box in the Drummer Boy the voice of Elvis Presley was no longer heard. *Why she had to go I don't know*, sang the Beatles, *she didn't say... I believe in yesterday*. And Eleanor Rigby entered people's lives, and Sergeant Pepper with her. The fantasies of secret agents, more fantastic than ever before, filled the screens of London's cinemas. Carnaby Street, like a jolly trash-can, overflowed with noise and colour. And in the bathroom of the Great Western Royal Hotel the love affair of Norman Britt and Marie was touched with the same preposterousness. They ate sandwiches in the bathroom; they drank wine. He whispered to her of the faraway places he knew about but had never been to: the Bahamas, Brazil,

Peru, Seville at Easter, the Greek islands, the Nile, Shiraz, Persepolis, the Rocky Mountains. They should have been saving their money, not spending it on gin and peppermint in the bar of the hotel and in the Drummer Boy. They should have been racking their brains to find a solution to the problem of Hilda, but it was nicer to pretend that one day they would walk together in Venice or Tuscany. It was all so different from the activities that began with Hilda's bedroom appetites, and it was different from the coarseness that invariably surfaced when Mr Blackstaffe got going in the Drummer Boy on an evening when a Travel-Wide employee was being given a send-off. Mr Blackstaffe's great joke on such occasions was that he liked to have sexual intercourse with his wife at night and that she preferred the conjunction in the mornings. He was always going on about how difficult it was in the mornings, what with the children liable to interrupt you, and he usually went into details about certain other, more intimate preferences of his wife's. He had a powerful, waxy guffaw, which he brought regularly into play when he was engaged in this kind of conversation, allying it with a nudging motion of the elbow. Once his wife actually turned up in the Drummer Boy and Norman found it embarrassing even to look at her, knowing as he did so much about her private life. She was a stout middle-aged woman with decorated spectacles: her appearance, too, apparently belied much.

In the bathroom all such considerations, disliked equally by Norman Britt and Marie, were left behind. Romance ruled their brief sojourns, and love sanctified – or so they believed – the passion of their physical intimacy. Love excused their eccentricity, for only love could have found in them a willingness to engage in the deception of a hotel and the courage that went with it: that they believed most of all.

But afterwards, selling tickets to other people or putting

Marie on her evening train, Norman sometimes felt depressed. And then gradually as more time passed, the depression increased and intensified. 'I'm so sad,' he whispered in the bathroom once, 'when I'm not with you. I don't think I can stand it.' She dried herself on the towel brought specially from Reading in her large red handbag. 'You'll have to tell her,' she said, with an edge in her voice that hadn't ever been there before. 'I don't want to leave having babies too late.' She wasn't twenty-eight any more; she was thirty-one. 'I mean, it isn't fair on me,' she said.

He knew it wasn't fair on her, but going over the whole thing yet again in Travel-Wide that afternoon he also knew that poverty would destroy them. He'd never earn much more than he earned now. The babies Marie wanted, and which he wanted too, would soak up what there was like blotting paper; they'd probably have to look for council accommodation. It made him weary to think about it, it gave him a headache. But he knew she was right: they couldn't go on for ever, living off a passing idyll, in the bathroom of a hotel. He even thought, quite seriously for a moment, of causing Hilda's death.

Instead he told her the truth, one Thursday evening after she'd been watching *The Avengers* on television. He just told her he'd met someone, a girl called Marie, he said, whom he had fallen in love with and wished to marry. 'I was hoping we could have a divorce,' he said.

Hilda turned the sound on the television set down without in any way dimming the picture, which she continued to watch. Her face did not register the hatred he had imagined in it when he rejected her; nor did bitterness suddenly enter her eyes. Instead she shook her head at him, and poured herself some more V.P. She said:

'You've gone barmy, Norman.'

'You can think that if you like.'

'Wherever'd you meet a girl, for God's sake?'

'At work. She's there in Vincent Street. In a shop.'

'And what's she think of you, may I ask?'

'She's in love with me, Hilda.'

She laughed. She told him to pull the other one, adding that it had bells on it.

'Hilda, I'm not making this up. I'm telling you the truth.'

She smiled into her V.P. She watched the screen for a moment, then she said:

'And how long's this charming stuff been going on, may I enquire?'

He didn't want to say for years. Vaguely, he said it had been going on for a just a while.

'You're out of your tiny, Norman. Just because you fancy some piece in a shop doesn't mean you go getting hot under the collar. You're no tomcat, you know, old boy.'

'I didn't say I was.'

'You're no sexual mechanic.'

'Hilda –'

'All chaps fancy things in shops: didn't your mother tell you that? D'you think I haven't fancied stuff myself, the chap who came to do the blinds, that randy little postman with his rugby songs?'

'I'm telling you I want a divorce, Hilda.'

She laughed. She drank more V.P. wine. 'You're up a gum-tree,' she said, and laughed again.

'Hilda –'

'Oh, for God's sake!' All of a sudden she was angry, but more, he felt, because he was going on, not because of what he was actually demanding. She thought him ridiculous and said so. And then she added all the things he'd thought himself: that people like them didn't get divorces, that unless his girlfriend was well-heeled the whole thing would be a sheer bloody nonsense, with bloody solicitors the only ones to benefit. 'They'll send you to the cleaners, your bloody solicitors will,' she loudly pointed out, anger still trembling in her voice. 'You'd be paying them back for years.'

'I don't care,' he began, although he did. 'I don't care about anything except – '

'Of course you do, you damn fool.'

'Hilda – '

'Look, get over her. Take her into a park after dark or something. It'll make no odds to you and me.'

She turned the sound on the television up and quite quickly finished the V.P. wine. Afterwards, in their bedroom, she turned to him with an excitement that was greater than usual. 'God, that switched me on,' she whispered in the darkness, gripping him with her limbs. 'The stuff we were talking about, that girl.' When she'd finished her love-making she said, 'I had it with that postman, you know. Swear to God. In the kitchen. And since we're on the subject, Fowler looks in here the odd time.'

He lay beside her in silence, not knowing whether or not to believe what she was saying. It seemed at first that she was keeping her end up because he'd mentioned Marie, but then he wasn't so sure. 'We had a foursome once,' she said, 'the Fowlers and me and a chap that used to be in the Club.'

She began to stroke his face with her fingers, the way he hated. She always seemed to think that if she stroked his face it would excite him. She said, 'Tell me more about this piece you fancy.'

He told her to keep her quiet and to make her stop stroking his face. It didn't seem to matter now if he told her how long it had been going on, not since she'd made her revelations about Fowler and the postman. He even enjoyed telling her, about the New Year's Day when he'd bought the emery boards and the Colgate's, and how he'd got to know Marie because she and Mavis were booking a holiday on the Costa Brava.

'But you've never actually ? '

'Yes, we have.'

'For God's sake where? Doorways or something? In the park?'

'We go to a hotel.'

'You old devil!'

'Listen, Hilda – '

'For God's sake go on, love. Tell me about it.'

He told her about the bathroom and she kept asking him questions, making him tell her details, asking him to describe Marie to her. Dawn was breaking when they finished talking.

'Forget about the divorce stuff,' she said quite casually at breakfast. 'I wouldn't want to hear no more of that. I wouldn't want you ruined for my sake, dear.'

*

He didn't want to see Marie that day, although he had to because it was arranged. In any case she knew he'd been going to tell his wife the night before; she'd want to hear the outcome.

'Well?' she said in the Drummer Boy.

He shrugged. He shook his head. He said:

'I told her.'

'And what'd she say, Norman? What'd Hilda say?'

'She said I was barmy to be talking about divorce. She said what I said to you: that we wouldn't manage with the alimony.'

They sat in silence. Eventually Marie said:

'Then can't you leave her? Can't you just not go back? We could get a flat somewhere. We could put off kiddies, darling. Just walk out, couldn't you?'

'They'd find us. They'd make me pay.'

'We could try it. If I keep on working you could pay what they want.'

'It'll never pan out, Marie.'

'Oh, darling, just walk away from her.'

Which is what, to Hilda's astonishment, he did. One evening when she was at the Club he packed his clothes and went to two rooms in Kilburn that he and Marie had found. He didn't tell Hilda where he was going. He just left a note to say he wouldn't be back.

They lived as man and wife in Kilburn, sharing a lavatory and a bathroom with fifteen other people. In time he received a court summons, and in court was informed that he had behaved meanly and despicably to the woman he'd married. He agreed to pay regular maintenance.

The two rooms in Kilburn were dirty and uncomfortable, and life in them was rather different from the life they had known together in the Drummer Boy and the Great Western Royal Hotel. They planned to find somewhere better, but at a reasonable price that wasn't easy to find. A certain melancholy descended on them, for although they were together they seemed as far away as ever from their own small house, their children, and their ordinary contentment.

'We could go to Reading,' Marie suggested.

'Reading?'

'To my mum's.'

'But your mum's nearly disowned you. Your mum's livid, you said yourself she was.'

'People come round.'

She was right. One Sunday afternoon they made the journey to Reading to have tea with Marie's mother and her friend Mrs Druk. Neither of these women addressed Norman, and once when he and Marie were in the kitchen he heard Mrs Druk saying it disgusted her, that he was old enough to be Marie's father. 'Don't think much of him,' Marie's mother replied. 'Pipsqueak really.'

Nevertheless, Marie's mother had missed her daughter's

contribution to the household finances and before they returned to London that evening it was arranged that Norman and Marie should move in within a month, on the firm understanding that the very second it was feasible their marriage would take place. 'He's a boarder, mind,' Marie's mother warned. 'Nothing only a boarder in this house.' There were neighbours, Mrs Druk added, to be thought of.

Reading was worse than the two rooms in Kilburn. Marie's mother continued to make disparaging remarks about Norman, about the way he left the lavatory, or the thump of his feet on the staircarpet, or his fingermarks around the light-switches. Marie would deny these accusations and then there'd be a row, with Mrs Druk joining in because she loved a row, and Marie's mother weeping and then Marie weeping. Norman had been to see a solicitor about divorcing Hilda, quoting her unfaithfulness with a postman and with Fowler. 'You have your evidence, Mr Britt?' the solicitor enquired, and pursed his lips when Norman said he hadn't.

He knew it was all going to be too difficult. He knew his instinct had been right: he shouldn't have told Hilda, he shouldn't have just walked out. The whole thing had always been unfair on Marie; it had to be when a girl got mixed up with a married man. 'Should think of things like that,' her mother had a way of saying loudly when he was passing an open door. 'Selfish type he is,' Mrs Druk would loudly add.

Marie argued when he said none of it was going to work. But she wasn't as broken-hearted as she might have been a year or so ago, for the strain had told on Marie too, especially the strain in Reading. She naturally wept when Norman said they'd been defeated, and so for a moment did he. He asked for a transfer to another branch of Travel-Wide and was sent to Ealing, far away from the Great Western Royal Hotel.

*

Eighteen months later Marie married a man in a brewery. Hilda, hearing on some grapevine that Norman was on his own, wrote to him and suggested that bygones should be allowed to be bygones. Lonely in a bed-sitting-room in Ealing, he agreed to talk the situation over with her and after that he agreed to return to their flat. 'No hard feelings,' Hilda said, 'and no deception: there's been a chap from the Club in here, the Woolworth's manager.' No hard feelings, he agreed.

For Norman Britt, as the decade of the 1960s passed, it trailed behind it the marvels of his love affair with Marie. Hilda's scorn when he had confessed had not devalued them, nor had the two dirty rooms in Kilburn, nor the equally unpleasant experience in Reading. Their walk to the Great Western Royal, the drinks they could not afford in the hotel bar, their studied nonchalance as they made their way separately upstairs, seemed to Norman to be a fantasy that had miraculously become real. The second-floor bathroom belonged in it perfectly, the bathroom full of whispers and caressing, where the faraway places of his daily work acquired a hint of magic when he spoke of them to a girl as voluptuous as any of James Bond's. Sometimes on the Tube he would close his eyes and with the greatest pleasure that remained to him he would recall the delicately veined marble and the great brass taps, and the bath that was big enough for two. And now and again he heard what appeared to be the strum of distant music, and the voices of the Beatles celebrating a a bathroom love, as they had celebrated Eleanor Rigby and other people of that time.

The Raising of Elvira Tremlett

My mother preferred English goods to Irish, claiming that the quality was better. In particular she had a preference for English socks and vests, and would not be denied in her point of view. Irish motor-car assemblers made a rough-and-ready job of it, my father used to say, the Austins and Morrises and Vauxhalls that came direct from British factories were twice the cars. And my father was an expert in his way, being the town's single garage-owner. *Devlin Bros.* it said on a length of painted wood, black letters on peeling white. The sign was crooked on the red corrugated iron of the garage, falling down a bit on the left-hand side.

In all other ways my parents were intensely of the country that had borne them, of the province of Munster and of the town they had always known. When she left the Presentation convent my mother had been found employment in the meat factory, working a machine that stuck labels on to tins. My father and his brother Jack, finishing at the Christian Brothers', had automatically passed into the family business. In those days the only sign on the corrugated façade had said *Raleigh Cycles*, for the business, founded by my grandfather, had once been a bicycle one. 'I think we'll make a change in that,' my father announced one day in 1933, when I was five, and six months or so later the rusty tin sheet that advertised bicycles was removed, leaving behind an island of grey in the corrugated red. 'Ah, that's grand,' my mother approved from the middle of the street, wiping her chapped hands on her apron. The new sign must have had a freshness and a gleam to it, but I don't recall that. In my memory there is only the peeling white behind the letters and the drooping down at the left-hand side where a rivet had fallen out. 'We'll paint that in and we'll be dandy,' my Uncle Jack said, referring to the island that remained, the contours of Sir Walter Raleigh's head and shoulders. But the job was never done.

We lived in a house next door to the garage, two storeys of cement that had a damp look, with green window-sashes and a green hall-door. Inside, a wealth of polished brown linoleum, its pattern faded to nothing, was cheered here and there by the rugs my mother bought in Roche's Stores in Cork. The votive light of a crimson Sacred Heart gleamed day and night in the hall. Christ blessed us halfway up the stairs; on the landing the Virgin Mary was coy in garish robes. On either side of a narrow trodden carpet the staircase had been grained to make it seem like oak. In the dining-room, never used, there was a square table with six rexine-seated chairs around it, and over the mantelpiece a mirror with chromium decoration. The sitting-room smelt of must and had a picture of the Pope.

The kitchen was where everything happened. My father and Uncle Jack read the newspaper there. The old Philips wireless, the only one in the house, stood on one of the window-sills. Our two nameless cats used to crouch by the door into the scullery because one of them had once caught a mouse there. Our terrier, Tom, mooched about under my mother's feet when she was cooking at the range. There was a big scrubbed table in the middle of the kitchen, and wooden chairs, and a huge clock, like the top bit of a grandfather clock, hanging between the two windows. The dresser had keys and bits of wire and labels hanging all over it. The china it contained was never used, being hidden behind bric-à-brac: broken ornaments left there in order to be repaired with Seccotine, worn-out parts from the engines of cars which my father and uncle had brought into the kitchen to examine at their leisure, bills on spikes, letters and Christmas cards. The kitchen was always rather dusky, even in the middle of the day: it was partially a basement, light penetrating from outside only through the upper panes of its two long windows. Its concrete floor had been reddened with Cardinal polish, which was renewed once a year, in spring. Its walls and ceiling were a sooty white.

The kitchen was where we did our homework, my two sisters and two brothers and myself. I was the youngest, my brother Brian the oldest. Brian and Liam were destined for the garage when they finished at the Christian Brothers', as my father and Uncle Jack had been. My sister Effie was good at arithmetic and the nuns had once or twice mentioned accountancy. There was a commercial college in Cork she could go to, the nuns said, the same place that Miss Madden, who did the books for Bolger's Medical Hall, had attended. Everyone said my sister Kitty was pretty: my father used to take her on his knee and tell her she'd break some fellow's heart, or a dozen hearts or maybe more. She didn't know what he was talking about at first, but later she understood and used to go red in the face. My father was like that with Kitty. He embarrassed her without meaning to, hauling her on to his knee when she was much too old for it, fondling her because he liked her best. On the other hand, he was quite harsh with my brothers, constantly suspicious that they were up to no good. Every evening he asked them if they'd been to school that day, suspecting that they might have tricked the Christian Brothers and would the next day present them with a note they had written themselves, saying they'd had stomach trouble after eating bad sausages. He and my Uncle Jack had often engaged in such ploys themselves, spending a whole day in the field behind the meat factory, smoking Woodbines.

My father's attitude to my sister Effie was coloured by

Effie's plainness. 'Ah, poor old Effie,' he used to say, and my mother would reprimand him. He took comfort from the fact that if the garage continued to thrive it would be necessary to have someone doing the increased book-work instead of himself and Uncle Jack trying to do it. For this reason he was in favour of Effie taking a commercial course: he saw a future in which she and my two brothers would live in the house and run the business between them. One or other of my brothers would marry and maybe move out of the house, leaving Effie and whichever one would still be a bachelor: it was my father's way of coming to terms with Effie's plainness. 'I wonder if Kitty'll end up with young Lacy?' I once heard him enquiring of my mother, the Lacy he referred to being the only child of another business in the town—Geo. Lacy and Sons, High-Class Drapers – who was about eight at the time. Kitty would do well, she'd marry whom she wanted to, and somehow or other she'd marry money: he really believed that.

For my part I fitted nowhere into my father's vision of the family's future. My performance at school was poor and there would be no place for me in the garage. I used to sit with the others at the kitchen table trying to understand algebra and Irish grammar, trying without any hope to learn verses from *Ode to the West Wind* and to improve my handwriting by copying from a headline book. 'Slow,' Brother Flynn had reported. 'Slow as a dying snail, that boy is.'

That was the family we were. My father was bulky in his grey overalls, always with marks of grease or dirt on him, his fingernails rimmed with black, like fingers in mourning, I used to think. Uncle Jack wore similar overalls but he was thin and much smaller than my father, a ferrety little man who had a way of looking at the ground when he spoke to you. He, too, was marked with grime and had the same rimmed fingernails, even at weekends. They both brought the smell of the garage into the kitchen, an oily smell that mingled with the fumes of my uncle's pipe and my father's cigarettes.

My mother was red-cheeked and stout, with waxy black hair and big arms and legs. She ruled the house, and was often cross: with my brothers when they behaved obstreperously, with my sisters and myself when her patience failed her. Sometimes my father would spend a long time on a Saturday night in Keogh's, which was the public house he favoured, and she would be cross with him also, noisily shouting in their bedroom, telling him to take off his clothes before he got into bed, telling him he was a fool. Uncle Jack was a teetotaller, a member of the Pioneer movement. He was a great help to Canon O'Keefe in the rectory and in the Church of the Holy Assumption, performing chores and repairing the electric light. Twice a year he spent a Saturday night in Cork in order to go to greyhound racing, but there was more than met the eye to these visits, for on his return there was always a great silence in the house, a fog of disapproval emanating from my father.

The first memories I have are of the garage, of watching my father and Uncle Jack at work, sparks flying from the welding apparatus, the dismantling of oil-caked engines. A car would be driven over the pit and my father or uncle would work underneath it, lit by an electric bulb in a wire casing on the end of a flex. Often, when he wasn't in the pit, my father would drift into conversation with a customer. He'd lean on the bonnet of a car, smoking continuously, talking about a hurling match that had taken place or about the dishonesties of the Government. He would also talk about his children, saying that Brian and Liam would fit easily into the business and referring to Effie's plans to study commerce and Kitty's prettiness. 'And your man here?' the customer might remark, inclining his head in my direction. To this question my father always replied in the same way. The Lord, he said, would look after me.

As I grew up I became aware that I made both my father and my mother uneasy. I assumed that this was due to my slowness at school, an opinion that was justified by a conversation I once overheard coming from their bedroom: they appeared to regard me as mentally deficient. My father repeated twice that the Lord would look after me. It was something she prayed for, my mother replied, and I imagined her praying after she'd said it, kneeling down by their bed, as she'd taught all of us to kneel by ours. I stood with my bare feet on the linoleum of the landing, believing that a plea from my mother was rising from the house at that very moment, up into the sky, where God was. I had been on my way to the kitchen for a drink of water, but I returned to the bedroom I shared with Brian and Liam and lay awake thinking of the big brown-brick mansion on the Mallow road. Once it had been owned and lived in by a local family. Now it was the town's asylum.

The town itself was small and ordinary. Part of it was on a hill, the part where the slum cottages were, where three or four shops had nothing in their windows except pasteboard advertisements for tea and Bisto. The rest of the town was fiat, a single street with one or two narrow streets running off it. Where they met there was a square of a kind, with a statue of Daniel O'Connell. The Munster and Leinster Bank was here, and the Bank of Ireland, and Lacy and Sons, and Bolger's Medical Hall, and the Home and Colonial. Our garage was at one end of the main street, opposite Corrigan's Hotel. The Electric Cinema was at the other, a stark white façade not far from the Church of the Holy Assumption. The Protestant church was at the top of the hill, beyond the slums.

When I think of the town now I can see it very clearly:

THE RAISING OF ELVIRA TREMLETT

cattle and pigs on a fair-day, always a Monday; Mrs Driscoll's vegetable shop, Vickery's hardware, Phelan's the barber's, Kilmartin's the turf accountant's, the convent and the Christian Brothers', twenty-nine public houses. The streets are empty on a sunny afternoon, there's a smell of bread. Brass plates gleam on the way home from school: Dr Thos. Garvey M.D., R.C.S., Regan and O'Brien, Commissioners for Oaths, W. Tracy, Dental Surgeon.

But in my thoughts our house and our garage close in on everything else, shadowing and diminishing the town. The bedroom I shared with Brian and Liam had the same nondescript linoleum as the hall and the landing had. There was a dressing-table with a wash-stand in white-painted wood, and a wardrobe that matched. There was a flowery wallpaper on the walls, but the flowers had all faded to a uniform brown, except behind the bedroom's single picture, of an ox pulling a cart. Our three iron bedsteads were lined against one wall. Above the mantelpiece Christ on his cross had already given up the ghost.

I didn't in any way object to this bedroom and, familiar with no alternative, I didn't mind sharing it with my brothers. The house itself was somewhere I was used to also, accepted and taken for granted. But the garage was different. The garage was a kind of hell, its awful earth floor made black with sump oil, its huge indelicate vices, the chill of cast iron, the grunting of my father and my uncle as they heaved an engine out of a tractor, the astringent smell of petrol. It was there that my silence, my dumbness almost, must have begun. I sense that now, without being able accurately to remember. Looking back, I see myself silent in a classroom, taught first by nuns and later by Christian Brothers. In the kitchen, while the others chattered at mealtimes, I was silent too. I could take no interest in what my father and uncle reported about the difficulties they were having in getting spare parts or about some fault in a farmer's carburettor. My brothers listened to all that, and clearly found it easy to. Or they would talk about sport, or tease Uncle Jack about the money he lost on greyhounds and horses. My mother would repeat what she had heard in the shops, and Uncle Jack would listen intently because although he never himself indulged in gossip he loved to hear it. My sisters would retail news from the convent, the decline in the health of an elderly nun, or the inability of some family to buy Lacy's more expensive First Communion dresses. I often felt, listening at mealtimes, that I was scarcely there. I didn't belong and I sensed it was my fault; I felt I was a burden, being unpromising at school, unable to hold out hopes for the future. I felt I was a disgrace to them and might even become a person who was only fit to lift cans of paraffin about in the garage. I thought I could see that in my father's eyes, and in my uncle's sometimes, and in my mother's. A kind of shame it was, peering back at me.

*

I turned to Elvira Tremlett because everything about her was quiet. 'You great damn clown,' my mother would shout angrily at my father. He'd smile in the kitchen, smelling like a brewery, as she used to say. 'Mind that bloody tongue of yours,' he'd retort, and then he'd eye my uncle in a belligerent manner. 'Jeez, will you look at the cut of him?' he'd roar, laughing and throwing his head about. My uncle would usually be sitting in front of the range, a little to one side so as not to be in the way of my mother while she cooked. He'd been reading the *Independent* or *Ireland's Own*, or trying to mend something. 'You're the right eejit,' my father would say to him. 'And the right bloody hypocrite.'

It was always like that when he'd been in Keogh's on a Saturday evening and returned in time for his meal. My mother would slap the plates on to the table, my father would sing in order to annoy her. I used to feel that my uncle and my mother were allied on these occasions, just as she and my father were allied when my uncle spent a Saturday night in Cork after the greyhound racing. I much preferred it when my father didn't come back until some time in the middle of the night. 'Will you look at His Nibs?' he'd say in the kitchen, drawing attention to me. 'Haven't you a word in you, boy? Bedad, that fellow'll never make a lawyer.' He'd explode with laughter and then he'd tell Kitty that she was looking great and could marry the crowned King of England if she wanted to. He'd say to Effie she was getting fat with the toffees she ate; he'd tell my brothers they were lazy.

They didn't mind his talk the way I did; even Kitty's embarrassment used to evaporate quite quickly because for some reason she was fond of him. Effie was fond of my uncle, and my brothers of my mother. Yet in spite of all this family feeling, whenever there was quarrelling between our parents, or an atmosphere after my uncle had spent a night away, my brothers used to say the three of them would drive you mad. 'Wouldn't it make you sick, listening to it?' Brian would say in our bedroom, saying it to Liam. Then they'd laugh because they couldn't be bothered to concern themselves too much with other people's quarrels, or with atmospheres.

The fact was, my brothers and sisters were all part of it, whatever it was—the house, the garage, the family we were—and they could take everything in their stride. They were the same as our parents and our uncle, and Elvira Tremlett was different. She was a bit like Myrna Loy, whom I had seen in the Electric, in *Test Pilot* and *Too Hot to Handle* and *The Thin Man*. Only she was more beautiful than Myrna Loy, and her voice was nicer. Her voice, I still consider, was the nicest thing about Elvira Tremlett, next to her quietness.

*

'What do you want?' the sexton of the Protestant church said to me one Saturday afternoon. 'What're you doing here?'

He was an old, hunched man in black clothes. He had rheumy eyes, very red and bloody at the rims. It was said in the town that he gave his wife an awful time.

'It isn't your church,' he said.

I nodded, not wanting to speak to him. He said:

'It's a sin for you to be coming into a Protestant church. Are you wanting to be a Protestant, is that it?' He was laughing at me, even though his lips weren't smiling. He looked as if he'd never smiled in his life.

I shook my head at him, hoping he might think I was dumb.

'Stay if you want to,' he said, surprising me, even though I'd seen him coming to the conclusion that I wasn't going to commit some act of vandalism. I think he might even have decided to be pleased because a Catholic boy had chosen to wander among the pews and brasses of his church. He hobbled away to the vestry, breathing noisily because of his bent condition.

Several months before that Saturday I had wandered into the church for the first time. It was different from the Church of the Holy Assumption. It had a different smell, a smell that might have come from mothballs or from the tidy stacks of hymn-books and prayer-books, whereas the Church of the Holy Assumption smelt of people and candles. It was cosier, much smaller, with dark-coloured panelling and pews, and stained-glass windows that seemed old, and no cross on the altar. There were flags and banners that were covered with dust, all faded and in shreds, and a Bible spread out on the wings of an eagle.

The old sexton came back. I could feel him watching me as I read the tablets on the walls, moving from one to the next, pretending that each of them interested me. I might have asked him: I might have smiled at him and timidly enquired about Elvira Tremlett because I knew he was old enough to remember. But I didn't. I walked slowly up a side-aisle, away from the altar, to the back of the church. I wanted to linger there in the shadows, but I could feel his rheumy eyes on my back, wondering about me. As I slipped away from the church, down the short path that led through black iron gates to the street at the top of the hill, I knew that I would never return to the place.

'Well, it doesn't matter,' she said. 'You don't have to go back. There's nothing to go back for.'

I knew that was true. It was silly to keep on calling in at the Protestant church.

'It's curiosity that sends you there,' she said. 'You're much too curious.'

I knew I was: she had made me understand that. I was curious and my family weren't.

She smiled her slow smile, and her eyes filled with it. Her eyes were brown, the same colour as her long hair. I loved it when she smiled. I loved watching her fingers playing with the daisies in her lap, I loved her old-fashioned clothes, and her shoes and her two elaborate earrings. She laughed once when I asked her if they were gold. She'd never been rich, she said.

There was a place, a small field with boulders in it, hidden on the edge of a wood. I had gone there the first time, after I'd been in the Protestant church. What had happened was that in the church I had noticed the tablet on the wall, the left wall as you faced the altar, the last tablet on it, in dull grey marble.

Near by this Stone
Lies Interred the Body
of Miss Elvira Tremlett
Daughter of Wm. Tremlett
of Tremlett Hall
in the County of Dorset.
She Departed this Life
August 30   1873
Aged 18.

Why should an English girl die in our town? Had she been passing through? Had she died of poisoning? Had someone shot her? Eighteen was young to die.

On that day, the first day I read her tablet, I had walked from the Protestant church to the field beside the wood. I often went there because it was a lonely place, away from the town and from people. I sat on a boulder and felt hot sun on my face and head, and on my neck and the backs of my hands. I began to imagine her, Elvira Tremlett of Tremlett Hall in the county of Dorset, England. I gave her her long hair and her smile and her elaborate earrings, and I felt I was giving her gifts. I gave her her clothes, wondering if I had got them right. Her fingers were delicate as straws, lacing together the first of her daisy-chains. Her voice hadn't the edge that Myrna Loy's had, her neck was more elegant.

'Oh, love,' she said on the Saturday after the sexton had spoken to me. 'The tablet's only a stone. It's silly to go gazing at it.'

I knew it was and yet it was hard to prevent myself. The more I gazed at it the more I felt I might learn about her: I didn't know if I was getting her right. I was afraid even to begin to imagine her death because I thought I might be doing wrong to have her dying from some cause that wasn't the correct one. It seemed insulting to her memory not to get that perfectly correct.

'You mustn't want too much,' she said to me on that Saturday afternoon. 'It's as well you've finished with the tablet on the wall. Death doesn't matter, you know.'

I never went back to the Protestant church. I remember what my mother had said about the quality of English goods, and how cars assembled in England were twice the ones assembled in Dublin. I looked at the map of England in my atlas and there was Dorset. She'd been travelling, maybe staying in a house near by, and had died somehow: she was right, it didn't matter.

Tremlett Hall was by a river in the country, with Virginia creeper all over it, with long corridors and suits of armour in the hall, and a fire-place in the hall also. In *David Copperfield*, which I had seen in the Electric, there might have been a house like Tremlett Hall, or in *A Yank at Oxford*: I couldn't quite remember. The gardens were beautiful: you walked from one garden to another, to a special rose-garden with a sundial, to a vegetable garden with high walls around it. In the house someone was always playing a piano. 'Me,' Elvira said.

My brothers went to work in the garage, first Brian and then Liam. Effie went to Cork, to the commercial college. The boys at the Christian Brothers' began to whistle at Kitty and sometimes would give me notes to pass on to her. Even when other people were there I could feel Elvira's nearness, even her breath sometimes, and certainly the warmth of her hands. When Brother Flynn hit me one day she cheered me up. When my father came back from Keogh's in time for his Saturday tea her presence made it easier. The garage I hated, where I was certain now I would one day lift paraffin cans from one corner to another, was lightened by her. She was in Mrs Driscoll's vegetable shop when I bought cabbage and potatoes for my mother. She was there while I waited for the Electric to open, and when I walked through the animals on a fair-day. In the stony field the sunshine made her earrings glitter. It danced over a brooch she had not had when first I imagined her, a brooch with a scarlet jewel, in the shape of a dragon. Mist caught in her hair, wind ruffled the skirts of her old-fashioned dress. She wore gloves when it was cold, and a green cloak that wrapped itself all around her. In spring she often carried daffodils, and once—one Sunday in June—she carried a little dog, a grey Cairn that afterwards became part of her, like her earrings and her brooch.

I grew up but she was always eighteen, as petrified as her tablet on the wall. In the bedroom which I shared with Brian and Liam I came, in time, to take her dragon's brooch from her throat and to take her earrings from her pale ears and to lift her dress from her body. Her limbs were warm, and her smile was always there. Her slender fingers traced caresses on my cheeks. I told her that I loved her, as the people told one another in the Electric.

'You know why they're afraid of you?' she said one day in the field by the wood. 'You know why they hope that God will look after you?'

I had to think about it but I could come to no conclusion on my own, without her prompting. I think I wouldn't have dared; I'd have been frightened of whatever there was.

'You know what happens,' she said, 'when your uncle stays in Cork on a Saturday night? You know what happened once when your father came back from Keogh's too late for his meal, in the middle of the night?'

I knew before she told me. I guessed, but I wouldn't have if she hadn't been there. I made her tell me, listening to her quiet voice. My Uncle Jack went after women as well as greyhounds in Cork. It was his weakness, like going to Keogh's was my father's. And the two weaknesses had once combined, one Saturday night a long time ago when my uncle hadn't gone to Cork and my father was a long time in Keogh's.

I was the child of my Uncle Jack and my mother, born of his weakness and my mother's anger as she waited for the red bleariness of my father to return, footless in the middle of the night. It was why my father called my uncle a hypocrite. It was maybe why my uncle was always looking at the ground, and why he assisted Canon O'Keefe in the rectory and in the Church of the Holy Assumption. I was their sin, growing in front of them, for God to look after.

'They have made you,' Elvira said. 'The three of them have made you what you are.'

I imagined my father returning that night from Keogh's, stumbling on the stairs, and haste being made by my uncle to hide himself. In these images it was always my uncle who was anxious and in a hurry: my mother kept saying it didn't matter, pressing him back on to the pillows, wanting him to be found there.

My father was like a madman in the bedroom then, wild in his crumpled Saturday clothes. He struck at both of them, his befuddled eyes tormented while my mother screamed. She went back through all the years of their marriage, accusing him of cruelty and neglect. My uncle wept. 'I'm no more than an animal to you,' my mother screamed, half-naked between the two of them. 'I cook and clean and have children for you. You give me thanks by going out to Keogh's.' Brian was in the room, attracted by the noise. He stood by the open door, five years old, telling them to be quiet because they were waking the others.

'Don't ever tell a soul,' Brian would have said, years afterwards, retailing that scene for Liam and Effie and Kitty, letting them guess the truth. He had been sent back to bed, and my uncle had gone to his own bed, and in the morning there had begun the pretending that none of it had happened. There was confession and penance, and extra hours spent in Keogh's. There were my mother's prayers that I would not be born, and my uncle's prayers, and my father's bitterness when the prayers weren't answered.

On the evening of the day that Elvira shared all that with me I watched them as we ate in the kitchen, my father's hands still smeared with oil, his fingernails in mourning, my uncle's eyes bent over his fried eggs. My brothers and sisters talked about events that had taken place in the town; my mother listened without interest, her large round face seeming stupid to me now. It was a cause for celebration that I was outside the family circle. I was glad not to be part of the house and the garage, and not to be part of the town with its statue and its shops and its twenty-nine public houses. I belonged with a figment of my imagination to an English ghost who had acquired a dog, whose lips were soft, whose limbs were warm, Elvira Tremlett, who lay beneath the Protestant church.

'Oh, love,' I said in the kitchen, 'thank you.'

The conversation ceased, my father's head turned sharply. Brian and Liam looked at me, so did Effie and Kitty. My mother had a piece of fried bread on a fork, on the way to her mouth. She returned it to her plate. There was grease at the corner of her lips, a little shiny stream from some previous mouthful, running down to her chin. My uncle pushed his knife and fork together and stared at them.

I felt them believing with finality now, with proof, that I was not sane. I was fifteen years old, a boy who was backward in his ways, who was all of a sudden addressing someone who wasn't in the room.

My father cut himself a slice of bread, moving the bread-saw slowly through the loaf. My brothers were as valuable in the garage now as he or my uncle; Effie kept the books and sent out bills. My father took things easy, spending more time talking to his older customers. My uncle pursued the racing pages; my mother had had an operation for varicose veins, which she should have had years ago.

I could disgrace them in the town, in all the shops and public houses, in Bolger's Medical Hall, in the convent and the Christian Brothers' and the Church of the Holy Assumption. How could Brian and Liam carry on the business if they couldn't hold their heads up? How could Effie help with the petrol pumps at a busy time, standing in her Wellington boots on a wet day, for all the town to see? Who would marry Kitty now?

I had spoken by mistake, and I didn't speak again. It was the first time I had said anything at a meal in the kitchen for as long as I could remember, for years and years. I had suddenly felt that she might grow tired of coming into my mind and want to be left alone, buried beneath the Protestant church. I had wanted to reassure her.

'They're afraid of you,' she said that night. 'All of them.'

She said it again when I walked in the sunshine to our field. She kept on saying it, as if to warn me, as if to tell me to be on the look-out. 'They have made you,' she repeated. 'You're the child of all of them.'

I wanted to go away, to escape from the truth we had both instinctively felt and had shared. I walked with her through the house called Tremlett Hall, haunting other people with our footsteps. We stood and watched while guests at a party laughed among the suits of armour in the hall, while there was waltzing in a ballroom. In the gardens dahlias bloomed, and sweet-pea clung to wires against a high stone wall. Low hedges of fuchsia bounded the paths among the flower-beds, the little dog ran on in front of us. She held my hand and said she loved me; she smiled at me in the sunshine. And then, just for a moment, she seemed to be different; she wasn't wearing the right clothes; she was wearing a tennis dress and had a racquet in her hand. She was standing in a conservatory, one foot on a cane chair. She looked like another girl, Susan Peters in *Random Harvest*.

I didn't like that. It was the same kind of thing as feeling I had to speak to her even though other people were in the kitchen. It was a muddle, and somewhere in it I could sense an unhappiness I didn't understand. I couldn't tell if it was hers or mine. I tried to say I was sorry, but I didn't know what I was sorry for.

*

In the middle of one night I woke up screaming. Brian and Liam were standing by my bed, cross with me for waking them. My mother came, and then my father. I was still screaming, unable to stop. 'He's had some type of nightmare,' Brian said.

It wasn't a nightmare because it continued when I was awake. She was there, Elvira Tremlett, born 1855. She didn't talk or smile: I couldn't make her. Something was failing in me: it was the same as Susan Peters suddenly appearing with a tennis racquet, the same as my desperation in wanting to show gratitude when we weren't in private.

My mother sat beside my bed. My brothers returned to theirs. The light remained on. I must have whispered, I must have talked about her because I remember my mother's nodding head and her voice assuring me that it was all a dream. I slept, and when I woke up it was light in the room and my mother had gone and my brothers were getting up. Elvira Tremlett was still there, one eye half-closed in blindness, the fingers that had been delicate misshapen now. When my brothers left the room she was more vivid, a figure by the window, turning her head to look at me, a gleam of fury in her face. She did not speak but I knew what she was saying. I had used her for purposes of my own, to bring solace. What right, for God's sake, had I to blow life into her decaying bones? Born 1855, eighty-nine years of age.

I closed my eyes, trying to imagine her as I had before,

willing her young girl's voice and her face and hair. But even with my eyes closed the old woman moved about the room, from the window to the foot of Liam's bed, to the wardrobe, into a corner, where she stood still.

She was on the landing with me, and on the stairs and in the kitchen. She was in the stony field by the wood, accusing me of disturbing her and yet still not speaking. She was in pain from her eye and her arthritic hands: I had brought about that. Yet she was no ghost, I knew she was no ghost. She was a figment of my imagination, drawn from her dull grey tablet by my interest. She existed within me, I told myself, but it wasn't a help.

Every night I woke up screaming. The sheets of my bed were sodden with my sweat. I would shout at my brothers and my mother, begging them to take her away from me. It wasn't I who had committed the sin, I shouted, it wasn't I who deserved the punishment. All I had done was to talk to a figment. All I'd done was to pretend, as they had.

Canon O'Keefe talked to me in the kitchen. His voice came and went, and my mother's voice spoke of the sheets sodden with sweat every morning, and my father's voice said there was terror in my eyes. All I wanted to say was that I hadn't meant any harm in raising Elvira Tremlett from the dead in order to have an imaginary friend, or in travelling with her to the house with Virginia creeper on it. She hadn't been real, she'd been no more than a flicker on the screen of the Electric Cinema: I wanted to say all that. I wanted to be listened to, to be released of the shame that I felt like a shroud around me. I knew that if I could speak my imagination would be free of the woman who haunted it now. I tried, but they were afraid of me. They were afraid of what I was going to say and between them they somehow stopped me. 'Our Father,' said Canon O'Keefe, 'Who art in heaven, Hallowed be Thy Name. . . .'

259

Dr Garvey came and looked at me: in Cork another man looked at me. The man in Cork tried to talk to me, telling me to lie down, to take my shoes off if I wanted to. It wasn't any good, and it wasn't fair on them, having me there in the house, a person in some kind of nightmare. I quite see now that it wasn't fair on them, I quite see that.

Because of the unfairness I was brought, one Friday morning in a Ford car my father borrowed from a customer, to this brown-brick mansion, once the property of a local family. I have been here for thirty-four years. The clothes I wear are rough, but I have ceased to be visited by the woman who Elvira Tremlett became in my failing imagination. I ceased to be visited by her the moment I arrived here, for when that moment came I knew that this was the house she had been staying in when she died. She brought me here so that I could live in peace, even in the room that had been hers. I had disturbed her own peace so that we might come here together.

*

I have not told this story myself. It has been told by my weekly visitor, who has placed me at the centre of it because that, of course, is where I belong. Here, in the brown-red mansion, I have spoken without difficulty. I have spoken in the garden where I work in the daytime; I have spoken at all meals; I have spoken to my weekly visitor. I am different here. I do not need an imaginary friend, I could never again feel curious about a girl who died.

I have asked my visitor what they say in the town, and what the family say. He replies that in the bar of Corrigan's Hotel commercial travellers are told of a boy who was haunted, as a place or a house is. They are drawn across the bar to a window: Devlin Bros., the garage across the street, is pointed out to them. They listen in pleasurable astonishment to the story of nightmares, and hear the name of an English girl who died in the town in 1873, whose tablet is on the wall of the Protestant church. They are told of the final madness of the boy, which came about through his visions of this girl, Elvira Tremlett.

The story is famous in the town, the only story of its kind the town possesses. It is told as a mystery, and the strangers who hear it sometimes visit the Protestant church to look up at the tablet that commemorates a death in 1873. They leave the church in bewilderment, wondering why an uneasy spirit should have lighted on a boy so many years later. They never guess, not one of them, that the story as it happened wasn't a mystery in the least.

A Dream of Butterflies

Various people awoke with a sense of relief. Sleepily, Colin Rhodes wondered what there was to be relieved about. As he did in the moment of waking every morning, he encased with his left hand one of his wife's plump breasts and then remembered the outcome of last night's meeting. Miss Cogings, alone in her narrow bed and listening to a chorus of house-martins, remembered it with the same degree of satisfaction. So did the Poudards when their Teasmade roused them at a quarter to seven. So did the Reverend Feare, and Mr Mottershead and Mr and Mrs Tilzey, and the Blennerhassetts, who ran the Village Stores. Mrs Feare, up since dawn with an ailing child, was pleased because her husband was. There would be peace when there might have been war. A defeat had been inflicted.

The Allenbys, however, awoke in Luffnell Lodge with mixed feelings. What to do with the Lodge now that it remained unsold? How long would they have to wait for another buyer? For having made their minds up, they really wanted to move on as soon as possible. A bridging loan had been negotiated at one point but they'd decided against it because the interest was so high. They planned to buy a bungalow in a part of Cornwall that was noted for its warmth and dryness, both of which would ease Mrs Allenby's arthritis. Everything that had been said at the meeting made sense to Mr and Mrs Allenby; they quite understood the general point of view. But they wished, that morning, that things might have been different.

*

'That's really bizarre,' Hugh said in the Mansors' breakfast-room.

'Dreams often are.'

'But butterflies – '

'It has to do with the meeting.'

'Ah, of course, the meeting.'

He saw at once what had been happening. He traced quite easily the series of his wife's thoughts, one built upon the last, fact in the end becoming fantasy.

Emily buttered toast and reached for grapefruit marmalade. 'Silly,' she said, not believing that it was.

'A bit,' he agreed, smiling at her. He went on to talk of something else, an item in *The Times*, another airliner hi-jacked.

The sun filled their breakfast-room. It struck the bones of his narrow face; it livened his calm grey hair. It found the strawberry mark, like a tulip, on her neck; it made her spectacles glint. They were the same age, fifty-two, not yet grandparents but soon to be. He dealt in property; she'd once been a teacher of Latin and Greek. She was small and given to putting on weight if she wasn't careful: dumpy, she considered herself.

'Don't let it worry you,' Hugh said, folding *The Times* for further perusal on the train. 'It's all over now.'

He was handsome in his thin way, and she was plain. Perhaps he had married her because he had not felt up to the glamour of a beautiful woman: as a young man, unproved in the world, he had had an inferiority complex, and success in middle age had not managed to shake it off. It wouldn't have surprised him if the heights he'd scaled in his business world all of a sudden turned out to be a wasteland. He specialised in property in distant places, Jamaica, Spain, the Bahamas: some economic jolt could shatter everything. The house they lived in, on the edge of a Sussex village, was the symbol of his good fortune over the years. It was also his due, for he had worked doggedly; only his inferiority complex prevented him from taking it for granted. It puzzled him that he, so unpromising as a boy at school, had done so well; and occasionally, but not often, it puzzled him that they'd made a success of their marriage in times when the failure rate was high. Perhaps they'd made a go of it because she was modest too: more than once he'd wondered if that could be true. Could it be that Emily, so much cleverer than he, had found a level with him because her lack of beauty kept her in her place, as his inferiority complex kept him? She had said that as a girl she'd imagined she would not marry, assuming that a strawberry mark and dumpiness, and glasses too, would be too much for any man. He often thought about her as she must have been, cleverest in the class; while he was being slow on the uptake. 'You're very kind' was what most often, in the way of compliments, Emily said to him.

'Have a good day' was what she said now, forcing cheer-fulness on to her face, for the dream she'd had still saddened her and the memory of the meeting worried her.

'I'll be on the five o'clock.' He touched her cheek with his lips, and then was gone, the door of the breakfast-room opening and closing, the hall-door banging. She listened to the starting of the car and the sound of the wheels on the tarmac, then the engine fading to nothing in the distance.

She felt as he did, that together they had not done badly in twenty-seven years of marriage. She'd been a Miss Forrest; becoming Mrs Mansor had seemed the nicest thing that yet had happened to her; and for all their married life – the worries during the lean years, the bringing up of their three children – she had regretted nothing, and in the end there'd been the reward of happiness in middle age. She missed their son and daughters, all of whom were now married themselves, but in compensation there was the contentment that the house and garden brought, and the unexacting life of the village. As well, there were the visits of their children and her memories of girls whom she had taught, some of whom kept up with her. It was still a pleasure to read Horace and the lesser Greek poets, to find in an experimental way a new interpretation in place of the standard, scholar's one.

Their house, in the style of Queen Anne though in fact of a later period, was hidden from the road and the surrounding fields by modest glades of silver birches. It was a compact house, easy to run and keep clean, modernised with gadgets, warm in winter. Alone in it in the mornings Emily often played Bach or Mozart on the sitting-room hi-fi system, the music drifting into the kitchen and the bedrooms and the breakfast-room, pursuing her agreeably wherever she went.

But this morning she was not in the mood for Bach or Mozart. She continued to sit as her husband had left her, saying to herself that she must come to terms with what had happened. She had raised her voice but no one had cared to listen to it. Only Golkorn had listened, his great tightly-cropped head slowly nodding, his eyes occasionally piercing hers. At the meeting her voice had faltered; her cheeks had warmed; nothing had come out as she'd meant it to.

*

Unladylike assortment of calumnies. In the train on the way to Waterloo he couldn't think of a nine-lettered word. As a chore, he did *The Times* crossword every day, determined to do better with practice. *There's none of the Old Adam in a cardinal* (6). He sighed and put the paper down.

It worried him that she'd been so upset. He hadn't known what to say, or to do, when she'd stood up suddenly at the meeting to make her unsuccessful speech. He'd felt himself embarrassed, in sympathy or shame, he couldn't tell which. He hadn't been quite able to agree with her and had been surprised when she'd stood up because it wasn't like her to do anything in public, even though she'd been saying she was unhappy about the thing for months. But then she was so unemphatic as a person that quite often it was hard to guess when she felt strongly.

With other suited men, some carrying as he did a brief-case and a newspaper, he stepped from the train at Waterloo. He strode along the platform with them, one in an army, it often seemed. In spite of how she felt, he really couldn't help believing that the village had been saved. Their own house and garden, and the glades of silver birches, would in no way suffer. The value of the house would continue to rise with inflation instead of quite sharply declining. There would be calm again in the village instead of angry voices and personal remarks, instead of Colin Rhodes saying to Golkorn's face that he was a foreigner. Thank God it was all over.

'There's been a telex,' Miss Brooks informed him in his office. 'That place in Gibraltar.'

*

In the breakfast-room Emily's thoughts had spread out, from her dream of butterflies and the meeting there had been the night before. She saw images of women as they might have been, skulking in the woods near the village, two of them sitting on the stone seat beside the horse-trough on the green, another in a lane with ragwort in her hand. They were harmless women, as Golkorn had kept insisting. It was just that their faces were strange and their movements not properly articulated; nothing, of course, that they said made sense. 'Anywhere but here,' snapped the voice of Colin Rhodes, as vividly she recalled the meeting. 'My God, you've got the world to choose from, Golkorn.'

Golkorn had smiled. Their village was beautiful, he had irritatingly stated, as if in reply. Repeatedly it had been said at the meeting last night, and at previous meetings, that the village was special because it was among the most beautiful in England. The Manor dated back to Saxon times, it had been said, and the cottages round the green were almost unique. But it was that very beauty, and the very peacefulness of the lanes and woods, that Golkorn had claimed would be a paradise for his afflicted women. It was why he had chosen Luffnell Lodge when it went up for sale. Luffnell Lodge was less impressive than the Manor, and certainly nothing like as old. It was larger and less convenient, colder and in worse repair, yet ideal apparently for Golkorn's purpose. In her dream Emily had been walking with him in a field and he had pointed at what at first she'd taken to be flowers but had turned out to be butterflies. 'You've never seen that before,' he'd said. 'Butterflies in mourning, Mrs Mansor.' They flew away as he spoke, a whole swarm of them, busily flapping their black wings.

She rose and cleared away the breakfast things. She carried them on a tray through the hall and into the kitchen. Her dog, an old Sealyham called Spratts, wagged his tail without getting out of his basket. On the window-sill in front of the sink, hot with morning sunshine, a butterfly was poised and she thought at once that that was a coincidence. Its wings were tightly closed; it might have been dead but she knew it wasn't, and when she touched it and the wings opened they were not sinister.

*

Of course it had been for the best when the Allenbys had realised that to sell Luffnell Lodge to Golkorn would have caused havoc: dealing with the telex about the place in Gibraltar, Hugh found himself yet again thinking that. Golkorn was a frightful person; it was Golkorn's presence rather than his sick women whom one might reasonably object to. Luffnell Lodge would put the village on the map, Golkorn had confidently promised, once it was full of his patients: in medical terms he was making a breakthrough. And Hugh knew that what he had offered the Allenbys was more than they'd get otherwise. You couldn't blame them, elderly and wanting to get rid of what they'd come to think of as a white elephant, for listening to Golkorn's adroit arguments. The Allenbys had done nothing wrong and in the end had made the sacrifice. They'd sell the Lodge eventually, it stood to reason, even if they had to wait a bit. 'You see, we don't particularly want to wait,' old Mr Allenby had said. 'That's just the trouble. We've waited two years as it is.' The Allenbys had asked Hugh's advice because they thought that being in the international property market he might know a little more than Musgrove and Carter, who after all were only country estate agents. 'Dr Golkorn is offering you a most attractive proposition,' he'd had to admit, no way around that. 'It could be a while before anyone matched it.' Mr Allenby had asked if he'd care to handle the sale, in conjunction with Musgrove and Carter, but Hugh had had to explain that property in England was outside his firm's particular field. 'Oh, dear, it's all so difficult,' Mrs Allenby had disconsolately murmured, clearly most unhappy at the prospect of having to hang on in the Lodge for another couple of years. Hugh had always liked the Allenbys. In

many ways, as a friend and as an expert, he should have told
them to accept immediately Golkorn's offer. But he hadn't
and that was that; it was all now best forgotten.

For Hugh that day passed as days did at the office. He
dictated letters and received telephone calls. He lunched
with a client in the Isola Bella, quite often he thought about
his wife. Emily was unhappy because of everything that had
happened. She felt, but had not said so, that he had let the
Allenbys down. She felt that she herself had let the inmates
of Golkorn's home down. Hugh tried not to think about it;
but in his mind's eye he kept seeing her again, standing up at
the meeting and saying that afflicted women have to live somewhere. Like mongol children, she had said, stammering; or
the blind. 'That's quite appreciated, Mrs Mansor,' the
Reverend Feare had murmured, and as if to come to her
assistance Golkorn had asked if he might address the meeting.
He had nodded his heavy razored head at Emily; he had
repeated what she'd said, that afflicted women, like mongol
children and the blind, have to go somewhere. He had
smiled and spread his hands out, impatient with those who
were protesting and yet oilily endeavouring to hide it. A
woman present, he'd even suggested, might one day need
the home he proposed for Luffnell Lodge. Hugh sighed,
remembering it all vividly. He would take Emily out to
dinner, to the Rowan House Hotel. He was about to pick
up the telephone in order to ask to be put through to her
when it rang. Odd, he thought as he picked up the receiver,
that she had dreamed so strangely of butterflies.

'It's a Dr Golkorn,' his secretary's voice said. 'On the other
line, Mr Mansor.'

He hesitated. There was no point in speaking to Golkorn; at
half-past ten last night Golkorn had lost his case; the matter was
closed. Yet something – perhaps just politeness, he afterwards
thought – made him pick up the other telephone. 'Yes?' he said.

'It's Golkorn,' Golkorn said. 'Look, Mr Mansor, could we talk?'

'About the Lodge? But that's all over, Dr Golkorn. The Allenbys – '

'Sir, they agreed beneath all this pressure not to let me have the house. But with respect, is that just, sir? At least agree to exchange another word or two with me, Mr Mansor.'

'It would be useless, I'm afraid.'

'Mr Mansor, do me a favour.'

'I would willingly do you a favour if I thought – '

'I ask you only for ten minutes. If I may come to see you for ten minutes, Mr Mansor, I would esteem it.'

'You mean, you want to come here?'

'I mean, sir, I would like to come to your very pleasant home. I would like to call in at seven tonight if that might be convenient. The reason I am suggesting this, Mr Mansor, is I am still in the neighbourhood of the village. I am still staying in the same hotel.'

'Well, yes, come over by all means, but I really must warn you – '

'I am used to everything, Mr Mansor.' Laughter accompanied this remark and then Golkorn said, 'I look forward to seeing you and your nice wife. I promise only to occupy ten minutes.'

Hugh telephoned Emily. 'Golkorn,' he said. 'He wants to come and see us.'

'But what for?'

'I really can't think. I couldn't say no.'

'Of course not.'

'He's coming at seven.'

She said goodbye and put the receiver down. The development astonished her. She thought that at least they had finished with Golkorn.

The telephone rang again and Hugh suggested that they should go out to dinner, to Rowan House, where they often went. She knew he was suggesting it because she'd been upset. She appreciated that, but she said she'd rather make it another night, mainly because she had a stew in the oven. 'I'm sorry about that wretched man,' Hugh said. 'He wasn't easy to choke off.' She reassured him, making a joke of Golkorn's insistence, saying that of course it didn't matter.

In the garden she picked sweet-peas. She sat for a moment in the corner where she and Hugh often had coffee together on Saturday and Sunday mornings. She put the sweet-peas on the slatted garden table and let her glance wander over lupins and delphiniums, and the tree geranium that was Hugh's particular pride. On trellises and archways which he'd made roses trailed in profusion, Mermaid and Danse du Feu. She loved the garden, as she loved the house.

At her feet the Sealyham called Spratts settled down to rest for a while, but she warned him that she didn't intend to remain long in the secluded corner. In a moment she picked up the sweet-peas and took them to the kitchen, where she arranged them in a cut-glass vase. The dog followed her when she carried it to the sitting-room. Was it unusual, she wondered, to pick flowers specially for a person you didn't like? Yet it had seemed a natural thing to do; she always picked flowers when a visitor was coming.

'Ten minutes I promised,' Golkorn said at seven o'clock, having been notably prompt, 'so ten minutes it must be.' He laughed, as if he'd made a joke of some kind. 'No, no drink for me, please.'

Hugh poured Emily a glass of sherry, Harvey's Luncheon Dry, which was what she always had. He smeared a glass with Angostura drops and added gin and water to it for himself. Perhaps there was something in the fact that he had rescued her, he thought, wanting to think about her rather than their visitor. Even though she loved the subject, she had never been entirely happy as a teacher of Classics because she was shy. Until she came to know them she was nervous of the girls she taught: her glasses and her strawberry mark and her dumpiness, the very fact that she was a teacher, seemed to put her into a certain category, at a disadvantage. And perhaps his rescuing of her, if you could so grandly call it that, had in turn given him something he'd lacked before. Perhaps their marriage was indeed built on debts to one another.

'Orange juice, Mr Golkorn?' Emily suggested, already rising to get it for him.

He waved a hand, denying his need of orange juice. 'Look,' he said, 'I don't want to beat about the bush. I want to come to the point. Luffnell Lodge, Mr Mansor. You're a man of business, you know those people wouldn't ever get that price. They'll lose a lot. You know that.'

'We've been through all of it, Dr Golkorn. The Allenbys do not wish to sell their property to you.'

'They're elderly people – '

'That has nothing to do with it.'

'With respect, Mr Mansor, it may have. Our elderly friends could be sitting there in that barracks for winter after winter. They could freeze to death. The old lady's crippled with arthritis as it is.'

'Mrs Allenby's illness cannot enter into this. The Allenbys – '

'With respect, sir, they came to you for advice.'

'That is so.'

'With respect, sir, the advice you gave them was unfortunate.'

'If they'd sold the Lodge to you they'd be hated in the village.'

'But they'd be gone, Mr Mansor. They'd have kicked the dust off their heels. They'd be imbibing the sun on some island somewhere. As their doctor advised.'

'They've lived in this village for more than fifty years. It matters to them what the village thinks of them. We've been all through this, you know. I can't help you, Dr Golkorn.'

Golkorn bent his head for a moment over clasped hands, as if praying for patience. He was slightly smiling. When eventually he looked up there was a glint in his dark, clever eyes which suggested that, despite appearances, he held the more useful cards. His black pin-striped suit was uncreased, his smooth black shoes had a glassy glow. He wore a blue shirt and a blue bow-tie with small white spots on it. The night before, at the meeting, he'd been similarly dressed except for his shirt and tie. The shirt had last night been pink and the tie a shade of deep crimson, though also with white spots.

'What do you think, Mrs Mansor?' he said in his soft, unhurried voice, still smiling a little. 'How do you see this unhappy business?' His manner suggested that they might have been his patients. Any moment now, Hugh thought, he might tell them to go out for a walk.

'I feel as my husband does,' Emily said. 'I feel the Allenbys have given you their answer.'

'I mean, madam, how do you feel about the people I wish to help? I do not mean the Allenbys, Mrs Mansor; I mean of course those who would one day be my patients in Luffnell Lodge.'

'You heard what my wife said last night, Dr Golkorn,' Hugh interjected quickly. 'She is sympathetic towards such people.'

'You would not yourself object to these patients in your village, Mrs Mansor? Did I understand you correctly when you spoke last night?'

'That is what I said. I would personally not object.'

'With respect, madam, you feel a certain guilt? Well, I assure you it is natural to feel a certain guilt. By that I mean it is natural for some people.' He laughed. 'Not Colin Rhodes of course, or Mr Mottershead, or Mr and Mrs Tilzey, or Miss Cogings. Not your clergyman, Mr Feare, even though he is keen to show his concern for the unwell. I think you're different, madam.'

'My wife – '

'Let us perhaps hear your wife, eh? Mrs Mansor, you do not believe the village would be a bear garden if a handful of unhappy women were added to it: that was what you implied last night?'

'Yes.'

'But the vote went against you.'

'No vote was taken,' Hugh said sharply. 'The meeting was simply to explain to you why the Allenbys had decided not to sell.'

'But there had been other meetings, eh? At which I naturally was not present. There have been six months of meetings, I think I'm correct in stating. You've argued back and forth among yourselves, and sides have naturally been taken. In the end, you know, the question we have to ask is should our elderly friends not be allowed to do what is best for them since they have done so much for the village in the past? The other question we have to ask is would it be the end of the universe to have a handful of mentally ill women in Luffnell Lodge? With respect, madam, you feel guilty now because you did not fight hard enough for justice and humanity. And you, sir, because in your efforts to see everyone's point of view you permitted yourself to be bulldozed by the majority and to become their tool.'

'Now look here, Dr Golkorn – '

'With respect, you misinformed the vendors, sir. They'll be in Luffnell Lodge till they die now.'

'The house will be sold to another buyer. It's only a matter of time.'

'It's what you call a white elephant, sir.'

'I think we'd rather you went, Dr Golkorn.'

Golkorn leaned back in his chair. He crossed one leg over the other. He smiled, turning his head a little so that the smile was directed first at Hugh and then at Emily. He said:

'You are both of you upset. In my profession, Mr Mansor, which has to do with the human heart as much as the human mind, I could sense last night that you were both upset. You were saying to yourself, sir, that you had made an error of judgement. Mrs Mansor was wanting to weep.'

'I admit to no error of judgement –'

'Shall we refer to it as a mistake then, sir? You have made a mistake with which you will live until the white elephant is sold. And even then, if ever it is sold in the lifetime of the vendors, the mistake will still be there because of the amount they will have forfeited. In good faith they called you in, sir, taking you to be an honest man –'

'You're being offensive, Dr Golkorn.'

'I apologise for that, sir. I was purely making a point. Let me make another one. Your wife, as long as she has breath to keep her alive, will never forgive herself.'

Emily tried not to look at him. She looked at the sweet-peas she'd arranged. Through her shoes she could feel the warmth of the Sealyham, who had a way of hugging her feet. She felt there was nothing she could say.

Hugh rose and crossed the room. He noticed that Emily hadn't touched her sherry. He shook the little bottle of Angostura bitters over his own glass, and added gin and water.

'Actually, sir,' Golkorn said, 'all I am suggesting you should do is to pick up the telephone. And you, madam, all that is necessary is to say how you feel to Mrs Allenby. She, too, has humanitarian instincts.'

His beadiness had discovered that they were the weak links in the chain. When he'd argued with the others the night before, trying to make them see his point of view, opinion had hardened immediately. And when he'd persisted, anger had developed. 'In blunt terms,' Colin Rhodes had shouted at him, 'we don't want you here. If you're going to be a blot on the landscape, we'd be obliged if you could be it somewhere else.' And Colin Rhodes would say it even more forcibly now: there'd have been no point in Golkorn's insinuating his way into the Rhodes's sitting-room, or the sitting-room of the Reverend Feare, or the sitting-room of Mr Mottershead or Miss Cogings. There'd have been no point in tackling the Poudards, or taking on the Tilzeys, or making a fuss with Mr and Mrs Blennerhassett in the Village Stores.

'My trouble is,' Golkorn said softly, laughing as if to dress the words with delicacy, 'I cannot accept no for an answer.'

She imagined telling him now that she had dreamed of butterflies in mourning. She imagined his cropped head carefully nodding, going slowly up and down in unspoken delight. Eventually he would explain the dream, relishing the terms he employed, telling her nothing she did not already know. He was a master of the obvious. He took ordinary, blunt facts and gave them a weapon's edge.

'Which comes first,' he enquired quite casually, 'the beauty of an English village, like a picture on a calendar, or the happiness of the wretched?' He went on talking, going over the same ground, mentioning again by name the Poudards and the Tilzeys and the Blennerhassetts, Mr Mottershead, Miss Cogings, Colin Rhodes and the Reverend Feare and Mrs Feare, comparing these healthy, normal people with other people who were neither. He made them seem like monsters. He mentioned the Middle Ages and referred to the people of the village as belonging to an inferno of ignorance out of which the world had hauled itself by its own bootstraps. He himself, he threw in for some kind of good measure, had been a poor man once; he had worked his way through a foreign university, details of which he gave; he was devoted to humanity, he said.

But the Poudards and the Tilzeys were not monsters. The Blennerhassetts just felt strongly, as the others, varying in degree, did also. Mr Mottershead would do anything for you; the Feares had had children from Northern Ireland to stay for two summers running; Miss Cogings cleaned old Mrs Dugdall's windows for her because naturally old Mrs Dugdall couldn't do it herself any more. Having sherry with Colin Rhodes after church on Sundays was a civilised occasion; you couldn't in a million years say that Colin Rhodes and Daphne were a pair of monsters.

'Listen, you've got this all wrong, Dr Golkorn,' Hugh said.

'I wouldn't have said so, sir.'

'Your patients would be all over the neighbourhood. You admitted that yourself. They would be free to wander in the village –'

'I see now, sir, I should have told a lie. I should have said these unhappy people would be safely behind bars; I should have said that no suffering face would ever disturb the peace of your picture-postcard village.'

'Why didn't you?' Emily asked, unable to restrain curiosity.

'Because with respect, madam, it is not in my life-style to tell lies.'

They had to agree with that. In all he had said to the Allenbys and at the meeting last night he had been open and straightforward about what he had intended to do with Luffnell Lodge. He might easily have kept quiet and simply bought the place. It was almost as if he had wished to fight his battle according to the rules he laid down himself, for if lies were not his style deviousness made up for their absence. He knew that if they approached the Allenbys with the second thoughts he was proposing the Allenbys would not hesitate.

Deliberately he had let the rowdier opposition burn itself out in righteous fury, and had accepted defeat while seeing victory in sight. His eyes had not strayed once to Emily's tulip-shaped birth-mark, nor lingered on her spectacles or her dumpiness, as such eyes might so easily have done. He had not sought to humiliate Hugh with argument too fast and clever.

'I think,' he said, 'all three of us know. You are decent people. You cannot turn your backs.'

In Luffnell Lodge the women would be comforted, some even cured. Emily knew that. She knew he was not pretending, or claiming too much for himself. She knew his treatment of such women was successful. He was right when he said you could not turn your back. You could not build a wall around a pretty village and say that nothing unpleasant should be permitted within it. No wonder she had dreamed of butterflies mourning the human race. And yet she hated Golkorn. She hated his arrogance in assuming that because his cause was good no one could object. She hated his deviousness far more than the few simple lies he might have told. If he'd told a lie or two to the Allenbys all this might have been avoided.

Hugh only wanted him to go. He didn't need Golkorn to tell him he had misled the Allenbys. In misleading them he had acted out of instincts that were not dishonourable, but Golkorn would not for a second understand that.

'I have my car,' Golkorn said. 'We could the three of us drive up to Luffnell Lodge now.'

Hugh shook his head.

'And you, Mrs Mansor?' Golkorn prompted.

'I would like to talk to my husband.'

'I was only hoping to save you petrol, madam.' He spoke as if, at a time like this, with such an issue, the saving of petrol was still important.

'Yes, we'd like to talk,' Hugh said.

'Indeed, sir. If I may only phone you from the hotel in an hour or so? To see how you've got on.'

They knew he would. They knew he would not rest now until he had dragged their consciences out of them and set them profitably to work. If they did not go to Luffnell Lodge he would return to argue further.

'You understand that if we do as you suggest we'd have to leave the village,' Hugh pointed out. 'We couldn't stay here.'

Golkorn frowned, seeming genuinely perplexed. He gestured with his hands. 'But why, sir? Why leave this village? With respect, I do not understand you.'

'We'd have been disloyal to our friends. We'd be letting everyone down.'

'You're not letting me down, sir. You're not letting two elderly persons down, nor women in need of care and love – '

'Yes, we're aware of that, Dr Golkorn.'

'Sir, may I say that the people of this village will see it our way in time? They'll observe the good work all around them, and understand.'

'In fact, they won't.'

'Well, I would argue that, sir. With respect – '

'We would like to be alone now, Dr Golkorn.'

He went away and they were left with the dying moments of the storm he had brought with him. They did not say much but in time they walked together from the house, through the garden, to the car. They waved at Colin Rhodes, out with his retrievers on the green, and at Miss Cogings hurrying to the post-box with a letter. It wasn't until the car drew up at Luffnell Lodge, until they stood with the Allenbys in the hall, that they were grateful they'd been exploited.